Glass House Books

The Signatory

Stuart worked for Saatchi & Saatchi in Sydney and London, before becoming the founding partner and CEO of South-East Asia's leading healthcare communications group, Ward6.

Alongside his career in advertising, Stuart is the author of two novels. In 2003, he had a manuscript shortlisted for the NSW Writers' Centre Popular Fiction Competition and, in 2009, published the psychological thriller *Shallow Water*.

Stuart's second novel, *The Signatory*, is based on his intimate knowledge of the international corporate world.

Stuart is married and has two children.

Glass House Books
Brisbane

THE SIGNATORY

Stuart Black

Glass House Books
Brisbane

Glass House Books
an imprint of IP (Interactive Publications Pty Ltd)
Treetop Studio • 9 Kuhler Court
Carindale, Queensland, Australia 4152
ipoz.biz/glass-house-books/
ipoz.biz/ipstore

First published by IP in 2023

Printed in 12 pt Adobe Caslon Pro on 14 pt Avenir Book

ISBN 9781922830289 (PB); ISBN 9781922830296 (eBook)

A catalogue record for this book is available from the National Library of Australia *to Kristi, Tom, and Maddy*

Acknowledgments

Cover design: Lisa Reidy
Book design: David P Reiter
Author photo: Toby Burrows

The idea for *The Signatory* came from the work I do. Advertising. To all those people who were working with me at the agency when I wrote this book, and to those who have inspired me along the way, thank you. But especially to Hugh Fitzhardinge, Grant Foster, and Paul Whitehead. When you decide to start your own agency, you know you have a wild ride ahead of you. Many start-ups fail, and often it's within the first twelve months. We have survived. For sixteen years, so far. At times, we have thrived. That's because we have always stuck by each other. And we have been a good team. To another one of my work mates, Steve Samuel, thank you for helping with the marketing message. You always know the right words to use, and I have always admired your sense of humour. To Bradley Moore, thank you for all your help with the digital assets. To Mark Worman, thank you for reassuring me that I wasn't saying anything in the novel that was breaking any laws or might cause any friends or colleagues too much offence.

To my family – Kristi, Tom, Maddy, Mum, Dad, Susie, and Ted – thank you for your patience, your guidance, and your love.

To my friends – Simon Martin, Angus Paull, Syd Evans, Michael Jarjoura, Pixie Shields, Kate Cato, and Peter Duncan – thank you for slogging your way through some of the early drafts and for your helpful suggestions.

To Toby Burrows, thank you for your artistry, and to Lisa Reidy, thank you for the wonderful cover design.

To Debbie McInnes, thank you for your bold advice and your help in general with all things relating to the launch and publicity.

To Irina Dunn, thank you for believing in the potential of the novel, for your valuable advice early on, and for sending the manuscript out into the world. Your positivity and your love of fiction have, for many years, provided a much-needed spark for the Australian publishing scene.

To my publisher, Dr David Reiter, thank you for your enthusiasm and your vision, especially when all you had to go on was an unedited draft that needed a huge amount of work. I could not have done this without you. And, finally, to my editor, James Devitt, thank you for your thoughtful and clever suggestions, and for generally making the manuscript better.

Contents

Chapter 1

Thursday, June 4

Chaz Bailley was naked, sitting tightly bound to a chair. His wrists and ankles hurt. They'd used thin white rope to tie him, the kind you might find on a small sailing boat. The room was nearly empty. Some kind of storage facility. It had a grey cement floor, faded brick walls, a stack of brown cardboard boxes in the far-right corner, no windows that he could see, and a pair of old-fashioned fluorescent lights. A steel table was pushed up against the wall beside him. The only clean thing around.

He heard a door opening behind him. Turned out to be Blondie, the same lady he'd seen outside the Imperial Hotel. Dressed like a cocktail waitress.

'You're in good shape,' she said, giving him the once over. Her accent had an Australian twang to it, but there was something else there, too. French or Swiss. 'I hope you stay that way.'

'Who are you?' Chaz demanded.

Blondie was pacing around the room. 'Doesn't matter.'

'Can you at least tell me why I'm here?'

'Come on, Chaaaazzzzzz. You know why.'

'I honestly don't. Maybe this is some kind of mistaken identity or something?'

She sat herself down on his lap and crossed her legs, placing a cigarette between her lips. 'Look at you. Putting it all together.' She lit the cigarette and leaned into him, her elbow resting on his shoulder.

'Please…'

'Can you hear that music out there?' she asked. 'It's one of those small Bluetooth speakers. They'll bring it in here, soon. Not for you, of course, but for themselves. They'll turn the volume up until the speaker distorts, and they'll pretend you're screaming along to it. Like you're some kind of rock star. Isn't that something?'

'What are you saying?'

'People make some awful noises in these…circumstances. I prefer the sound of music.'

'What is this – some kind of torture routine?'

'Chaz, you upset some people. Some very serious people. Now you have to give them what they want.'

'Look. I'm not fucking James Bond. What do they want?'

Blondie continued to pace. She played with her cigarette, like in some old black and white movie. The room was cold. Silence seemed to make it colder.

'So,' said Chaz, 'where are they?'

'Keep your pants on,' she winked.

Chaz couldn't believe it. Blondie didn't give a damn! She just kept walking around the room, like she was at a medical centre waiting to see the doctor, or the dentist, or a plumber, or – whatever. How did someone get that frosty?

The door opened again. Two men walked in. Steady. Deliberate. Eastern European types. Blondie tensed and left the room.

***

A solitary blonde locked eyes with Sam as he scanned the bar for any sign of his CFO. She was mouthing the words to a Vance Joy song playing in the background and playing with her drink. He'd noticed her looking at him before, when she still had another man's company, but now she seemed to be alone. Sam quickly looked elsewhere.

'Where are you Chaz...'

He said he'd be at the pub by seven, and it was now past eight. Sam checked his mobile again. He wasn't one to assume the worst, but it was becoming increasingly difficult to remain positive. He phoned Zoe Barnes, his business partner. The call went straight to voicemail.

'Great.' Sam finished the soft drink he'd ordered fifteen minutes ago. He was deciding whether to leave or order something stronger when the phone rattled:

WE HAVE BAILLEY

A thousand thoughts ran through Sam's head, but there was no time for any of them. The Clock Hotel was not the place for him to be, he knew that much. He raced downstairs and leapt into his car. He drove past the office, and a police station he probably should have stopped at, straight home to his cottage in Bondi.

The front door was open, as if Lauren were hurrying him inside. After leaving the car a little crooked on their driveway, Sam tolerated an enthusiastic greeting from their winsome black Labrador. 'Hi, Rax,' he said. 'Smells good out here, doesn't it?'

The rain had receded, leaving the musky fragrance of apricot-yellow roses floating in the air. Sam thought back to that first afternoon after their move, after all the boxes were unpacked and they'd drunk their only bottle of wine, digging up plots for two dozen roses with only a serving spoon from the kitchen, Lauren laughing and smiling at him all the while. When Sam walked inside, he was reluctant to close the door behind him.

'Hi, darling!' called Lauren from the kitchen. 'By the way, I think you're amazing.'

Sam mumbled softly, 'You might not think that when…'

He walked over to the dining table and sat down as she came to meet him. 'I've got to…' He looked up. 'There's something I've got to tell you.'

Lauren's face normally had the freshness of a model in a Myer catalogue, but now it was morphing into dread. 'What's wrong?'

'You remember Chaz Bailley?'

'Your finance guy?'

'He's missing.'

'What do you mean, *missing?*'

It was strange, but Lauren almost looked relieved to ask after Chaz, as if she'd been in fear of hearing something worse. 'Well…' Sam said. He thought about all those TV dramas they'd been watching together, how the stress was always short-lived and things would all resolve by the end of each episode. Should he tell Lauren how bad it was, how deep his own fears fell for Chaz? 'He's disappeared.'

'That clears things up,' she said sarcastically. She touched his nose and disappeared into the kitchen, calling out from there, 'You sound like you could use a drink.'

Sam stared wistfully at the partition while he waited for her to return. She was like a detective, seducing her hesitant witness into spitting out whatever he was hiding by sliding a glass of white wine into his hand.

'You look pale,' she said. He gazed at his wife in her floral-print dress, her head tilted to one side, hair falling around her shoulders. 'What do you think has happened?'

Sam couldn't recall how much he'd told Lauren about his conversations with Chaz and Zoe over the last few days. She knew most of what was going on, but nobody shares everything, do they?

Sam's mother had said there are two types of people in this world: those who sweep uncomfortable truths under the carpet and those who like to give them a good airing. Lauren always denied it but, just like her parents before her, she did the odd bit of sweeping. It was not driven by ill intent; rather, it was to avoid confrontation. Sam, on the other hand, liked to get everything out in the open.

'Zoe reckons…'

Lauren gave him her furrowed brow look. 'Reckons what? You're scaring me!'

Sam retrieved the mobile from his pocket but held off showing Lauren the text, telling her instead that, 'Zoe thinks someone from YRG wants Chaz – out of the picture.'

'Someone from America?'

Sam nodded.

'But why?'

'He wouldn't stop asking questions,' Sam explained. 'The deal seemed too good to be true – because it was.'

'The deal to buy the company?'

'That'd be the one.'

'To die for,' she said quietly. 'I remember you saying that.'

'Unfortunate figure of speech.'

Lauren shook her head, though Sam was pretty sure she realised this was not a problem one could just shake off. 'So, what now?'

Sam stood up and put his arms around her. 'I'm sorry.'

She pulled back from him. 'Don't be. It's not your fault.' He watched her certainty soften into hope the longer they stood there. 'Is it, Sam?'

Chapter 2

Three weeks earlier

Zoe Barnes' look was not exactly what Sam would classify as 'cool' or 'in' fashion. Zoe had once described getting herself dressed as a process of picking out shapes and colours that wouldn't suddenly disappear when she moved; her body never seemed to fit into them anyway. She walked strangely, wore thick-rimmed glasses, smiled rarely, and always smelled clean, like a bar of non-scented soap. But Zoe could write dazzling copy, probably backwards and in her sleep, with that insight into a stranger's soul that broached the paranormal.

'Don't look for a pun in an elevator,' she said, totally deadpan.

Sam foolishly looked around the elevator for clues before asking, 'Why not?'

'It'll let you down.'

Sam laughed despite the appalling joke. 'I thought puns were on the banned list for copywriters.'

'If you've got a banned list, I want to be on it,' Zoe said, paraphrasing Billy Bragg.

The sight of the security camera staring down at Sam made him self-conscious. He'd made no effort to dress up, thinking he was too cool to care, like Zoe, one of the quirky creatives, but now he suddenly regretted it. He wasn't cool like Zoe. He was the boss.

'You all good, Sam?' asked Zoe. 'You're glaring at yourself in the doors.'

'Just mentally preparing for this thing.'

Zoe raised her eyebrows above those thick-rimmed glasses. 'Oh? Are you planning one of your legendary Sam-Pride-speeches, maybe something about the Romans and their baths, you know, something to really get the party swinging?'

Sam smiled and said, 'Something like that.'

The doors opened. The thumping bass track was beating at a similar rate to his heart. He told himself to relax. The May breeze was surprisingly warm, so he brushed off his dress-code embarrassment.

The scene was impressive; the sun was yet to set in the west and the pool was a glistening pale blue. TBA occupied the first four floors of the Crown Street building and, on a rotational basis with the other tenants, all TBA staff had access to the rooftop with uninterrupted views of the city skyline. Tonight, it was all theirs and the TBA 'fun force' had gone to a lot of trouble to dress it up. The theme was fantasy.

Zoe, with her un-styled light brown hair skewed severely to one side, looked out of sorts. She wobbled a little while asking Sam, 'How many people are going to wind up in the pool tonight?'

Sam suspected Zoe had got a drink or two in before the event. He said, 'So long as I'm gone by the time the clients are drowning.'

A topless rainbow-coloured waiter who might have stepped off a float in the Gay and Lesbian Mardi Gras offered Sam and Zoe a blue cocktail that matched the water in the pool.

'They kind of look like those cheap shots we had at the Hollywood the day we started TBA,' said Zoe. 'No time to be churlish,' she added, taking a big gulp of hers.

'Remarkably sweet,' Sam said.

'Kind of you to say so,' quipped Zoe.

Sam and Zoe walked over to the area where a wide range of potted cacti were gathered, taking a seat on a padded white lounge. They were joined within a few minutes by Chaz, the agency's Chief Financial Officer. He was wearing sunglasses and a sharp black suit, bearing no resemblance to the stereotypical CFO.

'I see you're pacing yourself,' Chaz said, noting the lack of progress Sam had made with his cocktail.

'Was that your first or fifth?' Sam asked, glaring at Chaz's empty glass. 'When are the clients arriving?'

A young account exec named Kitty Zhang, dressed as the DC Comics' Avery Ho with a purple streak through the middle of her hair, was floating within touching distance of Chaz. She was flirting with him, and Sam worried about how Chaz might respond.

Chaz was lean and hard, with dark Latino looks and an infectious smile that popped out of nowhere. But behind the smile and those big almond eyes was a hint of loneliness. Maybe that's what the girls went for. Either way, he was a bit of a walking HR disaster and Sam hated playing the role of policeman around him. He was tempted to tell Chaz to keep his hands in his pockets but noticed Jenny Graham approaching from the pool area and swiftly finished his drink instead.

Jenny was an exceedingly confident thirty-three-year-old General Manager from TBA's Melbourne office, and one of the few hardcore desk jockeys with enough charisma to make their form-fitting superhero costume look like a piece from Atoir.

'I know you're a superhero,' said Sam, 'but I'm not sure…'

'Captain Marvel,' she said, giving Sam a quick hug. 'But everyone thinks I'm Wonder Woman.' She noticed Chaz looking at her sideways and said, 'You're looking rather sharp, Mr Bailley.'

'I'd like to think so,' he said.

'No, really,' she assured him. 'A suit, strangely enough, suits you.'

'And you look less pale than most Melbournians,' said Chaz.

'My tan's fake. Yours is real. Where have you been?'

'Port Douglas. Three days.'

'Lucky you!'

While those two bantered effortlessly, Sam's thoughts drifted to his impending speech. He hadn't prepared anything, and that might have scared him a few years ago, but now it only felt like a mild indolence. In an environment like this, surrounded by all his staff, and with one blue cocktail in his bloodstream, he felt as comfortable as a dolphin in the Palm Beach surf. The question in these situations was always how much of the truth should he hold back?

It was only six years after starting the agency that they'd been given an offer they couldn't refuse. Sam was conscious of the way agency valuations were typically done, high projections extracted from ideal to perfect conditions, but the numbers for TBA still threw him. Sam thought they'd only consider selling after ten years, but that was before Uri Weissman had joined him for coffee.

Uri was just another finance man from one of the big holding companies, and it was normal for a guy like Uri to poke his nose into a successful start-up like TBA. Those companies didn't get to where they were without keeping an eye on who was climbing up the ranks, and who was falling to their deaths, but Uri was something different. He was relentless. He'd started flagging Sam down whenever he'd step out of the office; he was bright enough to keep away from Chaz in the beginning. It all started with a coffee, but then it was lunch and numbers the next day. Uri was always sure to praise Sam's ingenuity, his accomplishments, his 'vision'. At first, Sam had to ask himself if he was just entertaining the guy because he enjoyed the flattery; he'd worked so hard, and he liked hearing someone tell him it wasn't all a waste.

Sam pulled Chaz to one side to make sure nobody else could hear what he was about to say. 'Do you remember that first meeting with YRG?'

'Uri Weissman?'

'I still can't believe it.'

'Seventy-four million,' whispered Chaz. 'And you kept a straight face.'

'I just kept thinking about those enormous houses on the waterfront owned by rock stars, bank CEOs...'

'Crime bosses,' added Chaz.

'My mother once told me how extravagant I was, buying a ready-to-eat pasta meal from an Italian deli when I could have bought ingredients from a supermarket for half the price.'

'And right she was.'

Their buyer was the world's second largest communications company. Their CFO hadn't had their books open for more than twenty-four hours before offering ten per cent up front and the rest over five years. After all the contracts were signed, 3.7 million dollars landed in Sam and Lauren's joint account. That was three weeks ago. Sam had already paid off the mortgage, and Lauren was looking at investment properties. Not because she ever desired to own real estate, but rather because she thought it was the thing for young, sensible, married millionaires to do. Their financial adviser agreed.

'You ready?' asked Chaz.

Sam nodded.

Chaz started gathering people around, asking the wait staff to help him out. When they weren't moving fast enough, he began barking orders. 'Hey, mate. Put the drinks down. Please. Tell them they've got thirty seconds to get their arses over to the bar area or they're fired. They'll move. I know these people.'

Sam walked over to a live microphone beside the bar, partly relieved to find their clients hadn't yet arrived. He didn't much like the optics of passing around money in front of them; it could be interpreted as a form of boasting, as if they paid too much for the work they received. It was better to do this part without them. Once YRG were on the scene, the evening needed to be all about them.

'Well, hello,' he began, looking out over a sea of familiar faces. 'I'm sure you were all anticipating, certainly not dreading, one of my classic speeches.' A few of them laughed. Some playfully jeered and raised their glasses. Sam caught Zoe watching him from between

Chaz and Kitty and said, 'Maybe something incredibly inspiring, and motivating, and symbolic, like the time I spoke about the way Romans used to build bathhouses. Wasn't that a gem?' He had them all laughing along now; he'd even gotten a short smile out of Zoe. 'You're probably expecting me to tell you how great you all are, like I usually do. But, tonight, we have something else in mind, something a little more like marble. First, though, I'd like to say a few things about the company itself.'

Sam paused and tried to collect them all. Those expectant faces. Keen. Hungry for knowledge. Hungry for advancement. He noticed Brie, the receptionist, looking up at him with the same bright smile she wore every day. She'd been in the job for just under six months and seemed happy with it. There had been a moment at an office function a couple of months earlier when Brie's hand had brushed against him in a way that seemed mildly sexual, but he couldn't be sure. He looked down at the mic and continued.

'You all know YRG. They're huge, they're in the trade press almost every day. They're one of only a few companies in the comms business that can forge a new direction for the industry. Chekhov said, "If you cry 'forward', you must without fail make plain in what direction to go". I think we know where we are headed – in the same direction as YRG. It's one built on looking to the future. Embracing new technology, not fighting against it. Thinking like a start-up, not a has-been.'

Sam's audience had grown studious. The more he spoke about YRG, the less they moved and muttered among themselves. He understood what they were feeling, the uncertainty that was bleeding into their trust. They needed to know what was in it for them. He liked that they were focused, maybe even concerned. They'd earned their good news. They'd worked hard for it.

'By partnering with them, we are giving each and every one of you a greater chance at promotion. A greater chance to explore new opportunities, both here and abroad. YRG offers us connectedness. It gives us arms around the world, the sort of global relationships with clients that we couldn't otherwise achieve on our own.'

Sam plucked the mic out of its stand and started walking back and forth in front of them as he got into his flow. He could see the runway now, where he wanted to land them.

'Obviously, there's something in this deal for us. And for TBA. There's a lot of somethings,' he said suggestively. 'But what about them? What about YRG? What are they looking for?'

'They want Sam Pride,' someone shouted.

Sam chuckled as his colleagues politely laughed. 'Not quite,' he said, turning to slowly pace again, 'but he's almost right, he's almost there. I thought, sure, they want us because we won a stack of awards at Cannes last year.' A few cheered and Sam gave them a smile. 'Or they want us because we have one of the highest profit margins in the sector.' They cheered louder. 'I thought, maybe they just want us because, hell, they're rich and they want to be richer. But they told me – and I believe them – that more than anything they want you.' Sam paused to let the point sink in. 'You,' he repeated. 'Every single one of you. Because you're not the same as the people working for the next agency. You're different. You're unique. You are – extraordinary.' He knew it sounded like a cliché, but it was true.

'Really,' he said for the doubters. 'We knew that when we hired you. And the reason you're still here is because you never fail to show it. We have the best agency team in the country. We don't just have a creative department, or a planning department, with one or two stars. We've got the most innovative team of creative thinkers in the Asia-Pacific. You guys are – there's no other word for it – brilliant!' They erupted with cheer. Chaz handed Sam a glass of champagne. He raised it high up in the air, and as the audience raised theirs back, he shouted, 'You are my family, and I fucking love you!'

Chaz grabbed the microphone out of his hand and yelled, 'Now, this one's for Sam!' He skulled a shot of vodka. The audience shouted back, 'For Sam!', and followed suit with their own drinks.

It was the perfect note on which to initiate the clunky process of inviting each of them up to receive their envelopes. At first, people didn't know what to make of what was inside, but, once a few more envelopes had been opened, squeals of excitement began ringing out; it was mayhem. Halfway through the kisses and handshakes, people started calling for extra shots from the bar.

'Remember, tonight is also about our clients,' Sam called out, but to no avail. He didn't have the microphone anymore and, with a cheque for forty thousand dollars in hand, everyone already knew exactly what tonight was about.

At eight, Sam had greeted the clients right out of the rooftop elevator and walked with them to the poolside, only to witness a white-laced bra fly over everyone's head. It was a fair warning, almost like a shot fired across the bow of propriety itself, but there was little Sam could do to turn the ship about now. By nine, half the crowd were either dancing or falling into the pool. There were no lifeguards on hand, no doctors or nurses, just a bunch of giggling drunks clinging to each other one moment and thrashing about the next.

After an hour of trying to appease the new clients, only to see them fall into the alcohol fuelled degradation along with most everyone else, Sam looked for his own escape from the noise. He took a newly filled glass of wine over to an empty-looking booth on the far end of the rooftop, only to have Ted Lansing, better known as Little Ted, approach him for an intimate chat.

'Mate...' started Ted. Sam waited. The two-metre-tall man with the wide-eyed gaze was not one to be rushed.

'Mate, I've just got to say, I think what you and Zoe have done is so impressive. I mean, you know, you created something from nothing. And now look at you. I don't know how much you got, and I don't expect you to tell me, but...'

'Ted, I suspect it will all be in the public domain before long.'

'Yeah, of course. Anyway, I just wanted to say, well done.' Ted raised his glass.

'You know,' said Sam, 'I was determined not to go into advertising as a teenager.'

'Your dad?'

'Yes. He always said the stress and long hours made it a lousy career.'

'And you managed to avoid it for how long?'

'Eighty days,' said Sam. 'The time it took to complete basic army recruit training out at Kapooka. I don't know why I thought the army would be good for me.'

'It wasn't because of your old school mate...'

'It certainly was, you bastard. When you told me you were going to do it, I stupidly jumped on the band wagon.'

'And lasted less than three months.'

'Enough time to hear that siren calling from *Adland*.'

'Speaking of drowned men,' said Little Ted, giving a subtle nod to someone over Sam's shoulder. It was some stocky young fellow that Sam had never been formally introduced to, probably from the Melbourne office. He was barely keeping himself upright as he staggered toward them both.

'Mind if I say something?' he slurred.

'Not at all,' said Sam.

'Thanks for the cash,' the guy said, turning his gaze to the half-consumed bottle of craft beer he was holding, like it was a beacon of truth.

'My pleasure,' said Sam.

'No, I mean, really!' He looked back up from his bottle. 'The way you shared all the money around so – so evenly.'

'Okay,' said Sam. He knew where this was going.

'So, you and Zoe got forty thousand out of the deal, same as the rest of us. Right?'

Sam stood up. 'Whatever it is you want to say, just spit it out.'

'I know I could get fired for… I don't care. You're full of shit. All due respect but, you are. You act like you're being so, so generous.' He threw his hands up in the air. 'You give us crumbs. You probably get fucking millions. We – we're the ones who actually – we do the work. We do the real work, and all we get is crumbs. You piece of—'

Little Ted had stood up, quickly and quietly, as if a switch had been flicked. The stocky fellow appeared to freeze, seemingly unable to finish his thought. His eyes drifted down to his beer bottle and back up to Little Ted. He looked like he'd found himself in a big mistake and quickly turned around to stagger off.

'Forget about it, Sam,' said Little Ted. 'Every other person here is super appreciative of what you and Zoe have done.' Sam wanted to sink back into the booth, but something about that fellow had gotten under his skin. He thanked Little Ted and told him he'd expected that reaction, maybe even feared it a little, especially from his own TBA staff. He knew he wasn't in the wrong for making a lot of money, and he'd prepared himself to face scrutiny, but it still hurt. 'Ignore him,' said Little Ted.

Easier said than done, thought Sam. 'I want people to be happy. That guy isn't. He's just been given forty grand, and he's angry.'

'Forty suits me just fine.'

'Thank goodness for you, Ted.' Sam hoped he'd be able to give his old friend, and all the other decent staff, a lot more cash down the track, as well as the best possible environment in which to work. 'You deserve more than that prick, that's for sure.'

Little Ted waved him off. 'Ahh, stop it. I don't deserve nothin'.'

Sam noticed a senior bank client named Felicity Barton standing by the pool. She appeared to be chatting with a mid-level copywriter that looked like Jackie, who might just as easily have been Jessie or Jenny, or even Lizzy, all sub-optimal options when Zoe was just a few meters away. 'Talk again soon, Ted,' he quickly said.

'Sure, buddy.'

Sam walked over to Felicity, catching Jackie in the tail-end of a tailspin.

'—and that's why I feel like we're just not being brave enough, you know, to push the right kind of campaign.'

'Felicity,' interrupted Sam with a gracious smile, 'I do hope you'll be leaving here tonight with a newfound respect for our award-winning writers, if not their passion and diplomacy.'

'Ah, Sam,' she said. 'No, no, Jackie is right. We do need to be braver. I'm happy to be told that. I completely agree.'

Phew, thought Sam. After giving his thoughts and talking up both ladies to each other, he politely retreated from the conversation, only to imagine a hundred similar conversations taking place around him, maybe a thousand by the night's end, all of them a new role of the vodka dice with otherwise happy clients.

'You okay?' asked Zoe, finding Sam by the rooftop fence. 'Getting some fresh air?'

He nodded. 'There's a nice breeze rolling in.'

'What about my first question?'

'Oh, that one,' said Sam reluctantly. 'Sure. Party seems to be going pretty well and I'm—' Sam felt an elbow in his back. It was only a gentle bump but enough for him to turn around. The culprit turned out to be Kitty, the account exec with the purple hair who'd been hanging around Chaz.

'I'm sorry,' she said.

'Don't worry about it,' Sam replied. 'No drinks spilled. All good.'

Kitty gave Zoe a surprisingly stern look. 'Can I talk to you?'

'Of course,' said Zoe, her voice calm. 'What is it?'

'I'd rather… Could we speak downstairs? In private?'

Sam didn't say anything, only exchanging a mildly perplexed look with Zoe before she'd turned to leave with Kitty. He wondered if Chaz might have done something. But Kitty still looked as impeccably dressed as she did when the party began. Maybe it was something verbal, or maybe it was drugs, or maybe it was about the money.

Sam pressed his temple up against the safety glass and stared down at the street below.

What would someone do if they had a concern about their forty thousand dollars? Sam figured they'd talk to Chaz. But if Chaz had already taken his shot? They'd probably talk to Zoe.

He started to hope it was about the money. He could fix that.

'Downstairs, as in, somewhere completely confidential?' asked Zoe.

Kitty nodded and followed her into the lift. 'Yes. If that's okay with you?'

'Of course,' said Zoe, pressing for the third floor. The silver doors closed. She saw Kitty standing directly behind her in their reflection. 'We can use the meeting room near my desk. That'll be completely empty right now.' She turned to Kitty. 'Does that sound—'

Kitty lunged forward, pressing Zoe up against the doors and reaching for a kiss. Zoe instinctively raised her hands as a defence, pushing back to try and create immediate distance, but Kitty's hands were so active over her body that fighting against them started to feel like a wrestling match.

'I've wanted this so much,' breathed Kitty. 'The way you've looked at me.'

'Wait…' Zoe tried to turn herself away, feeling Kitty's lips graze up over the side of her neck. 'Kitty – stop.'

'Come on, Zoe. Miss Creative Director.'

Zoe felt Kitty's hand slide between her thighs. 'You've been driving me crazy all night.'

'Stop! Stop!' The lift doors opened behind Zoe. She fell away, pushing Kitty back into the elevator. 'Kitty,' she said, quietly this time, her hands still high and already shaking with adrenaline. 'What are you doing?'

Kitty wiped at the corner of her mouth where the lipstick was slightly smudged from Zoe's push; she'd done it incidentally while getting away. She watched Kitty's posture change as she began to fix her hair. She'd straightened herself up and was staring coldly at Zoe as the lift began to close. 'I think I'll go back up to the party,' she said, stabbing at the console and folding her arms. 'That was not cool, Zoe.'

The doors pressed together. Zoe saw herself in their silvery reflection and steadily lowered her guard. She stared blankly at herself for a moment before twisting around and asking the empty third floor foyer, 'What just happened?'

***

Chaz didn't realize he'd stopped listening to a junior staffer until it was too late to make any sense of their conversation. 'That's cool,' he said. He was really watching Little Ted, wondering what he was doing lounging out like a silverback gorilla on one of the white sofas, alone, without a drink or a phone in his hand. Chaz turned back to the staffer. 'I mean the way you put it, I never thought about it like that, but that's cool.'

'So, you *would* like to grab another drink, or…'

'Oh. No. I'm okay.' Chaz shifted his weight to the other leg, looking back over at Little Ted while cautiously sipping from his drink. 'This one's still going.' He sensed something short and sweet-smelling brush up beside him and rolled his eyes. 'No, really, I better finish my drink before—'

'Who hired that guy?' Kitty asked.

'Oh-hi-ho,' he blurted. 'I mean, hi, Kitty. Who do you mean?' Chaz felt like he'd gotten away with calling Kitty a Ho, as in the Avery Ho character from DC, but he wasn't entirely certain. 'Do you mean Ted?'

'Yeah. He's such a downer,' she said.

'Sam hired him,' said Chaz, 'almost as soon as he got out of jail. Nobody else would have touched the poor bugger.'

'For good reason,' she said. 'Who hires an ex-con to work in an ad agency?'

'Who wouldn't?' Chaz had said it like it was the obvious thing to do, that anybody with any sense of loyalty would hire their friend out of jail. But Kitty just rolled her shoulders and slowly shook her head. 'He's as committed as they come. Sam says he was much more upbeat when he was younger but that the stint behind bars changed him. Made him a lot more subdued.'

'Subdued, hey? He's certainly big.'

'And tough. Used to be a mixed martial arts fighter. Broke a guy's jaw once. But that was before.'

'What did he go to jail for?' asked Kitty, tilting her head to one side. 'Breaking someone's jaw?'

'He was working as a driver for a crook named Marco Bianchi.'

'Bianchi? The stockbroker?'

'Yeah. Someone told me he was a crook but… Hey, you have a scratch on your neck.' Kitty straightened up, looking at Chaz while she reached for her neck. 'Is that from tonight?'

'It's nothing,' she said. 'So, what did Ted do to land himself in prison?'

'Assault. A bad one. Left a guy unconscious with loads of broken bones. That's what Ted told me, although Sam's version is slightly different. Either way, I don't think he did it. Not sure why he took the fall. There were no witnesses. The victim didn't see what happened. He was hit from behind. But, for some reason, Little Ted went down for it. He was seen drinking at a nearby pub right after the attack. The victim was a supposed threat to Bianchi. And I guess—'

'Seems too miserable and lethargic to beat anyone up these days,' said Kitty, cutting him off. 'I can't imagine any of our clients liking the guy.'

'You're partially right,' admitted Chaz. 'Some clients find him sullen. But to those who are happy with a hard-working and diligent account manager, he's just the thing. Of course, some people assume he'd be axed if it wasn't for his friendship with Sam.'

'Fair assumption, no?'

'Come on, Kitty. Give the guy a chance.'

'Enough of him,' she declared. 'How about a swim!'

Chapter 3

Alliance Security was the name of a Chicago-based firm owned and controlled by two men, Viktor Tomic and Robert Miller. They liked to call themselves 'Ambassadors of Protection'. From day one, both Viktor and Robert knew it made sense for Robert to be the face of the firm. He was a fit thirty-eight years old, had been a successful athlete and scholar at one of the most prestigious high schools in Illinois, had a law degree from the University of Chicago, had never done drugs, and he rarely drank alcohol. He had great contacts and instilled trust in everyone he met.

But that alone would not have been enough to make the firm super profits. From a business point of view, Robert lacked aggression and hated risk. He liked good clean clients and, as Viktor occasionally reminded him, he couldn't negotiate his way out of a paper bag.

'Viktor to the rescue,' the older partner would say. His was not such a handsome face, and his body was more like a large boulder that had fallen off the side of a mountain than the handiwork of a Renaissance sculptor. Born in Dubrovnik, he had moved with his family to the States when he was in pre-school. He was now forty-one, though a history of hard drinking made him look a decade older. His high school had been free to attend, which was lucky because nobody in their right mind would have paid to go there, and he'd never set foot inside a university. He came from what he fondly called 'the school of brutally hard knocks' and loved taking on the kind of clients Robert didn't want to know about.

Viktor had once been asked by Robert as to where he 'drew the line', to which Viktor replied, 'What line?' For Viktor, there were no boundaries, no lines not to be crossed. Business was war, and he was happy to be a soldier. What mattered was whose side you were on. If you were a large client like YRG, then Viktor was on your side.

An hour had passed since Robert watched Viktor step into the lift from where he'd be heading to the garage and his Porsche 911 Speedster. It was late. Robert was the only employee left in the building. He didn't normally go near any of Viktor's cases and wouldn't have now were it not for one throwaway comment Viktor had made earlier that day.

Viktor had said that he had a feeling the Australian case could get messy. *Messy*. As far as Robert was concerned, that was a euphemism for operating on the wrong side of the ethical (and perhaps legal) line. It'd struck Robert as odd because the client was one of the biggest communications companies in the world, and all Alliance was doing was giving security advice on the purchase of a small ad agency. There was nothing untoward about the takeover, no reason to take unnecessary risks. Why should anything get messy in sunny Sydney? It wasn't like they were operating in a cartel-controlled region of Mexico or Colombia. They were working for a publicly listed company with a reputation for transparency and integrity.

Robert unlocked the door to his partner's office and quickly surveyed the spacious room. No sign of hidden cameras. No sign of any changes since he'd been in the room two days earlier for a chat. He felt anxious because he knew Viktor would be furious if he thought Robert was snooping. But he was a fifty per cent owner of the company, so he had every right to know what was going on within it.

The first two desk drawers he checked contained nothing of interest. However, the bottom one was locked. Robert had no idea where the key might be and considered giving up, but his curiosity got the better of him. He went to the kitchen and fetched a knife. Despite knowing there was nobody else around, Robert kept the blade concealed within his pocket until he reached the desk.

The wood splintered when he forced the drawer open. He tried to prod it back into shape, praying that it was not something Viktor would notice. But, of course, Viktor *would* notice, because Robert could not lock the frigging thing up again once he was finished; there were others before Robert that Viktor should suspect of the misdemeanour.

Sure enough, inside the drawer sat the YRG files neatly bundled into two folders. Robert opened the dossier on Chaz Bailley, CFO of The Bold Agency. It must have been two centimetres thick, crammed full of data, written in a small font, with images of Bailley from when he was a teenager through to very recent photos taken in offices and restaurants. It had been prepared by Darius Pisula, Viktor's go-to researcher. Viktor obviously hadn't felt he could entrust the work to a local, despite Alliance having an affiliation with a security network that covered Australia and the region. Viktor wanted to keep it close.

In the early days, Viktor would have spoken to Robert before sending an Alliance staffer abroad on a job like this. Sometimes Robert missed the days when the business felt like more of a partnership. He and Viktor were chalk and cheese, but they had once got on very well. They had fun. Now it was just work.

Robert read that Chaz Bailley studied accounting at the University of New South Wales before going on to do a master's at Monash in Melbourne. He'd worked for Price Waterhouse for seven years, then moved to Ogilvy for his first stint in advertising. No wife, no kids, no long-term girlfriend, though plenty of short-term ones. He'd smoked marijuana, occasionally, in his late teens and early twenties, and was thought to have had ecstasy at an industry function last Christmas. He drank alcohol four to five times per week, often to excess. He owed the Australian Tax Office thirty thousand dollars but had never missed a repayment. He had forty thousand dollars' worth of blue-chip shares, eighteen thousand in a Westpac trading account, owned an apartment in Balmain (negatively geared with a nine hundred thousand dollar mortgage), which was rented out to a newly married English couple, and he himself rented a two-bedroom terrace in Paddington, less than a fifteen minute walk from the office.

Robert lingered on a photograph of Bailley at a fine-dining restaurant with a tall, well-dressed woman, probably in her mid-twenties. She was laughing at something. Bailley the comedian? There were two more photos in the file where Bailley appeared to entertain attractive women. Bailley the womaniser?

Another image showed him sitting in an English-style pub, drinking beer with a bespectacled, brown-haired woman who looked tired and possibly hungover. No-one was laughing. The woman's head was circled in yellow marker pen, and the name Zoe Barnes was written beside it.

Robert moved to Sam Pride's file. Perhaps Sam was the man Viktor was concerned about, the reason he'd sent Darius to Sydney. The file was of a similar thickness to that of Bailley. Three pages in, Robert's impression was that Pride would not be a threat to anyone: dux of his school, distinction grades at university, brief stint in the army before advertising, thirty-four years old, just the one marriage to a banking executive named Lauren Pride, née Waters, owns a three-bedroom house in the affluent suburb of Bondi, no children, no religious affiliations, no criminal record, no points lost on driver's licence. This guy was as straight as an arrow. From a YRG point of view, he sounded like a dream leader for their newly acquired business. Nothing *messy* here. Why was Viktor so concerned?

A sharp noise startled Robert. He quickly put away the files and moved away from his partner's desk. It was the cleaners.

'Oh, I'm sorry,' said the older of the two women who had suddenly appeared. 'You're still…'

'No, please,' said Robert. 'I'm just finishing up.'

Chapter 4

'Want to pop out for a coffee?' asked Chaz.

Sam shrugged. 'Sure.'

'Maybe a bacon and egg roll, too?' Chaz added, clearly suffering from a hangover.

Sam had left the party when it was still going strong, and he knew Chaz would be able to give him a reasonable debrief. They took a table in the corner of Fred's Café in Crown Street, their usual spot, and were served by Ginny, a red-headed teen who attended acting classes when not suffering for her art.

'You boys don't look too bad,' she said. 'Couple of the girls who came in earlier said the party was a big one.'

It was true that Chaz didn't look too bad, despite the excesses of last night. Sam suspected it was something to do with his olive complexion and the fact that, mentally, he refused to be beaten. Whether it was business competitors, alcohol, or lovers, Chaz was never the loser. This morning, he'd probably have jumped out of bed and said, *Fuck it! It's a new day. Here I come!*

On the other hand, Sam knew Ginny was lying about him. When he'd passed the bathroom mirror at 6.45am, he'd caught the pallor of a refrigerated corpse. And he'd left the party early! Chaz was better at the partying lifestyle; Sam could live with that – at least – after a double shot of decent coffee.

'You okay?' said Chaz. 'You don't look good.'

'Thanks for the insight, pal!' Sam shook his head and was glad when the drinks arrived. 'What time did you finish up?'

'About three, I guess. You?'

'Bit after midnight,' he said. 'Any goss?'

'Not really.'

'You get lucky?'

'Nah. But it was good fun.'

'People seemed to be enjoying themselves.'

'Forty grand a piece. That helps!'

'No doubt.'

Chaz called Ginny back over and asked for an egg and bacon roll. He looked at Sam. 'You want one?'

'Why not?' Sam noticed Jenny Graham from the Melbourne office sitting on the opposite side of the café with someone he didn't recognise.

'You talk to her last night?' asked Chaz.

'No more than, hello. Did you?'

'I did, actually. She had some interesting things to say about YRG.'

'Like what?'

'Like, *watch out*. She reckons they're ruthless bastards. Friend of hers sold their production company, Eastern, to YRG a few years back. Lots of sweet talk leading up to the deal. Then they seriously fucked her over.'

'Fucked her over how?'

'Apparently, they made promises they didn't keep. The extent to which they'd help with working capital, an agreement to buy the remainder of the company... Shit like that.'

'Hopefully our contract's airtight. Maybe theirs wasn't?'

'I don't know,' said Chaz. 'I just don't like it when I hear that kind of thing.'

Soon after their food arrived, Chaz leaned across the table to whisper, 'Something happen between Zoe and Kitty last night?'

'I don't think so. Why? What did you hear?'

'Just something Kitty said.'

'What?'

'She kind of implied that Zoe tried it on with her.'

'Are you kidding?' Sam said. 'For Christ's sake.'

'It might have happened in the lift,' smirked Chaz. 'I imagine Kitty's a good kisser.'

'Zoe wouldn't have kissed Kitty,' Sam said, more loudly than intended.

'Okay, take it easy. If Zoe says she didn't, she didn't.' Chaz drank some more coffee and then added, 'But Kitty *was* looking cute in that super-hero outfit.' A self-satisfied grin crept over his face.

'I think you deserve a punch for that,' Sam declared. 'And I'm seriously tempted.'

Chaz laughed and responded, 'I'm sure you are.'

***

Sam wanted to pick Lauren up and take her to Rushcutters Bay to buy their *first-ever* new car, but a last-minute pitch meeting was all it took to spoil the romance. By the time he'd finished at the office, there was only enough daylight left to meet her at the dealership in McLachlan Avenue. They drove Japanese cars that were over ten years old so, buying two new BMWs would be a big step up. They'd worked hard to get to this position. Lauren was superb at locking a large portion of her salary into a savings plan, and Sam had certainly put in the hours at work. So, it felt good. Selling the agency wasn't just about a paper profit. It meant they got to be like kids on Christmas Eve again, imagining – even obsessing over – what their presents might look like. Feel like. Smell like.

When Lauren stepped out of the Uber, Sam wasn't the only one who noticed. The clothes, the hair, the earrings, the make-up. She looked stunning, and she was immediately copping pervy glances from every salesman in the vicinity. But, when she first saw Sam, for just that brief moment, he thought she looked unsure of herself. He couldn't imagine why.

Forty-something Gareth, salt and pepper lick of hair and a neat goatee, was the man to show them around. He had a soft English accent and seemed less pushy than most salesmen. His job, as far as Sam could tell, was simply to reveal the truth. And the truth would set them (and their credit cards) free.

The 7 Series. 'Self-assured presence,' declared Gareth. 'And, of course, it's got the twin power turbo eight under the bonnet, so...'

They had no need for a car that big, unless they were about to become a family of four overnight, but Sam thought the features were outstanding. He touched the leather upholstery, first with his finger, then he laid his palm flat on it. 'Oh, my god,' he whispered. He looked up at Lauren. She seemed impressed, but not as much as him. He took a deep breath, sucking in the aroma. It smelled like money.

Sam remembered the foul odour of his mum's old Hyundai before she had to sell it. It smelled like dirty, wet washing had been left on the back seat. He was going to have to buy her a new car, too. She'd caught public transport for the last five or six years, but things would be different now, for all the family.

Lauren looked in the back. 'Big enough for Rax?'

Sam hadn't considered that. But the smell of their crazy black beast could be removed with a quick spray of air freshener – he hoped.

Sam and Lauren spent the next half hour test driving three different models. When they were done, Gareth asked them to sit down in the cafeteria and discuss the pros and cons. 'Take all the time you want,' he said. 'When you're ready, I'll just be over there.' He pointed to a spotless white desk with an open laptop on it about eight metres away.

In the end, Lauren decided on the 3 Series convertible. 'It felt so good to drive,' she told Sam. 'And how good will it be in the summer?'

'You don't want one of the bigger cars? A 5 Series, or a 7?'

'Not really, no,' she said. 'I think the 3 is perfect.'

Sam went completely mad and committed to the 7. In the back of his mind, he had considered the idea of a baby taking pride of place in the backseat.

Gareth offered to take them upstairs to meet with Darren, who could help them with the finance. 'You'll find he does a much better rate than the banks. In fact, the first twelve months will be at zero per cent.'

'We won't be needing any finance,' Sam explained.

'You won't get a better rate…'

'No, I don't think you understand. We'll pay cash.'

'For *both* cars?'

'That's right.'

Gareth's face lit up like a lottery winner. Sam filled in the paperwork and agreed to come back in two days for the cars. Then he and Lauren walked back down to McLachlan Avenue, where he offered to drive her into town.

'Don't be silly,' she said. 'I'll just get an Uber.'

'You sure? I don't mind.'

She nodded and kissed him. When she pulled back, she said, 'You know you didn't have to buy me that car.'

'I know,' he said. But he was left wondering what the distressed look on her face was about. Was it that she felt guilty about buying a new luxury vehicle, were they being too indulgent, or was there something else going on?

'I always thought you'd be successful,' she said, 'but I'd love you just as much if you didn't have a dime.'

'Darling, I'm glad to hear it. But I like the fact that I can buy you nice things, now.'

'I'm not complaining.'

'I think you're a more balanced person than me,' he said. 'Better able to cope with life's ups and downs.'

'Really?'

Sam saw that look again. An insecurity lurking behind that beautiful face? 'Is there something you're not telling me? You are happy, aren't you?'

'Of course I'm happy. You just bought me a brand-new car!'

***

Sam tried to get back to sleep, but he kept opening his eyes and looking over at Lauren. There was something so effortlessly beautiful about her, and yet she'd gone the extra mile – really dressing up – for their big moment at the dealership. He loved that she'd gone to the effort to celebrate with him in style. It wasn't exactly how he'd imagined it all, as such things never are, but Lauren didn't seem her usual, happy self. He knew when she was happy, and there were moments yesterday when that part of her seemed to change places with something else. Maybe it was the feeling of achieving something great. The chase being more thrilling than the kill. He remembered Chaz once saying to him, 'Mate, you've got to embrace the concept of blissful ignorance. No man ever understands what the fuck's going through his wife's mind. Don't try.' The insight of a proud bachelor.

Sam decided it was time to let it go and drive Rax up to Christison Park for some exercise. After a quick run, Sam did a few exercises on the outdoor machines, and then eased off with a brisk walk past the lighthouse towards South Head. Half-way to The Gap, he stopped and said to his four-legged friend, 'Had enough?'

Rax barked loudly in defiance.

'I don't care,' said Sam. 'One of us needs to earn a living!'

By the time Sam got back to the house, Lauren had made him a coffee. 'You didn't need to do that,' he said.

She kissed him gently. 'I know.' She was wearing nothing but her skimpy underwear. Seeing how he was looking at her, she proclaimed, 'I've got to get to work.'

They said farewell to Rax and were on their way. Unfortunately, the roads were busier than usual. Stuck behind an advertisement-soaked bus in the slow crawl up Old South Head, Lauren said, 'Did I tell you Simon Karim got a job at the bank? He's our data analyst.'

'Your childhood sweetheart?'

'It's true, I did have a crush on him.'

'Until you realised all those rich private school boys were pathetic.'

'You know your class warfare rhetoric doesn't ring true anymore? You're in the richest one per cent of the population now.'

The traffic began moving, and they closed in on the junction. 'I'll always be a working-class man at heart.'

'You've never been a working-class man. I don't think you even know the lyrics to the song!'

'Simon Karim. You and he didn't…?'

'How many times have you met him?' Lauren asked. 'Twice?'

'Something like that. Why?'

'You didn't notice anything? Anything that might preclude…?'

Sam laughed at his own lack of insight. 'You mean I might have been more his type than you?'

'You're quick!'

They sat in silence for a couple of minutes, soft rock playing on the radio. Then Lauren asked him, 'Do you feel proud of what you've achieved?'

Sam had no idea how they'd got from Simon Karim's sexuality to whatever goals he might have kicked at TBA. 'Why do you ask?'

'You should feel good about yourself. I hope your staff appreciate you.'

'The way you do?'

'I do, you know!'

'You just like your new BMW.'

'I mean it.'

Sam nodded and put his hand on her knee. 'We are a good team.'

When they'd arrived at the station, Sam winked and said, 'Say hello to Simon for me.'

'Sure,' said Lauren. 'I'll give him one of these from you.' She leaned across and gave Sam a slow and passionate kiss.

'Be gone!' he yelled.

Chapter 5

Chaz and Sam had a Zoom call scheduled with Margaret Whitfield, the Global Chief Executive of YRG. Sam had been impressed by her in their previous meetings. She was a smart, serious woman, not to be mistaken for a Margie or a Marg. It was nearly 3pm, so he popped around to Chaz's desk to make sure the CFO wasn't running late.

Chaz looked indignant. 'Call me what you like,' he said. 'Wild? Reckless? But never late.'

The two of them caught the lift to the level three conference room where a large TV screen was set up for the call.

'Know what country she's in?' Chaz asked.

'No idea,' Sam replied. He'd been told by someone who knew her well that Margaret was on an aeroplane at least half of the year. Today, she could have been in Tokyo or Moscow just as easily as her head office in Chicago. Prior to their first meeting, Sam had begun following her on LinkedIn. She was born in New Zealand but had spent most of her life in the UK. He remembered being struck by her surprisingly posh accent the first time they spoke.

Sam walked over to the windows and closed the shutters. He asked Chaz if he wanted some water. When he declined, Sam poured some for himself. He and Chaz both had their laptops open, ready to quote numbers, though Sam suspected Margaret would be doing almost all of the talking.

'Can you hear me?' Margaret asked. The Zoom frame showed the top half of her body. She had a large muscular frame and had once been an A-Grade tennis player. Even sitting down, Sam felt her gravitas.

'Yes, thanks, Margaret, all good from this end.'

'How's the surf, today?'

Margaret always tossed in a light-hearted quip early in their meetings. It was disarming. 'Closing out,' said Sam.

'Is that a good thing or a bad thing?'

'Oh, it's bad,' said Sam. 'But don't worry. Chaz and I will cope.'

Margaret had been central to the negotiations over the last couple of months and, from Sam's point of view, her character and integrity – she always seemed genuine – were crucial for the deal to go through.

He didn't feel like he knew the finance guys based in Chicago and London. Of course, they were involved, but Sam preferred to steer the dialogue towards Margaret wherever possible. She seemed more like an agency person. An operations person. The finance people were all white men in their fifties and sixties, obsessed by spreadsheets, while Margaret was forty, and she genuinely seemed to care about Sam's modest, Aussie start-up. He felt like he'd be able to talk to her if something went wrong after the deal was done. And, in this business, something almost always goes wrong – eventually.

'Where are you today?' asked Chaz.

'Paris.'

'Is it early there?'

'I always wake up early when I'm in Europe. Apart from Madrid. The people from the Spanish office don't eat until, well, you know what it's like. How was Thursday night's party?'

'I left early,' Sam explained, 'but the first half seemed to go pretty well.'

Chaz added, 'And I can confidently declare that the second half was better than the first.'

'Glad to hear it,' Margaret said. 'Now I'm going to cut to the chase. I'm not sure how much you know about the Pointer White Agency?'

Sam and Chaz looked at each other, wondering where this might be going. 'I know a little about sharks,' said Sam with a smile. It had always amused him that such an historically successful business shared its name with a predator so feared by most Australians. 'Roz Clayton's still the MD there, isn't she?'

'Yes, she is,' said Margaret.

Sam had seen Roz on quite a few occasions five years ago when she was leading the media planning for one of TBA's biggest clients. They changed media agencies, through no fault of Roz's (simply a new global alignment), and that was the end of their dialogue.

'Now, I'm a fan of Roz's,' continued Margaret, 'but she's having a tough time there right now. The numbers are not – what our friends in Chicago might have hoped for. We need to make a few changes.'

'Right,' said Chaz.

'One of those changes,' said Margaret, 'is a merger with TBA.' Her words hung in the air uncomfortably. Eventually, she continued by saying, 'I know this probably comes as a bit of a shock.'

'A shock?' said Chaz, in a mocking tone that Sam was very uncomfortable with.

'You're currently paying, what, 6.5 per cent of revenue in rent?'

'Yes,' said Chaz, 'but that's only because the owners of the building put the rent up nine per cent last year. It's locked in at the current level for the next three years, and with our rev going up, the rent-to-rev ratio will obviously come down.'

'I know it's not ideal,' said Margaret. 'But Chicago are very keen to make it work. You move into Angel Place, which is a great location in my opinion, and you'll both be down to around four per cent rent-to-rev. They also think there'll be some useful synergies.'

Oh, no, Sam thought to himself. That word. He didn't expect Margaret to use it but there it was. Not enough to use synergy the singular, it was always a more vacuous business cliché when used in plural form. Sam had seen plenty of mergers involving great 'synergies'. They rationalised great profits and even greater bonuses for senior management, but soon guaranteed the gutting of 'non-essentials'; human beings who would also witness their friends getting fired in a year's time when projections inevitably fell short.

'Have you been to Angel Place?' Margaret asked.

'Yes, we have,' said Sam quickly, depriving Chaz of the time to say something sarcastic.

As Margaret carried on about cost savings and a potentially stronger margin across the group, as well as new opportunities, Sam pondered whether selling his agency to a big global company had been a mistake. Margaret was not a bad person. The YRG deal meant he, Zoe, Chaz (despite him not having equity), the consulting firm that managed the logistics of the deal, and a few people from YRG would make lots of money (not compared to Elon Musk or Jeff Bezos but certainly by ordinary people's standards). Maybe Sam was motivated by greed? He didn't like to think so. Sure, he loved the idea of keeping his family safe from financial stress. But if he thought lots of staff were going to get sacked because of the deal, whether they were TBA employees or YRG staff from another agency (such as Pointer White), then he would *not* have gone through with it. He'd started the agency because he wanted to build something. To grow something, something from nothing. Not to diminish a company. Not to have people's futures disappear.

'Margaret, is this merger with Pointer White something we have a say over?' Sam straightened in his seat; Chaz had just asked the question he'd been hesitating to ask himself. While Margaret glanced to her left, as if there was someone else in her room, Chaz added,

'If we said we thought merging at this time was a bad idea, would that hold some weight?'

Sam thought he heard someone whispering over the call, a deeper voice, but he couldn't be certain. This time, Margaret kept her eyes forward. 'I'm not sure it would,' she said. 'It's not because you fellows wouldn't do perfectly well on your own. I'm sure you would. It's just that for YRG, there's a problem in Sydney that needs fixing. Pointer White. There's no basis on which to think their revenue is going to shoot up anytime soon, so they need to cut costs. This is the obvious solution. A path to greater profitability.'

Chaz's body language made it clear he wasn't happy. Sam was secretly glad his CFO was shaking his head and looking pissed off because it meant that he didn't have to himself. Sam had to remain positive in his dealings with Margaret. He'd just been given all that money, and he was trying to consider things from a YRG perspective, though, after the call, he was quick to let Chaz know how unhappy he was. 'It's disappointing. I'm just not sure there's anything much we can do about it.'

'There was no mention of timing,' said Chaz.

'Maybe we could try to delay it?'

'Delay it?'

'We could say we're on board. And that we're going to spend the next little while talking to Roz and Idham about how to best execute the plan.'

'Pretend to be going along with her?'

'Yeah. Why not?'

'You really think that would work?'

'It might give us a few weeks. Maybe even a month or two.'

'Screw that. We need to delay this thing for at least the next ten fucking years!' yelled Chaz, finally allowing himself a half-smile in Sam's direction. He might have got angry and loud from time to time but Sam thought it not in his nature to dwell on the negative.

'Did you get the sense there was someone else in the room?' Sam asked.

'Fuck yeah. And it's not the first time they've pulled that shit. They are a secretive bunch of arseholes. Remember that hook-up with Chicago and London a fortnight ago? There was someone on the line they weren't telling us about that time, too.'

Sam did remember. 'Someone with the power to pull a few strings,' he said.

***

A little after five, Sam decided to give his mum a quick call. She'd had a doctor's appointment in the morning, one where she'd be getting the results of her eye test.

'Everything okay?' Sam asked.

'Yes, yes, I'm fine,' she said.

'What's the diagnosis?'

'Umm…'

'Mum?'

'Do you want to pop in for a cuppa on your way home?'

'Sure,' Sam said. 'I can be there in an hour?'

'That would be lovely.'

Sam's mum lived in a small flat in Rose Bay. By the time he arrived, she'd had dinner and was settled in front of the TV, watching the nightly news. She turned off the volume and said, 'Your father never wanted you to go into advertising.'

'I know, Mum.'

'He always said you should do medicine or architecture or, you know…'

'Anything but what he'd done.'

'I miss him, you know?'

'And so do I, Mum.'

She got up from her seat in front of the TV and walked over to where Sam was sitting. She remained standing. 'What do you miss?'

'Lots. It would have been great to compare notes with him, hear how things have changed since his day. I sometimes imagine having conversations with him.'

'You can talk to me. I was an agency person, too!'

'I know you were. And I do talk to you.'

'Occasionally, you do.' She turned towards the window and looked out over the golf course.

'Mum, if you're ever lonely, you know…'

Sam's mum sat down again and finished her tea.

After a moment's silence she said, 'I saw Charlotte this morning.' The second she mentioned his little sister's name, Sam knew where the conversation was going. 'She had Edward with her. You know he's starting to talk now?'

'Yes, Mum. Lauren and I went around to Charlotte and Jacob's place two weeks ago.'

'Isn't little Edward a darling?'

'Yes, Mum. Just divine.'

'Have you and Lauren talked about…?'

'I've told you before. We want to have kids. It's just a matter of—'

'You can certainly afford it now.'

'Yes, we can,' Sam said calmly.

When he and Lauren first got married, his mum had been concerned about whether he was earning enough money to have a family. She didn't want Lauren to have as hard a time as she'd had.

'You do know about decreasing fertility rates and—'

'And ageing,' said Sam, nodding his head. 'Yes, mum, I do. But don't worry. Lauren and I will be okay. Now, tell me what the doctor said about your eye test.'

His mum looked at him like he was asking her to confess to a terrible crime. 'I've got wet AMD. Whatever that means.'

'Macular degeneration. I know a few people who have it.'

'You do?'

'Zoe's father. It's a chronic eye disorder. The macula's part of the retina.'

'The – what?'

'So long as they detect it early,' Sam explained, 'which they hopefully have in your case, then, with the latest treatments, the outcomes tend to be very good.'

She looked sceptical. 'You know they get paid off by the big pharmaceutical companies?'

'And your evidence for that is?'

'It's what I've heard.'

'Mum, if they break the law, they get fined and maybe even arrested. Worry about it when you see the execs in handcuffs.'

'Well, you wouldn't lie to me…'

'No, Mum, I wouldn't lie to you.'

Sam also tried not to lie to anyone in business. He suspected the same couldn't be said of all those he dealt with in the agency world.

***

Lauren was playing with Rax in the back garden.

'How was your day?' she asked.

'Not crash hot,' Sam confessed.

They went inside to the lounge room and Lauren poured Sam a glass of wine. Norah Jones was playing softly in the background. Lauren was wearing a perfume Sam liked – he thought it was the English Pear and Freesia one he'd given her for her last birthday – which made him think of the romantic dinner they'd had that night, and the fun they'd had afterwards.

'What happened?' Lauren asked.

'Margaret said she wanted us to merge with an agency called Pointer White.'

'I've heard of them. Media agency, aren't they?'

'That's right. Anyway, it came as one hell of a surprise. We've been talking to YRG for months about the sale and the path ahead for TBA, and there was never a mention of the possibility of us having to merge with another agency. I think it's a betrayal.'

'And you've always trusted Margaret.'

'That's why it was such a shock.'

'I guess she has people she has to answer to. Maybe she had no choice?'

'Maybe,' Sam conceded.

'What would it mean? In practice?'

'Top of the list, moving into the Pointer White offices in Angel Place.'

'Very different to Crown or Oxford Street.'

'That's for sure. I'm not keen to break it to the staff.'

'Can you fight it?'

'I suppose we could try. But they own us now.'

'But you're still the boss of TBA.'

'Yes, but I have to answer to Margaret now. I knew it'd be tough giving up control of the agency, but I didn't think it would start so soon. I don't know. Their words, what they actually said to us, suggested...' Sam was looking down at the table. He shook his head. 'I really expected the next couple of years to be – that I'd be kind of – left alone, so we wouldn't lose any of the culture that's made the business successful.'

'I bet this isn't the first time they've shafted an agency they bought,' said Lauren, her innate cynicism kicking in. She might have worked for a big bank herself but that had only assured Lauren that high-flying corporate execs wouldn't hesitate to tread on the little guys to get what they wanted.

'I'm sure it's not,' Sam said.

Chapter 6

It was Tuesday morning and most of the staff were at their desks or in meetings. The pervasive buzz of the office diminished when Sam closed the glass door to the small meeting room on the second floor. He wasn't in there to meet anyone; he just needed quiet time away from the troops. He exhaled deeply, flipped open his laptop, and began checking emails.

'Holy cow!' he said out loud. He nearly fell off his chair, unable to comprehend what he read. It was an email from Chaz to Margaret:

> Hi Margaret,
>
> Thanks for the zoom catch-up. I've just got to say – you probably gathered this from the conversation – that we're not exactly thrilled with the idea of merging with Pointer White. We don't want to be difficult, of course. You guys have been so great with the acquisition and everything. It's just that there hadn't been any mention of a thing like this being on the cards prior to yesterday. And given we've been speaking for some months about the future of TBA, and how keen you were to maintain the culture, how you believed in our leadership...
>
> Well, the suggestion came as a big shock. Anyway, to cut a long story short, we do not want to be part of any merger with PW – a very different sort of agency to ours (or yours, as it is now, but the one we built into what it is today). We think it's very important for TBA to remain a separate entity from PW and that, at least for the next few years, we stay in our current Crown Street premises. That's how we can deliver the revenue and profit numbers we promised you and the rest of the YRG team. We hope you understand our perspective.
>
> Many thanks,
> Chaz

Sam had barely finished reading that email when another came through; Chaz doing a follow-up:

> PS. I should probably mention that I spoke with finance at Pointer White. It's very clear they're in trouble. They didn't spell out all the details, but their P&L is obviously in bad shape and their cashflow is a disaster. I'm going to be frank with you here when I say my gut feeling was, merging with them could actually cripple TBA, a hitherto very successful business that YRG paid a lot of money for. To remain a very successful business, I'd have thought.
>
> Thanks again,
> Chaz

'Oh, no!' Sam could barely breathe. Sitting there, facing Oxford Street, he looked down at the black desk as if into the abyss. Just when things had been going so well. He raised his head and stared out the window at the Darlinghurst streetscape. He knew Margaret was not the kind of woman to take this lightly. She'd not made it to where she was by having her instructions questioned, certainly not by having them rejected outright.

Sam raced down to Chaz's office on the first floor, opened the glass door and waited for him to get off the phone.

There was nothing terribly unusual about Chaz's office, apart from the Siamese fighting fish recently imported from Thailand. A month ago, Sam had been introduced to four fish, two pairs of two in a split tank, swimming harmoniously on each side. Now there were only two, looking twice as big as before, and staring at each other through the glass; Sam didn't want to ask what had happened to the others.

For a moment, Sam thought he could smell cigarette smoke. The New South Wales government banned smoking in enclosed areas in 2001. That's a flaming long time ago.

Chaz hung up, and looked at Sam.

'Don't give me that look,' Sam said. 'You know exactly why I'm here. What were you thinking?'

'I said what needed to be said. Now, take a seat, stop being so uptight.' He directed Sam towards the white couch.

'No, I think I'd rather stand. You're one of the smartest guys I know but this was dumb. *So* dumb! It puts everything we've worked so hard to build in jeopardy. It puts the rest of our seventy-four million dollars in jeopardy. Contract or no contract, a company as big as YRG, with all its legal and financial might, could mess us around for years if they wanted to. When you're facing a 360Kg Grizzly that can rip your head off, you don't poke it!'

'Hey, Sam, it had to be said. Okay? And I knew you wouldn't do it. Sometimes you're too soft.'

'It's not about being soft,' Sam said. 'You just told my new boss – *your* new boss – that we wouldn't do what she'd instructed us to do. She expects us to merge with Pointer White. End of story!'

Chaz looked over at the fish tank. 'I'm thinking of putting in some rainbow fish. How do you think they'd go?'

Sam shook his head, knowing it was time to leave.

He headed back upstairs to his desk and sent a note to Zoe. Sam wanted his creative director to join him for a coffee or a beer. The company was half Zoe's – at least it had been – so she deserved to know what was going on. The rest of her payout from YRG was on the line, as was Sam's.

Zoe called him back a short time later. 'You want to grab a drink at The Dolphin?'

'Yes.'

'Say, five?'

'I'll meet you out the front of the building.'

Sam wouldn't normally finish up so early, but these times were fast becoming abnormal. At the appointed hour, he and Zoe sauntered up the road, the creative director wearing an old Hugo Boss number.

'Isn't that the suit you wore when you picked up your first Gold at Cannes?' asked Sam. 'For the anti-gambling campaign, right? I was so proud of you.'

'The year Jono Swift was on the Jury,' said Zoe.

'Jono's done well for an Aussie, hasn't he?'

'Global Chief Creative Officer. That's not bad. Especially at YRG.'

'Our company, now.'

'Don't I know it,' she said.

'Jono is a big fan of your work.'

'Not sure he'd remember me.'

'I don't know. I got a text from him a couple of weeks ago. I think he's a good guy.'

Zoe coughed a few times.

'Alright?' asked Sam.

'It's because of the plane trees,' she said. 'Christ, I hate it. Little bit of wind, and we get all the... Actually, it's not just pollen in the air. Look at this stuff.' Zoe pointed up ahead. 'There's dirt and whatever else off the ground. These swirly gusts. I hate Surry Hills!'

Sam loved Surry Hills. It was a typical autumn day, the breeze gentle, the sky a uniform blue, and he was unaffected by whatever was in the air. More than a handful of staff suffered spring allergies, but Zoe seemed to suffer all year round. She looked pale and unwell.

'Apart from swirly gusts,' he said, 'how are you doing?'

'Okay, I guess.'

'Only okay?'

Zoe looked at Sam like she felt guilty for complaining. 'I know we've got the money and everything. I just... I don't know. It's weird.'

'What?'

'I'm not sure what I'm working for now, what my goals are.' Zoe produced a snivel bordering on the orchestral. 'We worked fricking hard to get here.'

'Don't worry,' Sam said. 'It's pretty normal. You go through an event like this and you question everything. It's like we've been on a mission and the mission's ended. What's next? I don't know. I said to Lauren that once the buyout's finalised we should take a year off. Sail around the Bahamas or something.'

'Sailing, hey?' Zoe looked unconvinced. 'Makes me think of sunburn and seasickness. Suppose I shouldn't complain. I know my present misery is of my own making.'

With Zoe sounding so down, Sam was tempted not to tell his friend what he knew about Chaz. But that wouldn't have been fair.

The public bar was half empty. Without hesitation, Zoe plonked herself on the nearest barstool making it clear whose duty it was to procure the first round. Two schooners later, Sam mustered up the courage to tell her about Chaz's emails; Zoe just listened, her sad brown eyes saying all that needed to be said.

'I'd never want to lose Chaz,' said Sam, 'but he does make life difficult at times.'

'He's not the only one.'

'What do you mean?'

'How about that Kitty girl?'

'Seriously, Zoe, you shouldn't worry about that. I know you and I know you wouldn't have done anything wrong. I'm sure it will just disappear.'

'Maybe I should confront her. Face to face. See what she says then.'

'Please, Zoe, don't. You're in the right.' He'd said it as though there could be no doubt whatsoever, but there were no witnesses, so it was impossible to be one hundred per cent sure. 'Just sit tight.'

'I don't know. I feel like I've got to do something.'

Sam didn't think it would help to repeat himself. 'What are you working on at the moment?'

'Oh, it's this new brief. You remember the *Crocodile Inside* campaign for Lacoste? I thought maybe we could do something a bit like that for the bank. You have a couple, maybe with a baby? The world's collapsing around them...' Zoe was off and running, and Sam was happy to let her carry on uninterrupted. To her credit, Zoe never let the noise, or what she called her 'eternal rain of crap', stop her from delivering for her clients.

Chapter 7

When the lift doors opened at the top floor, Viktor led Darius forward into a glorious, but to any newcomer a somewhat mysterious, world of pale pastels. Viktor was met by a girl in light pink, her G String and skimpy bra in furious agreement with the club's colour code. Viktor was usually impressed when he came here because it allowed him the luxury of focussing entirely on the present. But not tonight. He'd only just finished his last cigarette and already wanted another. Ridiculous, he chided himself. *Look at the gorgeous creature standing before you!* She was all tits and ass, just the way he liked it. He could see Darius wasn't about to complain. 'Stop gawking,' he told the youngster.

Darius turned his gaze to the floor.

The buxom blonde led them up half a dozen stairs to a table that looked down on the central platform where a tall Eurasian girl was dancing topless. The dancer had a hard face, operating in a world of her own, impervious to the stares of surrounding men in suits.

Viktor's upper-level table was for VIPs only. He had earned the right to be there, to look down on the general-entry punters. Not only had he spent a small fortune at the club, but he also knew the owner: Russian-born, also now calling the United States home. A bottle of Beluga Noble lay waiting on their table.

'Annika and Tash will be with you in a few minutes,' said the blonde. 'Now, is there anything else I can get for you?'

Viktor knew this girl would be able to source anything his heart may desire: a hooker of any colour, any age, who'd be happy to satisfy whatever fetish he fancied; drugs of any description; the best booze money could buy. But now was not the time for kink or narcotics. That would come later. Now, he wanted Darius to relax into his new environment. He'd done well on his first overseas job, so he deserved to be rewarded and brought in a little closer to the family.

A familiar man in an unbuttoned silk suit approached them, looking like he'd eaten so many chocolate donuts he'd become one. Viktor was not about to criticise him for his waistline. The man raised his gold Rolex-clad right hand to press down his greased-backed hair, as if it were possible a strand might have fallen out of place. The dirt under his fingernails was a curious mismatch for the watch.

'You don't like my vodka?'

'Boris, my dear friend,' said Viktor, standing to greet the club's owner. 'I love your vodka. I just haven't had the chance to drink any yet. I was so taken with this gorgeous girl who showed us to our seats.'

Boris joined them for a shot and then Viktor watched him ooze off down a corridor to share the love with his other precious VIPs. Cash registers would be ringing throughout the night; Boris was a difficult man to say no to.

Viktor sent the blonde on her way, filled his and Darius' glasses with a second shot of vodka, and prepared for a toast. He looked Darius in the eye and said, 'To beauty everywhere.'

'To beauty everywhere,' Darius repeated.

Viktor placed his shot glass back down on the table and said, 'Tell me, how were the Australian girls?'

'Mister Tomic, I don't honestly know.'

'No, no, you call me Viktor now.'

'Thank you, sir. The girls in Sydney were pretty, I guess, but I didn't really...'

'I understand. You didn't have time to get to know them the way you'd have liked.'

'That's right, sir.'

'No, not sir. Viktor.'

'Yes, I'm sorry. Viktor.'

'Now, this is good. It is good you are here. We will enjoy the good life together. You are part of the family now and we look after our family, don't we?'

'Yes, Viktor.'

'Tell me about that man in Australia, Sam Pride. I have read the file you put together but want to hear in your own words.'

Darius took an anxious breath before answering. 'Pride is what he seems to be. A family man. He's worked hard. Done well for himself. Still committed to the business, even though he now has quite a lot of money. Gets into the office early. Hasn't had a sick day in years. Even when he's on holiday, he's still on call. Treats his staff well. Takes the seniors for coffees and drinks, sometimes meals. I spoke to a lot of people about him. They were all quite positive. Apart from one woman who said he was stuck up. But she'd been fired two months earlier.'

'Yes, I understand. And what about the finance one? Chaz Bailley?'

'He may be a problem,' said Darius. 'He is not so straightforward. And not so straight. Some people like him but many distrust him.'

'Why?'

'I'm not sure. He is much more reckless than Mr Pride. More volatile. He has been successful in his career, but he goes out partying and…' Darius held back when he saw Annika and Tash arriving at the table.

Annika had a bottle of 2009 Cristal in her hand. 'From Boris,' she said.

'Thank you,' said Viktor. 'We appreciate it.'

'You must be Viktor. I hear you're a big man.'

'Sit down here, honey,' he said motioning toward his lap. 'You tell me.'

'Ah,' she said, quietly lowering herself down onto Viktor's lap. He knew she could feel his erect penis pressing against her as she teased him with her movement. She must have been with all manner of men in her time, all shapes and sizes. She gently stroked his thigh. 'I see you're also a hard man.'

Darius looked away. Viktor felt his phone vibrate under Annika's thigh and give her a startle. 'Sorry, honey,' he said, pushing her off. 'Maybe later, eh?' He read the text:

7am tomorrow? Usual place.

It was from the one man for whom Viktor was prepared to interrupt proceedings. The man who called himself the Special Counsel. Viktor wondered what the qualification for that might have been. A little knowledge of the law and a lot on how to break it? He was the man to give your company a competitive edge, if you seriously wanted to screw the competition.

***

The next day, Viktor approached the designated meeting place, Metric West Fulton, at 6.55am, just before its opening. He felt hungover, irritable, but not tired, even though he'd parted ways with Darius and the club roughly four hours ago. The meth Annika had given him would tide him through until the afternoon. Then he would crash out big time and that would be fine.

'Hellion Cold Brew,' he told the petite, young waitress.

Viktor could feel his heart beating too fast. Ten minutes later, Don Brandis arrived; Viktor considered him a riddle. Why would a man so obviously smart and successful choose the combover approach to manage his thinning grey hair? It was such a bad look. He should speak to Annika. She'd set him straight. Viktor reached out to shake his hand but there were no smiles on this occasion.

'I need you to go to Sydney yourself this time,' said Brandis. 'Your kid was okay for the last trip, but the situation has evolved. This Bailley character. Jesus! The guy doesn't know when to shut up. We gave those TBA weasels a small fortune. They should have taken their money and either done their jobs or fucked off. Either would have been fine by me. But raising questions about Pointer White is a no-go.'

'I can go to Sydney,' said Viktor. 'Happy to.'

Chapter 8

Thursday had been a long time coming for Lauren. The sonographer, clean shaven, sharp eyes, moved a transducer slowly over Lauren's abdomen while she studied his face like her life depended on it.

'So?'

'As you suspected.'

'I'm definitely pregnant?'

He pivoted the transducer's monitor around so Lauren could see for herself. 'It mightn't look like much right now, but that squiggly mass, there, is a developing baby.'

'Oh my...' Lauren let out a pent-up sigh, but it wasn't enough to fully relieve the tension. 'Thank you.'

'Don't thank me. Now, is there anyone else you'd like to tell?' He looked down at the one-and-a-half carat diamond ring on her wedding finger as Lauren reached for a tissue and wiped away the tears. He asked, 'Is something wrong?'

Lauren would have liked to tell him the truth, but it was hard enough to admit that to herself. Front of mind were images from her past she'd tried hard to forget. The betrayal she'd wanted to tell Sam about for what felt like an eternity but had never managed to.

She made her way down to the carpark. Back into the sunlight, stuck in traffic, she called her best friend, Mia, and tried to explain her dilemma. 'The affair meant nothing. If you could even call it an affair. One stupid night! That was my view then and it's my view now.'

'Who?'

'Some chisel-jawed guy I know from the gym.'

'How old?'

'Late twenties. His name is Noah.'

'Ah, okay. You mentioned him a few weeks ago. Muscles like Hercules, I think you said. But you didn't say you slept with him.'

'It happened once. And then I told him it was over. When I spoke to you – I guess I was pretending it never happened.'

'That's a mature way of—'

'Mia, don't lecture me.'

'So, why did you do it?'

'I honestly don't know. Sam had been really busy with work; I'd been doing lots of things on my own, and—'

'You weren't having sex with Sam at that time?'

'Not as much as usual.'

'So, you *were* having sex with Sam around the same time as you – had sex with this guy?'

'Um…'

'I take that as a *yes*?'

'Yes, okay, the baby could be Noah's. Unlikely, but possible.'

'Do I need to…' Lauren heard Mia take a breath. 'You've got the obvious moral dilemma to address, whether or not to keep the affair a secret from Sam. If Sam's not the father, would you tell him, or would you tell the real father?'

'I don't know, Mia. What's the answer?'

'Depends how compelling you think their right to know is. If you say nothing, and the baby is not Sam's, what if he finds out?'

'Do you know the weird thing?' said Lauren. 'That stupid one-nighter was the thing that made me know for sure, in the most absolute sense, that Sam's the only man I'd ever want to spend my life with. Maybe I should have known that before I married him. But when I was falling into bed with Noah, it wasn't that obvious.'

Mia sighed but said, 'I get it.'

'I told myself that Sam wouldn't *want* to know. That he'd want me to keep it to myself'.

'Of course, you did.'

'That was a lie, I know. Time passes. And then it feels like it's too late to reveal the truth. Things have been so good lately. Why would I want to spoil that?'

'Oh, Lauren, this is awful. I don't mean the pregnancy, I mean…'

'I know what you mean.'

'You want to tell Sam about the pregnancy but not the affair, don't you?'

'I think so. Telling him about the affair would make him angry and incredibly sad. Not telling him will make him happy. That's the best gift I can give him.'

'That and a blowjob.'

Lauren laughed through her tears. 'Just more blowjobs, huh?'

'Every day. Like clockwork.'

'It's why I seek your counsel, Mia. You've got all the answers.'

Ian Caldwell had worked for NetGen for four years and had been consulting to TBA for two of them. He spent one and a half days per week in the Crown Street offices and the rest onsite at other company locations. People at TBA were generally friendly, though he sometimes got terse emails from the more senior members when they wanted something sorted impossibly fast. IT was one of those areas of business where it takes as long as it takes. You can work around the clock to try to address an issue, but you can't defy the laws of physics.

Brie Allinson had always been Ian's favourite TBA employee. She was the receptionist. She looked at him, and indeed spoke to him, like he was important, like he mattered, even when he wasn't fixing something for her. For some of the others, he might as well have been the garbage man. They always looked right through him, if they'd bothered to look in his direction at all.

So far, today hadn't been anything unusual for Ian. He was up to task number three: fix Kitty Zhang's problem with the agency's finance software. He'd met Kitty a few times before, but they'd never engaged in a conversation beyond 'How long's this gonna take?'.

As he approached Kitty's desk, he noticed the skirt she was wearing was, well, very short. She looked up at him and smiled. She'd never done that before; his day just took an upward swing. 'Hey, Ian,' she said.

Oh, Lord, she was hot, thought Ian. Smoking, as they say. 'Hey, Kitty, how are you?'

'I'm great. So glad you're here. I need your help with something.'

'Whatever I can do to—'

'But the problem is slightly more complicated than the one I logged. Can you just come with me?'

Kitty stood up and didn't wait for Ian to respond. She obviously knew he would follow. Like an obedient pup, he entered the meeting room after her, and then she locked the door.

'Please, sit down,' she said.

Ian did as he was instructed. Kitty leaned back against the boardroom table, right beside him, making her skirt ride up even higher. He tried not to look, but she seemed to want him to. This was too good to be true, like some crazy schoolboy fantasy.

'I'm going to ask a favour of you,' Kitty said.

Her hand reached down and stroked his inner thigh. She had long, slender arms, and exquisitely petite wrists. He could feel himself becoming aroused. The few girls he'd been with were not even close to Kitty's league.

'You know the security cameras?' she said. 'Like the one in the lift?'

'Of course,' said Ian, his voice trembling. 'What about them?'

'How is the video footage stored?'

Kitty got down on her knees and began undoing Ian's belt. He wanted to resist; he really did. But this was too good to pass up. His blood was boiling, and his balls were about to explode.

***

Sam and Zoe arrived at Marilyn's office together, unsure of why she'd asked to see them both. Sam admired Marilyn. She'd been with the agency just over three years and always came across as very professional. One of those people who just seemed to understand the way the world worked – and how the human brain worked.

'It's been a week now,' said Marilyn. 'Zoe, I know you gave me your potted version of what happened at the party last Friday, and that was all I needed from you at that time, but there's been a development. Kitty hasn't made a formal complaint, but she has told another account exec that she was harassed by you, Zoe. That exec has spoken to me, in confidence.'

Panic-stricken, Zoe quickly went through every detail of what occurred in the lift, as well as the minutes that followed. 'I haven't spoken to or seen Kitty since.'

'Well, if everything you've told me is true, I don't think you need to worry.'

'Of course, it's true,' said Zoe.

'Sorry, yes, I didn't mean to suggest otherwise. Look, you just need to be prepared. You're a company director, and she's a junior employee. If she makes a complaint, we must be seen to act on it.'

'You're right, Marilyn,' said Sam. 'Zoe hasn't done anything wrong. We just need to play it by the book.'

'It's ridiculous,' Zoe scoffed. 'All I did was say *no*.'

'Do you know what time it is?' Marilyn asked her.

Zoe looked at her watch. 'Quarter past seven.'

'What's your husband's name?'

'What's that got to do with—'

'I suggest you go home and tell him how you feel about him.'

'What do you…'

'When awful stuff like this happens, it's good to be reminded of who matters in this world; it's the people you love, not those who seek to bring you down.'

***

Buds and Bowers in Crown Street was Sam's favourite flower shop, and the only one he went to these days. Their flower arrangements looked sublime, but it was their attitude he particularly liked. He remembered JJ, the founder, explaining that, while they might have great designs, if they didn't have customers, they didn't have a business. Service. JJ got it. Sam wished the man had been an account handler for TBA.

'What are you thinking?' asked a friendly young woman with a shiny nose piercing.

Sam looked at the different flowers on show against the northern wall. 'A bit of pink, maybe some purple…'

'And some blue?' she said, hinting at the Agapanthus.

'Sold,' Sam said with a smile.

Watching the woman wrap the pretty flowers in the shop's signature black paper and use twine to attach his card, Sam remembered the very first bouquet he bought for Lauren. It was long before he planted the roses in the front garden of their current home. She'd been living in a share flat in Bronte. Sam had invited her out for dinner, then realised he couldn't afford to go to the restaurant he'd booked, so he suggested that he cook for her instead. Her flatmate was away for the weekend, so it would be just the two of them. It was a Saturday. Sam picked up the ingredients in the morning, got to Lauren's in the late afternoon, stuck like glue to a snapper recipe he'd dug up online, and started talking about movies.

That was when Lauren told him she'd never seen *Casablanca*. 'You're kidding?' Sam said to her, shocked. Not because it was strange that someone might not have seen a black and white movie released in 1942, but because Lauren struck him as the sort of person who would have been drawn to it. He knew she was a romantic, despite the lengths she went to trying to cover it up. 'Bankers are like robots,' she once said to him. Maybe so, but not Lauren. She loved a bit of drama, a bit of intrigue.

From the very first time he'd met Lauren, Sam would hear stories about the private lives of her friends and acquaintances, their conflicts and resolutions. She had a warmth and enthusiasm for talking about people. She seemed to enjoy being in the thick of things. Sam thought she would have liked Ilsa, the role played by Ingrid Bergman. Lauren had told him she was always in search of a noble cause, her version of Laszlo, but was never in a rush to deny herself the pleasures of ignobility.

Lauren's flatmate had paid for a streaming service, so, after dinner, they opened a second bottle of shiraz and watched the movie. Sam kept quiet during his favourite scenes. He wanted Lauren to see what he saw in the film. He suspected she did.

Within minutes of Rick saying to Louis, 'I think this is the beginning of a beautiful friendship', Lauren and Sam were making love. The caresses began on the large white sofa, their tangled bodies soon dislodging cushions and blankets, two as one, totally oblivious to the TV still playing in the background or, indeed, any other activity on Earth at that moment. Then Lauren took him by the hand, leading him upstairs to her cosy, sweetly cluttered bedroom. It had been one of the best nights of his life. One where he asked himself, as he would many times subsequently, 'Am I the luckiest guy in the world?'.

***

'Come on, Darius. I need your help here,' said Viktor.

He'd just shot a couple of idiots who'd tried to double cross one of Alliance's major clients, a real estate guy who also trafficked drugs. Now the bodies needed to be taken to their friendly crematorium. He'd already rolled out the two body bags, but Darius remained frozen. 'What? They're dead. They can't hurt you now.'

'Sorry, Viktor.'

Darius wrapped the male while Viktor got going with the female. The zipper on the second bag was broken and kept getting stuck, making Viktor even more cranky. His mobile rang. He could see it was his second most lucrative client. 'Yes?'

'You're still in Chicago?' asked Brandis.

'I had to clean up some mess before leaving.'

'The thing in Sydney can't wait.'

'Don't worry. My flight's booked. I'll be on the plane shortly.'

'I'm counting on it.'

Turning the corner to their street in Bondi, Sam wondered if Lauren might be preparing dinner. He was hungry and felt guilty for not having spoken to her earlier in the day. He called most days, just to check in and see how things were going, and to hatch a plan for the evening, but today he was busy, caught up in meetings. Time had run away from him.

'Hi darling,' he yelled out, once inside the house. 'And hello to you, too,' he said to Rax.

Lauren stepped into the hallway from the kitchen.

Knowing very well how cheesy it would sound, Sam sang, 'And when two lovers woo…'

Lauren gave him three words, 'They still say…'

'What do they still say?'

Lauren held off for a beat, before finally uttering, 'They still say, I love you. You crazy man.' He could see a tear in her eye. 'Oh, my God, they're beautiful!' She kissed him and removed the bouquet from his hand. 'When I didn't hear from you, I was worried.'

'Yes, sorry, I meant to call.'

Sam followed Lauren into the kitchen and watched her open the cupboard to retrieve her favourite glass vase.

'Give a girl flowers, and she'll forgive you anything. Isn't that what they say?' She cut the stems and filled the vase with water. 'Wine?'

'That'd be great,' he said, noticing there was only one glass on the bench next to the open bottle. 'You're not having any?'

'We're having Vietnamese,' she said. 'That okay?'

'You know I love Vietnamese.'

Sitting down with glass in hand, Sam asked Lauren about her day.

'Nothing out of the ordinary,' she said, after hesitating.

'Did Nick give you a hard time again?' Sam was referring to Lauren's immediate boss who, on any given day, was highly likely to have done something to annoy her. Sam wondered if that was causing the skerrick of angst he was sensing.

'No, no, Nick was fine. Actually, I barely even saw him today. What about you, darling? How was your day?'

'Pretty good. No more crazy emails from Chaz.'

'Thank Heaven. Any response from Margaret about what happened yesterday?'

'No. Which is why I am still worried about it.'

'Well, maybe Chaz said what needed to be said.'

'Don't scare me.'

'What do you mean?'

'You're starting to sound like him.'

The banter continued over dinner, but Sam sensed there was something Lauren wasn't telling him. 'Do you know what tells are?' he asked.

'Like, in poker?'

'It's a change in behaviour that tells your opponent what your hand is. In poker you're always trying to cover up the truth. So, a tell, in theory, reveals the truth.'

'Why are we talking about poker?' Lauren asked with a touch of nervous hysteria. 'What have you been up to?'

'The most obvious one is when you act weak to disguise a strong hand,' continued Sam. 'You shrug, or sigh. Look miserable. That kind of thing. Trying to hide the truth.'

'Okay.'

'Posture,' said Sam. 'That's another. When someone straightens their back, sits upright, it usually means they have confidence in the play they're about to make. It's supposed to be a signal of a good hand.'

'How do you know all this?'

'One of our qual researchers told me. She's always studying the way people behave. Whether their body language is matching their words.'

Lauren got up and walked around the table to kiss Sam. 'I never knew there was so much depth to your work,' she mocked.

He wondered what her sudden flirtation was all about. Was she hiding something or was he being the dumbest husband in the world? With an adorable wife making moves on him, only a fool would be thinking about hands of poker.

Chapter 9

Early morning, May 22, with his face drenched in sweat, his T-shirt sticking to his back, Sam ran breathlessly along the cold sand, past the idling middle-aged women having a chat, and up to the rocks at the south end of Bondi Beach. As usual, he finished with a sprint. Superfluous, he imagined Lauren saying, given that he wasn't competing against anyone other than himself. The sun was about to rise but it needed to climb above a small bank of clouds before it would have any impact. There was a chill in the air, one that cut through Sam's thin layer of clothing as soon as he stopped running. He noticed a man in sunglasses and a cap standing by the rocks. The guy looked out of place and when Sam got closer, he turned to face the other way. It was his collared shirt that seemed particularly odd. Nobody wears a collared shirt on the beach at this time of the morning.

Earlier, when he was leaving the house, Sam could see that Rax wasn't happy; what was Sam doing heading off in running gear without him? But he needed some alone time. The run helped him clear his head. He'd woken up worried about Chaz's comments to Margaret, but with the run came the clarity that it would be okay. It was the same for his concern regarding Lauren's unusual behaviour. He was just inventing another thing to worry about. Even the Kitty and Zoe incident felt like less of a problem.

***

Sam had been at his desk for twenty minutes when Little Ted appeared; he was just standing there, waiting to be invited to sit down.

'Go on, then,' Sam said. 'Take a seat, big guy.' Ted lowered himself down onto a nearby stool as delicately as a rugby league forward in a child's nursery. 'I don't think they had you in mind when they were designing the furniture.'

Little Ted chuckled. 'I just wanted to say thank you. Again. That was so generous of you guys. You know, the cheque and everything.'

'Hey mate, it's me who should be thanking you, and the rest of the team. You guys earned every cent. You've done an incredible job. You make me look good, every day of the year.'

'What's that Churchill quote you always say?'

'Continuous effort, not strength or intelligence, is the key to unlocking our potential.'

'That's it,' said Ted. 'I love the way you remember all those things. Anyway, everyone knows who the star of the show is around here. That's all I wanted to say.' He stood up, but then stopped for a final word. 'Ever you need anything, you know where I am.'

'I do.'

Sam thought it good of Ted to thank him again like that, but completely unnecessary. The guy was so, damn loyal. Since his stint in jail, Ted had become kinder and more thoughtful. 'You still helping out at the Exodus Foundation in Ashfield?'

'When I can, yes.'

'It's great work, you do. There's a lot of homeless people out there.'

'Gotta do what you can,' said Little Ted.

Later, Chaz had come up to Sam's desk and told him they were going for lunch with Roz and Idham from Pointer White. 'I know you've met Roz before,' he said, 'but do you know Idham?'

'I know of him,' said Sam, 'but we haven't actually met. He's their CFO, isn't he?'

'That's right. I know him quite well from an industry committee we sat on together.'

'Do I have to go?'

'You can't tell me you're too busy. I've looked at your diary. You're clear!'

***

The restaurant was light and breezy, a marked change from the dark and moody wine bar it had replaced. Its big-flavoured middle eastern cuisine brought something new to the area, which Sam was happy about. The only problem he'd had on the two occasions he'd been there recently was eating too much warm hummus and flatbreads before getting to the falafel crumpet and grills. Today, the place was humming with a relatively young but well-heeled Surry Hills crowd. Roz and Idham were sitting at a table near the front window. 'You don't muck around,' said Chaz, looking at the half-empty bottle of Pinot Gris.

Sam looked at his watch. They weren't late. Roz and Idham must have arrived early.

'It's Friday!' said Idham. 'Now, can I pour you a glass? We've just ordered some flatbreads.'

Chaz gladly accepted and sat down opposite Idham, while Sam took the seat opposite Roz. They spoke for ten minutes about how the industry was going, the changes since covid first hit in 2020, Sam wondering when they'd get to the point. He gave Chaz a glaring look, to which his CFO responded by asking Idham, 'Do you mind if I just ask, what's going on with your books? We've been told you're in a spot of bother.'

'We probably need to go back to the start,' said Roz, her voice warm and fluid. Considering the difficulty that they were in, she seemed remarkably level-headed. She explained, with more detail than Sam was expecting, the history of their sale to YRG. 'If my theory is right,' she said, 'it's all about the receivables and the payables. Or, Sam, for you, the aged debtors and the aged creditors. I'm guessing in your role you see those each week?'

'I do.'

Roz had a look around at the other diners, possibly concerned that someone might overhear what she was going to say next. But she was safe; there was plenty of space between tables, and the restaurant was noisier than most. 'Okay, so imagine in the sale of Pointer White to YRG, that people got a bit lost in determining exactly what was owed and what was owing.'

'What do you mean?' Sam asked. 'How could that happen?'

'It happens when your account service guys are not close to your finance guys.' She had a gulp of wine. 'You do Job Cost Report meetings with your account directors each month, don't you?'

'Sure.'

'Well, we've stopped having those meetings. One month it was because everyone was too busy, so everything was done over email. Next month, finance cuts more corners and tells the account service guys to just email a list of the jobs they want closed.'

'I see where this is going,' said Chaz.

Roz continued. 'About two months after the merger, when we're all trying to come to terms with how much money we owe to suppliers, and how much is owed to us by our clients…' She stopped and looked each of them in the eye.

'Go on,' Sam said.

'That's when a large amount of money – almost eight million dollars – goes missing.'

'What do you mean, missing?'

'It just, kind of, gets lost.'

'How can that happen?'

'The finance guys were going through hundreds of pages of mess,' Roz said, 'going back months, even years in some cases. On the books, it looks like certain media operators are owed hundreds of thousands of dollars, but, for some reason, they've not been asking for the money.'

'What?' said Chaz.

'Media always ask for the money if you've run ads on their channels or in their publications, right? So, you start asking if our clients' ads actually ran?'

'And did they?' Sam asked.

'In some cases, yes. But, in others, no.'

'So, the agency had taken money from clients for ads that never ran, and the media company hadn't asked for the money – because the ads never ran?'

'That's right.'

'Get the fuck outta here!' said Chaz.

'When they bought us,' Idham explained, 'the finance guys from YRG took over responsibility for everything as you'd expect. Their company, so they can do what they want.'

'Of course.'

'Then eight million bucks moves from our bank account to a UK bank account.'

'To YRG's?' said Chaz.

'Now that's the thing,' said Roz. 'The account the money went into wasn't YRG's. Or, at least, not as far as we can see.'

'You contacted the bank?'

Idham nodded. 'They only gave us the account name. Premier Enterprises.'

'And they are?'

'We started doing a little digging, but then were told by YRG's CFO to leave it alone.'

'Leave it *alone*?'

'Their tone was more like *leave-it-the-fuck-alone!*' said Idham. 'Claimed it was all legit. And there was no consequent cashflow issue for Pointer White because there had been that eight million taken from clients for media buys that never happened.'

Sam had heard of small-scale media buys that were suspicious in the past but nothing like this. 'So, the media fraud had created a spare eight million in cash. Which was transferred to a bank account unconnected to YRG or any of its known subsidiaries?'

'That just about sums it up. Look, I can't prove that a crime was committed. Hell, I probably shouldn't be saying any of this to you.'

'How was the transfer of money to Premier Enterprises authorised?'

'A memo. Clear instructions.'

'YRG letterhead?'

'Yes.'

'Who was the signatory?'

'A guy named Don Brandis.'

'YRG's Special Counsel,' nodded Chaz.

'You know him?'

'He was lurking in the background when our deal was being done. We think he's been on some telecons with us, but not introduced and not mentioned in the attendee list. You'd suddenly hear the voice of someone you didn't know, wonder who the fuck it was.'

'A mysterious dude,' said Idham.

'You have a copy of that memo?' asked Chaz.

'I do.'

'Original, and signed?'

'Yes.'

'Can I see it?'

Idham looked at Roz, who nodded. 'Okay,' he said. 'But there's something else you should know. I was the recipient of the memo from Brandis and I'm expecting my position will be made redundant post the merger. They want me gone. I get the sense they don't trust me.'

'You may be right,' said Roz. 'Or it may be that they are simply doing housekeeping. Your name is on the memo, Idham. With you gone, it's almost like the memo never existed.'

'The memo never existed,' said Chaz, 'and the eight million dollars never existed.'

'What eight million dollars?' said Roz.

Chapter 10

Viktor and Darius arrived in Sydney on QF8 at 6.25am, having left O'Hare International twenty-one hours earlier. 'Thank goodness for vodka,' Viktor said as they waited to exit the plane.

'And Ambien,' said Darius.

'You slept for fourteen hours!'

'I was tired.'

'No more late nights at strip clubs for you, young man.'

'Come on, boss. I was just warming up.'

'That's what worries me.'

Viktor liked his young protégé. The kid had attitude, which was a plus these days. 'What do you want to do with your life, Darius?'

'What do you mean?'

'Do you want to be a boss? Do you want to start your own company? What is it you're after?'

'I don't know. I feel like I'm only just getting started.'

Viktor shook his head. 'You stick with me, son. I'll look after you.'

'Thank you, Viktor. I really appreciate your support.'

'I never had anyone looking out for me when I was young. I nearly didn't make it.'

'Really?'

'A couple of times, I thought, this is it; I'm a dead man.'

'What happened?'

'I found a way to survive.'

Once they were through Customs, a man in a black suit introduced himself as Michael Haddad, Managing Director of Triple S Security. Haddad was tall, well over six foot, with pockmarked skin and grey eyes that appeared tired and soulless, like the humanity had been sucked out of them. 'Good flight?' he asked, voice deadpan.

'Good enough,' said Viktor.

Haddad followed the current of the crowd out into the morning sunlight, leading his guests to a black Lexus. He opened the boot for their luggage. 'We've done what you asked,' he said. 'Do you want me to show you?'

'All right,' said Viktor. 'But I want to make one thing clear. For most of what we're doing here in Sydney, Darius and I will be working alone.' Viktor considered various possible scenarios, and then added, 'But if we need to call on you, how many men have you got at your disposal?'

'Thirty permanents,' said Haddad, 'and then another forty or so casuals.'

'Good to know.'

'They're at your disposal, Mr Tomic.'

Haddad drove the speed limit, changing lanes like a precision driver, only overtaking when it was safe to do so. On Southern Cross Drive, they passed the Lakes Golf Club and the Botany Dams on their right, then onto Zetland and Waterloo with their shiny high-rise apartment buildings on the left. 'The place you're staying is pretty central,' he said. 'You should like it. The observation room we've set up is in Surry Hills, just a few minutes from the hotel.'

It was a twenty-minute drive to the Sheraton Grand, a five-star hotel sitting directly opposite Hyde Park in Elizabeth Street. After checking in, Viktor and Darius were back in the Lexus in less than ten minutes.

'Okay, gentlemen,' said Haddad. 'The building I'm taking you to is in Riley Street. From there, it's just a few blocks to the TBA offices – in case you want to do a walk-by or whatever.'

As they drove south, Viktor spotted two men holding hands. One looked in his forties, the other about twenty years younger. 'Ugh,' he muttered, shaking his head.

'What?' said Darius.

Viktor gave him a look of disdain.

Arriving at the property owned by Triple S, Haddad pressed the remote and turned into the driveway of a three-storey structure on the city side of the street. The garage door opened to reveal a modern parking space with multiple security cameras that belied the well-aged and ordinary exterior of the building. They disembarked from the car and watched Haddad use his security pass to open a metal door. It opened to a cement-walled corridor, beyond which lay a windowless room, about forty square metres, with half a dozen large screen TVs facing a walnut melamine desk with four chairs behind it.

'All live feeds, as per your instructions,' said Haddad. The screen on the far left showed people coming and going at the entrance to a multi-storey building. A tag was taped below it which said TBA building. The next screen was inside a TBA lift, and after that, a display of an empty office. It was labelled Bailley's office. 'He's not there at the moment.'

'I'm not blind,' said Viktor.

'Sorry, of course, Mr Tomic. I didn't mean…'

The next two screens were exteriors of the homes of Chaz Bailley and Sam Pride; the final screen on the right was the interior of Bailley's apartment.

'These are fine,' said Viktor. 'But I also want feeds from the interior of Pride's home and…'

'And?'

'What's the creative one called?'

'Barnes. Zoe Barnes.'

'Yes. Her.'

'Sure,' said Haddad. 'We'll get onto that right away.'

Viktor also told Haddad he'd require a rental car for the duration of his stay in Australia. 'Something with grunt. But I don't want to look like a cock-sucking drug dealer. You understand?'

Haddad nodded. 'I'm on it.'

'One other thing,' said Viktor. 'Put a tail on Bailley.'

'No problem.' Haddad thought he might even handle a few shifts himself. Get a feel for this Bailley bloke. He seemed to be the one Viktor cared most about. Must be a reason.

***

Robert Miller touched the splintered wood with his forefinger. The lock on the drawer had not been fixed. Could Viktor have missed it? Unlikely. Maybe he just didn't have time to get it fixed before he left. Robert opened the drawer to discover the YRG files exactly as he'd left them. At least they *looked* untouched. Was he walking into a trap? This time he wore gloves – hardly making him immune from discovery – but surely better than nothing. He picked up right where he'd left off, sifting through the documents, one by one.

There was that man's name again. The one constant in all Viktor's dealings with this client. Don Brandis. The Special Counsel. There was a lot to digest, with dozens of meetings between Viktor and Brandis over the years. But in terms of YRG's interest in Australia, the only project of any significance – at least as far as Alliance was concerned – was the takeover of The Bold Agency. Apart from the personnel files

Robert had looked at last time, there were reams of data on the business performance of TBA. Financial spreadsheets, market reports, client listings, performance reviews, and so on. But at the end of it all, he could not spot any sign of illegal activity, or even anything that looked ethically dubious. The only thing grabbing his attention was a short note he recognised as Viktor's handwriting. Only six words, but they seemed significant:

Find the Memo

Destroy all copies

What *memo*? There were no memos in any of the soft or hard copy files, not even a reference to one.

Robert took a photo of the note with his phone. Earlier, he'd looked through all the electronic files on the Alliance computer network relating to YRG. And now he'd checked every shelf, every drawer, and every filing cabinet in Viktor's office. There was nowhere else to look. Perhaps – in fact, almost certainly – there were secret files on Viktor's hard drive, but those flew with him to Sydney.

Annoyingly, despite his best efforts, Robert felt he'd learned very little about what Viktor was up to. He still didn't know what was so important that both Viktor and Darius had to suddenly jump on a plane and fly halfway across the world. He just had a feeling about this note. The word, *Destroy*, was concerning. And the suggestion that a memo needed to be found, which meant it had somehow gone missing.

Robert felt his phone vibrate. There was a message from Viktor in Australia:

Anything interesting?

Robert spun around the room, looking for cameras. How could he know? Was Viktor watching him from Sydney?

Chapter 11

It was late Tuesday morning and Sam had just finished going through some job cost reports with the account service leads when he got a text from Chaz asking him to come to his office. 'Urgent' had been used. Unusual for Chaz. Sam guessed it had something to do with the memo they'd discussed with Roz and Idham at lunch. Instead of stewing over the matter, Sam went straight down.

'You might want to close the door,' Chaz said.

Sam obliged and took a seat.

'It's Kitty. She hasn't turned up for work.'

'She's sick?'

'Not in the way you might think. Says she's suffering emotional trauma.'

'What?'

'She's going to make a claim.'

'She said that?'

'No, but I can tell. For what happened at the party.'

'Zoe didn't do anything to her.'

'I know, I know.'

Sam imagined all kinds of horrendous scenarios, and some of them included Chaz. 'Wait,' he said. 'How do you – did you speak to Kitty yourself?'

'She spoke to Brie Allinson and Brie spoke to me.'

'You're suddenly Brie's confidant?'

'I don't know about confidant, but – we're friendly, all right?'

Sam closed his eyes and gritted his teeth. He really didn't want to consider the implications of his CFO being *friendly* with the receptionist. One problem at a time, he said to himself. 'What did Brie think?'

'She just told me what Kitty told her. No judgment.'

'There's always judgment. Doesn't matter if Zoe's version is one hundred per cent true, some people will side with Kitty. We'd have to assume a fair number of staff have now heard Kitty's version of the story through the grapevine. If the blooming receptionist knows…'

'It's ridiculous.'

'If Zoe had actually done something wrong, that would be different. What do you think we should do?'

'Can we leave it to Marilyn?' said Chaz.

'She's the expert. And we assume Kitty hasn't gone to the police?'

'That's right. So, it's not a criminal matter.'

Sam needed time to think. 'It's just so — when there are so many genuine cases of…'

'We'll sort it out. Liars get found out in the end.'

'I hope so.'

***

Michael Haddad was sitting in his car, watching a live feed of Chaz Bailley meeting Sam Pride on his mobile, when he heard a tap on his driver's window. It was a cop.

He lowered his window. 'What's the problem?'

'Can't park here, mate.'

Haddad looked over at the No Stopping sign and apologised. 'I'll move, right away.'

Two blocks down Crown Street he found a one-hour spot, pulled out his phone again and watched Bailley leave his office. He turned around to look back at the TBA building and observed Bailley hailing a cab. He followed the taxi down Crown Street, past Bar Reggio and the East Sydney Italian Village, and down to the roundabout on Sir John Young Crescent. The traffic stalled near the art gallery. Once it got moving again, Haddad followed the taxi to the centre of the city, where Bailley finally disembarked. It was a thirty-five-storey commercial tower with frontages onto Ash Street and Angel Place. Haddad got out of the car and scurried across the road to see whose office Bailley was attending.

The lift Bailley was in only stopped at two floors. Level 5 housed a company called CVZ Capital, and Level 7 was some mob named Pointer White; Haddad googled them both. CVZ was a private equity firm, established in 1995, and had raised over three billion dollars across eight different funds. Pointer White, on the other hand, was a media planning and buying agency. The latter seemed to be a little more closely connected to the business of TBA, but Haddad still wasn't certain which of the two Bailley was visiting. He'd include both in his report and let Viktor work out which one made more sense.

When Bailley stepped out of the lift an hour later, he was carrying an A4 envelope. He'd gone into the building carrying nothing, so Haddad thought he must have been given the envelope by whomever he met with. Probably just another random business document. Maybe he'd be able to determine its importance when he watched the video feed of Bailley opening the envelope back in his office.

'Fuck,' Haddad mumbled. Had Bailley just clocked him? The target was staring right at him, like he was about to run over and launch some sort of assault. Haddad turned and raced out of the building. There was no way Bailley could have known who he was. He'd been incredibly careful when tailing him in the Lexus.

Haddad hurried down a side street and waited, whispering to himself, 'Maybe not careful enough.'

***

For the second time that day, Chaz called Sam down to his office. Sam felt like telling him to come up to his floor this time but couldn't be bothered challenging the request. Anyway, it would do him some good to get away from the computer screen for a while.

'You've got news?' Sam asked.

'I met with Roz and Idham,' said Chaz. 'They had lots to say about YRG. None of it good.'

'Go on.'

'Idham gave me the memo.'

'A copy of it?'

'No, he gave me the original.'

'Why?'

'He seemed to think it would be safer with me than with him. He has this theory. I initially thought it was all a bunch of conspiracy bullshit.'

'Now, you're not so sure?'

'I think we might be dealing with some unscrupulous cunts.'

'Don't we deal with those on a daily basis?'

'Very funny. This bloke the memo's from, Don Brandis, you remember Idham mentioning him at lunch?'

'He's the most unscrupulous of them all?'

'You're not taking this nearly as seriously as you should be.'

'Sorry, Chaz, but – I don't know. One minute, I think we've landed ourselves somewhere deep in the underworld and that we're dealing with hardened criminals, and then I read the business press and think that YRG is a very successful, fully above-board, blue-chip company, worthy of investors' loyalty.'

Chaz handed Sam the memo. He read it carefully, wondering who its author really was. What kind of man was Brandis? Did he have a family? Was he cruel to animals?

Chaz said, 'Roz and Idham have made it very clear that someone from YRG took money from Pointer White, using the memo signed by Brandis. Did they move it to legitimately put cash into another part of the YRG business or to go towards dividends for shareholders? That's what you'd think, right? Were it not for the slippery way YRG management have obfuscated and tried to cover it up...'

'And Roz and Idham think that's because the money wasn't just moved, it was stolen?'

'Yes,' said Chaz.

'But, if so, how could others at YRG not have known about it?'

'That's what Roz and Idham are trying to work out.'

'What do you think Margaret's role is in all this? Is Brandis following her orders?'

'How the fuck would I know?'

Sam certainly didn't. Margaret and Brandis could well have been in it together. Or maybe there was a dozen corporate heavies all stealing from the YRG coffers. Maybe they'd started off small, and it had just grown and grown, so that now it was simply the way they did business. Like the mafia – impossible to stamp out.

***

'What document?' asked Viktor.

'I don't know. I watched on my mobile, but, you know, it's hard to tell.'

'I want you to go back over the footage and blow it up or whatever you have to do.'

'It was probably just some regular work thing,' said Haddad. 'Pointer White is a media buying agency and they probably share some clients with TBA. I don't think it's all that strange.'

'When I want your opinion,' said Viktor tersely.

'Okay,' said Haddad. 'Understood. I'll check the footage more closely.'

Viktor ended the call.

Haddad whacked the steering wheel with the palm of his hand, smouldering as he cursed all Eastern European gangsters. They were a breed unto themselves, and, despite the large financial rewards, it was not a breed Haddad liked to spend more time with than absolutely necessary.

***

Back at his desk after a 9am meeting, Sam decided that he and Chaz really needed to talk to Zoe about that eight-million-dollar transfer. Zoe was a creative and often seemed oblivious to the financial and legal side of their operation, but she was Sam's business partner and she needed to know what was happening. So, he gave her a call.

She answered, 'Pride cometh before…'

'Zoe, that wasn't funny ten years ago, and it hasn't improved with age.'

'Wait. Hey, Holly, what do you think? When Sam calls me, it's usually about a problem. Holly agrees with me. So, is it?'

'Zoe. Please.'

'Okay, okay, don't get all worked up. What is it, Oh Powerful One?'

'Lunch. At the Dolphin. You, me, and Chaz.'

'I need to consult Holly.'

'Zoe! I'm coming by your desk at twelve forty-five.'

'Or else?'

'Shut up. I'll see you then.'

To Sam's great surprise, Zoe actually came and got him, just before the appointed time. Damn creatives, he thought. They never do what you expect.

The three of them wandered up Crown Street together, Sam and Zoe in jeans and casual collared shirts, Chaz in a dapper suit. Sam was clearly erring on the side of being creative. The cool air made him think he probably should have worn a jacket, but today he wanted – in fact, needed – to adopt a ballsy persona. He wanted to get on the front foot with this missing money from Pointer White. If there was something illegal going down with this Don Brandis bloke, he had to be on top of it. Sam couldn't be bothered dealing with arseholes anymore. Especially not criminal ones.

When they entered the pub, Chaz led them to a stark white table at the far end of the dining room, right beside the floor-to-ceiling glass windows.

Sam stopped and stared. 'You can see there are only two other people here, right?'

'We need privacy.'

'Chaz, there is nobody here. We could have sat anywhere and been unheard.'

'Crowd's just about to arrive.'

'You hear the echo in my voice?'

'Sam, you dragged us here,' said Zoe, breaking up the interlude. 'I'm guessing it wasn't to talk about the lack of patrons in the Dolphin dining room?'

'Chaz and I have heard some pretty ugly accusations from Roz and Idham,' said Sam. 'You know, from Pointer White? About someone at YRG pinching eight million bucks. Money duped from clients who thought they were paying for media.'

Chaz chimed in. 'The thing is, Roz and Idham have given us this memo that provides evidence of who ordered the money to be transferred to a suspicious account.'

'Which account?' asked Zoe.

'Premier Enterprises.'

'Who?'

'They're a registered company in the UK. We haven't done the paid-for company search thing yet to check on the shareholders and directors, but we will. And I bet Don Brandis, the guy who wrote the memo, or a relative or friend of his, is one of the Directors. We've been slow to follow up because, well, what if this eight million is just a small fraction of what Brandis and his cronies have misappropriated? Maybe they do this sort of thing all the time?'

'But all we know about is the eight million,' said Sam.

'I need a drink,' said Zoe. 'Here comes the waiter.'

'I suppose we should order.'

'Why are you looking at the menu?' said Zoe. 'You're famous for your photographic memory. Well, that and your ridiculous goddam ear for languages. Nothing will have changed since we were here last week.'

'You never know,' said Sam. But a few seconds later he admitted, 'You're right, nothing's changed. Risotto verde, again.'

'You know what I think?' said Zoe. 'We should stay the fuck out of it. What does it matter if this guy Brandis is skimming a bit of cash from YRG? It's not our job to solve some crime that has nothing to do with us.' She took a quick breath. 'And I don't understand what it's got to do with our agency. Roz and Idham have told you something bad went down at Pointer White. We don't work for Pointer White.'

'If we know about it,' said Chaz, 'and we look the other way, does that make us enablers?'

Zoe's voice became louder, 'Enablers? Really? Now you're using the language of people who allow drug addicts to carry on with their habit? What the... Just let it go, guys. It's not our problem.'

They ate their meals, drank some wine, and talked about other things. They had just ordered coffees when Chaz turned to Sam. 'Is it okay to talk about that other thing?'

'What other thing?'

'The Kitty thing.'

'Yes,' said Zoe. 'Jessie Thorne, the art director – we had a few drinks on Monday night – she said she'd heard about it.'

'Heard what?'

'That I sexually harassed Kitty at the party.'

'Trial by gossip,' said Sam. 'Marilyn told us there's been no complaint to HR, and yet we've got Kitty blabbing to anyone who'll listen.'

'We know it's bullshit,' Chaz said.

'But that doesn't stop it being a problem,' said Zoe. 'It's a bad look for me, and it's a bad look for TBA.'

'Doesn't help that YRG owns us now,' said Chaz. 'They wouldn't like a story getting out about a director of their newest subsidiary assaulting a powerless young girl.'

'It's blackmail,' said Zoe.

'Kitty is a fucking extortionist!' agreed Chaz, the wine now colouring his vernacular.

'She hasn't asked for any money,' said Sam.

'Give her time,' said Chaz.

'I'll speak to Marilyn again. If Kitty gossips about the incident to anyone else, then that could amount to malicious intent.'

'There's no doubt about her intent!' said Zoe.

Chapter 12

Sam switched on his laptop to discover an email sent at 10pm Thursday London time, or 7am Friday morning Sam's time:

Sam

I have enormous respect for you as a leader. We would not have bought your agency if that were not the case. Now I need you to exercise that leadership. Please bring Chaz into line on the merger with Pointer White. This is about making the Australian business stronger, and I am not convinced Chaz realises it is finalised. Whether he believes it a good idea or not is no longer relevant. I leave it to you to ensure he's one hundred per cent on board. It would be a great pity were he not to feature in the Australian operation moving forward.

Thanks,
Margaret

Sam's first concern was that Chaz might have had contact with Margaret since the email he'd sent her last Tuesday. And, as Sam read her words, he also wondered about her relationship with Don Brandis. Would Brandis have known about Chaz's reluctance to jump into bed with Pointer White? Sam had no idea. He hated feeling like he didn't know what was going on. This was serious and had the potential to spoil everything. Bloody Chaz.

Sam phoned him and Zoe and arranged to meet the pair in Chaz's office at noon. He immediately forwarded them Margaret's email, so there would be no confusion about why they were meeting.

Sam began the discussion by asking Chaz if he'd sent any more emails in the last week to Margaret or anyone else at YRG that Sam didn't know about. Chaz insisted he hadn't.

Zoe said, 'She's not mincing her words, is she?'

'No,' Sam replied. 'We've got no options here, guys.'

'Sam, it's your company, so it's your decision,' said Chaz. 'But I think you should fight it. What's she going to do? Fire you? I don't think so.'

'She might fire *me*,' said Zoe.

'Fuck off, Zoe,' said Chaz. 'She's not firing anyone. This is the company you two idiots built. YRG might have bought the shares but it's still your agency. If you two left, they'd be fucked. Remember that. You have more power than you think.'

Sam wasn't so sure. They were small fry for a company as big as YRG. If they wanted to, they could sack Zoe and all of the senior management. It would hurt the local TBA business but, in Chicago, would anyone even notice?

***

Ian Caldwell spent from 9am until 10am Wednesday working from home, huddled over a coffee-table in his studio flat in Parramatta, not far from the river. Out the window, he could see one of the new residential developments. His current place was clean and convenient – he'd never complained about it – but he would not be there for long. He was going places and determined to do whatever it took.

He knew a girl like Kitty Zhang would never go out with a guy who was stagnating. An overweight loser with no aspiration. He stood up, walked to the bathroom, and studied himself in the mirror. Yes, he needed to get fitter. And, okay, he ought to eat less fatty food. But that was all doable for a prize like Kitty. Never before had he been with a girl who made him feel like that. Those songs sprang to mind where they say that love is a drug. It really did feel like that. He'd had a taste and he wanted more.

Come eleven, Ian was at the desk of Bob Cooper, a TBA art director who managed to break his laptop at least once every few months. He always claimed that it wasn't his fault but the cracked screens and faint booze smell wafting up from the keyboard suggested otherwise. There were even little bits of food stuck in there from time to time; Ian wondered if they deducted the cost from Bob's pay.

As he went through the usual checking routine, Ian wondered whether Kitty would be at her desk now. She wouldn't be expecting him, but he simply had to see her again. He would catch the lift and then walk past her desk, as if on his way somewhere else. A casual drop-in, one might say. He hoped it wouldn't embarrass her. But how could he? She certainly didn't show any signs of embarrassment when they were at it in the meeting room last week.

11.40am. He'd been thinking about it all morning. The moment when words are hollow, and action is sacrosanct. Had he a chorus of trumpeters, this would be their time to play. He stepped out of the lift, and there she was, working at her computer.

He approached her desk. 'Hey, Kitty.'

She looked up. 'Oh, Ian. Hi there.'

'Everything okay?' he asked.

'Yeah, just super busy. Catch you later?'

And that was it. Nothing more to be said. He couldn't hang around. It wasn't like a nasty brush off or anything. She was just – busy. There'd be another time.

***

Chaz leaned back in his chair, sucking in the oxygen. 'I was right!' he said out loud to no one. He had been digging into Premier Enterprises and had finally discovered who the company's officeholders were.

CURRENT COMPANY EXTRACT:
PREMIER ENTERPRISES PLC
6th Floor, 88 Wood Street, London, EC2V 7QR

Officeholders and Other Roles
Director Name: DONALD JAMES BRANDIS
Address: 125 Ledbury Road, London, W11
2AQ
Born: 16/07/1981, INVERURIE, UNITED
KINGDOM
Appointment date: 23/08/2016

Secretary Name: LEO STEPHEN TAYLOR
Address: 81 Great Portland Street, London,
W1W 7LT
Born: 04/05/1969, OXFORD, UNITED
KINGDOM
Appointment date: 01/09/2017

So, there were only two of them. Brandis and some guy named Leo Taylor. No mention of Margaret. And these guys were also the only two shareholders. That made it even more suspicious. There was no way a YRG-affiliated company would have only two officeholders (who also happened to be the shareholders).

Chaz tried finding background information on Brandis and Taylor on the usual social media channels, but these guys were not easy to trace. He called Sam's mobile.

'Don't you think it's odd that Brandis, in an important role like Special Counsel for a big public company, isn't featured anywhere on YRG's various digital channels?'

'I do,' agreed Sam.

'They're a bunch of self-serving fuckwits. I just want TBA to remain the way it's always been.'

'Wishful thinking, Chaz.'

'I tell you what, you better not bloody leave, Sam.'

'I'm not planning to.'

'Whether or not Roz and Idham are correct in thinking Brandis and others acted corruptly doesn't really matter – in one sense. YRG is a shipwreck of a company either way. Even if there was a legal reason for Brandis moving the money, it still involves eight million dollars being taken from the coffers of Pointer White for a reason not understood by or ever explained to the agency's CFO or CEO.'

'And it's something that could send them bankrupt,' said Sam. 'Particularly if it was simply the first of what might turn out to be many such inexplicable financial transactions.'

Chaz finished his call with Sam, wondering what to do next. He needed to relieve the tension. Best way to do that? Sex. He might not have had a willing participant right this minute, but with a little planning...

Lunch! He decided to toss a coin to determine whom he should invite. If heads, it was the cute new account manager reporting to Little Ted, and if tails, Brie at reception. He got out of his chair to throw the coin high up into the air, and then watched it land on the carpet. Tails. 'The gods have spoken!'

He sent a text to Brie:

Lunch?

Instead of texting back, Brie called him on the landline. 'Today?'

'It won't ever come again,' said Chaz.

'You're crazy.'

'And?'

'I finish my shift at one.'

'See you then,' said Chaz.

One o'clock meant that if Chaz decided to have a few drinks – and there was little doubt that drinks were on the cards today after the unbelievable UK money trail discovery – then Brie could kick on with him. And Brie was fun, not like some of the other whingers around the office. He'd never seen her in a bad mood. Receptionists would have every right to be pissed off on any given day considering the way some fuckers gave them shit, often for things that were never their fault. Yeah. Brie was great. And she had a hot little body. Great legs. Like she'd been a gymnast or something.

Chaz received a text back:

Where are we going?

He texted:

Surprise

Brie responded with a heart emoji.

Chaz did a little fist pump from behind his desk. The day was certainly looking brighter than it had thirty minutes ago. He looked down at his pocket, remembering he still had a little pick-me-up left from earlier in the week. He'd not tested the waters with her, but he figured Brie would probably be into it. Oh, yes, this was looking like a fucking bright, sunshiny day!

***

Halfway along Syd Einfeld Drive, Sam's standard route home, he was driving faster than usual. All four windows were down, and the cool evening air was blowing hard against his face. The new BMW felt powerful, which gave Sam a kick, but it also made him conscious of what had changed recently. It was a product of the sale of the agency to YRG. The deal that had seemed so perfect, so too-good-to-be-true perfect.

He shot past a guy doing seventy in an old Mazda, much like the one Sam had driven for the last ten years. He tried to get a look at the man's face. Probably just his imagination playing tricks on him, but this bloke looked eerily like a younger version of Sam. Weird. Forget that!

Sam accelerated for a few hundred metres but then had to slow down for the speed cameras as he went through the lights.

At home, Rax was desperate to be fed. 'Come on, you monster,' said Sam, leading the black lab out the back. Sam threw the ball around the yard with him for about ten minutes, and then went into the kitchen to prepare a roast.

Once it was in the oven, he looked at his phone and spotted an email from Chaz. 'Oh, no!' he said out loud. 'Not to bloody Margaret again!'

Just then, Lauren walked in. 'Who are you shouting at?'

'Sorry, sweetheart. Just a crazy work email.'

'Another one?' she said, putting her bag down on the kitchen table.

'To Margaret. From Chaz.'

'Must have been a doozy for you to start shouting.'

'You don't want to know,' Sam said, pouring Lauren a glass of white from the open bottle.

'Try me.'

'Okay. But only because you asked.' He moved next to her and showed her his screen:

dear margaret

i don't want you to take this the wrong way
but – we won't be merging with pointer white. i
know you want us to. but i'm going to be frank
here. we know some stuff about the way you
operate. and you and i both know some of it
isn't good. we know about the money that went
to premier enterprises. yeah, we know all about
that. and we know about the memo from don
brandis which authorised it. in fact, i have that
memo. yes, idham gave it to me. so please
do not try and bully us. we're australian. we
don't take kindly to being bullied. we're born of
convicts. we're mostly polite but if you try and
hurt us, we'll hurt you back. oh, by the way,
did I tell you the australian media would love a
story like this. they'd just lap it up. you'd make it
out of the trade press and into the mainstream
press. really big story. go viral around the
world. good friend of mine is a journo with the
australian. she'd love this story. actually, i'm
seeing janet on friday night. it's not my intention
to sound threatening. look – sorry for the heavy
language but someone needed to speak frankly
about this. tba is a fabulous agency. don't mess

with it. i mean, why would you? there's no
need. you and yrg can make plenty of money
out of us. just not by merging the agency with
pointer white. thank you and goodnight.

sincerely, chaz.

'He says it's not his intention to threaten,' said Lauren. 'But it is as threatening as it gets. And this business about the money that went to Premier Enterprises? Sam, you look ill.'

'I feel ill.' Sam noticed that Lauren hadn't touched her wine.

'You going to call him?' she asked.

'I tried, but it went straight to his voicemail.'

'The whole message is in lower case.' said Lauren. 'You think he was drunk?'

'I'm sure he was, and more.'

'What are you going to do?'

'Try my best to salvage things.'

'I like Chaz,' said Lauren, 'but he really doesn't make it easy, does he?'

Sam shook his head. 'I'm tempted to email Margaret right away to apologise. But maybe that would only inflame things.'

'Probably best to wait until morning, sweetheart.'

'After a cooling off period? Right now, I feel like drowning myself in tequila. Or jumping on a plane to some remote village in the Amazon. Possibly both!'

'Don't let me stop you.'

Chapter 13

Thursday, June 4

Sam had barely slept but that didn't stop him getting to the office at his usual time to stew over all that had happened. He still hadn't spoken to Chaz, but he knew he'd have to contact Margaret promptly. Dread was getting the better of him.

Little Ted came over to ask how he should handle an issue with their solar energy client. 'The client wants us to carry them for a month or two. Says he'll have loads to spend come the new financial year.'

Sam felt completely distracted but was determined not to let down Little Ted, or indeed anyone else in his team. 'He wants creative work done now?'

'That's right,' said Little Ted. 'What should I say?'

'Tell him we'll do it, just this once.'

'You understand that we can't bill him until July?'

'We can live with that, so long as we have a purchase order.'

Little Ted walked off with a smile on his face. Sam was relieved. When the big man wasn't pleased, everyone in the office felt it.

Nine o'clock arrived with no sign of Chaz, so Sam emailed Margaret. He tried his best to make the tone sound warm and conciliatory, but he knew she'd still be mad.

At ten, one of the other finance guys told Sam that Chaz was in the building but caught up in meetings. Sam wasn't sure if he believed that, but he had a client meeting himself which he needed to get to. He picked up his phone to ring Zoe to check if she knew what was going on, but then an SMS came through from Chaz:

> meet me at the clock at seven.
> gotta talk

Sam thought about phoning him to find out what on earth he was up to, but finally just texted a reply.

***

Chaz glanced behind him and saw a tall swarthy-looking bloke pull back and duck into a retail outlet. Chaz picked up his pace. He was sure the man was following him. Was this the sort of man Brandis and his cronies might set upon him?

Chaz had first spotted him when passing Vinnies. He'd noticed the dark suit and sunnies. Could have been a security guy at a nightclub, Chaz thought, but these were far from nightclub conditions.

It was just after twelve thirty, bright sunshine, and Chaz was on his way home to meet Brie for a bit of lunchtime action. After yesterday's fun, he was supercharged for more. He hadn't told anyone else about her yet but, if he had, he would have included a declaration that she was the lay of the century. Without a fucking doubt. Lord, was she a fun girl!

Chaz came to an abrupt halt in front of the Stonewall Hotel in Paddington. He needed to capture an image of his stalker. He held his phone up, as if to take a selfie, but by the time he'd hit the photo button, the tall guy had slipped out of shot – somewhere near Mr Crackles.

At the Beacham traffic lights, Chaz leaned forward and jogged across South Dowling Street. He thought about popping into the Palace Verona and waiting to see if Mr Swarthy followed him in there. No, fuck that! He wasn't going to be hiding in a corner, waiting to be searched out. Who cared if he was being followed? Swarthy wasn't going to actually do anything. He was just observing. In fact, now he'd drifted out of sight.

By the time Chaz reached the Town Hall, he was fairly certain the guy was gone. Good riddance.

Chaz turned down Underwood Street and noticed a blonde woman staring at him. Just standing there in front of the Imperial, nicely dressed, eyes attentive. Blondie removed her mobile from her handbag and focused on that. Maybe she'd just been flirting when she looked at him. Or perhaps she was near-sighted and didn't even know she was looking at him. Anyway, his worries were over, and the walk home was nearly complete. Now his mind returned to Brie and that awesome sex that was soon to be soaking up his senses.

***

'Go!' said Viktor.

He and Darius flew out from behind a black windowless van and tasered Chaz before he could react. Fifty thousand volts later, they bundled his limp mass into the back of the van.

'Good job, my son,' Viktor said to Darius. He started the engine and pulled out from behind a red Toyota. 'You've got balls.'

Chapter 14

Sam looked over at the locked filing cabinet beside his desk. It was filled with legal and finance documents, most of which didn't move around much. He had to hang onto them for seven years as part of TBA's client contracts. In the middle drawer, in an unmarked white envelope, was the memo from Chaz. 'Why are you giving it to me?' Sam had said to him.

It made no sense. Chaz was the one Idham had given the memo to initially, and Sam didn't see why it wasn't still in Idham's hands. It was a Pointer White document, not a TBA one. What was Idham so afraid of? Would it be the subject of a subpoena if things ever turned nasty? But, if so, surely he could just have handed it over to his lawyer to let them deal with it. It was rarely wise to hide documents like that from the courts. Sam had made a copy and couriered it to the TBA lawyers. He would need to certify it in front of them if he wanted it taken seriously, but that didn't need to be done right this minute.

The landline rang. It was Marilyn Banks. 'Sam, I'm calling about Chaz,' she said. 'Do you know where he is?'

'No. Why?'

'I've just had a call from Brie. Apparently, Chaz was meant to be meeting her for lunch and never showed.'

'Maybe he double-booked?'

'Chaz usually keeps his appointments in the shared TBA Finance calendar,' said Marilyn. 'But the last couple of days, he's been ducking in and out at times when there's not been anything marked. It's not like him to be so – unpredictable.'

'Okay. Let me make a couple of calls,' said Sam, already checking for Brie's mobile number before hanging up the phone. What was Chaz doing, going for lunch with Brie? He'd said before that the two of them were friendly. Seriously, Chaz. The receptionist!

Now, what to do with that original memo?

***

Sam had not heard back from Margaret, which was reasonable, given the London time difference, but it still worried him, on top of the call from Marilyn Banks. He'd left a message on Chaz's mobile but there'd been no response.

He felt a bit weird ringing Brie. If Chaz was having a thing with her, Sam didn't want to get caught in the middle. He had other problems to deal with, namely Kitty Zhang. Sam hoped to God that would just go away. He felt he should tell Lauren about it, if for no other reason than to make sure she heard it from him first and not from social media.

Meanwhile, he was trying to read through a pitch brief which a client had given him a week ago. Normally he'd have been completely on top of it by now, but today he kept losing track of the information, having to re-read paragraphs after he'd just finished them.

His mind went back to Chaz. The email Chaz wrote to Margaret was completely over the top and extreme, even by Chaz's standards. He must have been high as a kite to have even sent it. If Chaz upset YRG enough, the money they owed Sam and Zoe could be held back.

He sent a text to Chaz:

All ok for tonight?

***

Sam arranged to meet Zoe in the boardroom at 5.30pm. On the way, he grabbed two beers from the nearby fridge.

'You're worried, aren't you?' Zoe said.

Sam sat down and took a swig of beer. 'Bloody Chaz,' he mumbled.

'Have you spoken to him?'

'Not today. You?'

'Last night,' said Zoe. 'He was pretty wasted.'

'Was he with…'

'Brie? Yeah. Fessed up pretty quick. I think he was having so much fun he didn't care who knew.'

'Where was he?'

'His place.'

'You think he's still there?'

'I don't know,' said Zoe. 'I've left more than one message for him. Nothing back. I spoke to Brie; she told me about their plan to meet up at lunchtime. She waited, he didn't arrive. She called, but no word. Not a lot of time between noon and when he went missing.'

'Time to?'

'You know,' said Zoe, 'for him to have suddenly come up with a new plan for his afternoon, for him to have been called away for a legitimate work reason.'

'What about Idham? Is it worth calling him?'

'Great minds. He hasn't heard. But I told him about that email to Margaret, and it made him all jumpy. I know it sounds ridiculous, but he actually thought Chaz could be in serious danger.'

'Really? Over a *memo*?'

'It's not just that,' said Zoe. 'Remember, Idham thinks there's much more to it than the eight million we know about. He thinks Brandis is…'

'What?'

'I don't know. One of those high-level sort of crooks. Mafia type.'

'Zoe, have you ever come across a less mafia-style company than YRG? Not a lot of Italian names on that board of directors.'

'Okay, not the actual mafia. Not Italian crims. But big bloody organised ones. You know what I mean? Like you get with corrupt governments, and cops and all that.'

'Sounding like a work of fiction to me, Zoe.'

'Well, tell me where Chaz is, then.'

'I'll tell you when I see him at seven.'

Sam went back to his desk and tried to adopt a business-as-usual mindset, but it didn't work. Seven o'clock loomed large. He rang. No answer. He left a message. 'Chaz, it's me. I'm assuming we're still on for seven. Call me. Otherwise – I guess I'll just see you there.'

Then Zoe had called again. 'I'm kind of freaking out. I think Chaz is in trouble.'

'Have you heard something?' asked Sam.

'I spoke to Idham again. He told me he thought someone had been following him. A big Middle Eastern looking dude.'

'Seriously?'

'He's afraid to be alone.'

'A *Middle Eastern looking dude*! You and Idham need to stop the racial profiling. Brandis is a senior YRG—'

'You didn't see the man who was following Idham.'

'And neither did you,' Sam pointed out.

'I know, but from what Idham said…'

'Look, I'm leaving now. Chaz said he'd meet me, and that's what I expect him to do.'

'If he's not dead, already.'

'Zoe, Chaz is not dead.'

Chapter 15

Chaz would have preferred Blondie to have remained in the room, as a witness to whatever was about to go down.

One man was dressed in black from head to toe, his eyes cruel. He took off his leather jacket and threw it on the table. That brought his holstered handgun into plain sight. 'Worried about the gun?' he asked Chaz, in what sounded like some kind of Eastern European accent. The man kept twisting his head around, like he'd just got out of bed and had a sore neck. 'Don't be. If we don't get what we want, it'll be much worse for you than being shot.'

Chaz glanced at the other man, younger, dressed in a blue patterned shirt. He was leaning against the table and had a small backpack.

'Look at *me*!' said the Man in Black, yanking Chaz's face. 'He can't help you.'

'Just tell me what you want,' Chaz said.

'What do you know about the eight million dollars?'

'I don't know anything—' The Man in Black had removed his gun from its holster and grazed Chaz's head with the butt. 'Augh!' Chaz felt new blood beginning to trickle from his scalp.

'If I'm asking you something, then you must know something about it.' The Man in Black motioned over to the younger guy, who opened his backpack to reveal a knife; it looked like a fishing knife, a blade large enough to slice through flesh and bones with ease. 'If you say I don't know again, I will cut off your finger.'

'Okay, okay!' said Chaz. 'Eight million dollars was transferred from Pointer White to Premier Enterprises in the UK.'

'That's better. How many people know about this?'

Chaz didn't want to say anyone's name, but he had to say something. While he was thinking, the Man in Black raised his gun again. 'Wait! Roz and Idham, the C-suiters at Pointer White.'

'Who else?'

Chaz hesitated again. 'Maybe someone else in finance. I don't know.'

The Man in Black brought down his gun, this time a little harder. 'What about your friend, Sam?'

Chaz felt groggy, felt blood pooling onto his shoulder, a trickle rolling down his back. 'I thought,' he said, taking a pained breath, 'I thought you meant from Pointer White.'

'Oh?' The Man in Black shrugged at the younger man waiting with the knife. 'I guess I wasn't being clear. Maybe I should hit him again?'

'No, no,' hurried Chaz. 'I can tell you; Sam doesn't know about it.'

The Man in Black nodded at the younger guy, who proceeded to remove a small speaker from the backpack. There was a moment of quiet, while the Man in Black and Chaz both watched the young man fiddle with his mobile, and then the Eagles' "Hotel Californa" could be heard.

Chaz's mind was spinning. Blondie had told him what the music was for. Nothing about this was good. Time had slowed down for a moment but there was no escaping the nightmare. How did people with missing fingers do any of the things he liked to do in life?

'Apart from the memo,' said the Man in Black, 'is there any other evidence of Don Brandis' involvement in the transfer of the money?'

'No. Not that's been shared with me.'

'Shared by?'

'Roz and Idham.'

'And the memo? Where is it now?'

'I don't have it.'

The Man in Black nodded to the young guy. The response was immediate. Chaz felt his ribcage implode; the young man's punch was harder than any knock Chaz had felt before. And then he did it again.

'What do you want from me?' Chaz begged.

'Where *is* it?'

'I told you! I don't have it.'

The Man in Black walked away for a few seconds, returning with the fishing knife to hand, pushing the blade right up against Chaz's throat. 'Feels sharp, doesn't it?' Chaz tried to pull free from his binds, but they were much too tight. 'I think we'll start with your little finger, then work our way around.'

'I don't know where it is,' said Chaz.

'You're lying!'

The man's movement was swift. The fifth finger of Chaz's right hand was on the floor. Blood everywhere. The younger man pulled a cloth from his backpack and put it over the wound.

Chaz was barely conscious now. He wondered if this might be the end. But then a part of him, a part buried deep inside wanted revenge upon these people – if he did manage to somehow survive.

***

Viktor looked closely at Chaz's face. He was passed out, both eyes shut, blood from his scalp wounds starting to coagulate. Viktor checked for a pulse. Still alive. That was useful.

'Tell me,' Viktor said to Darius. 'What did you see?'

'He wasn't weak.'

'No, he wasn't weak. He only pretended to be weak.'

'There was one name he didn't give up.'

'Yes. Sam Pride.'

'They're friends, right? Probably felt guilty.'

'It was more than that.'

'He – knows where the memo is?'

'Yes. And if we woke him up and threatened to take another finger, he'd confess, but there's no need for that.'

'Because you think it's with Pride?'

'Very good, Darius. Now, call Haddad.'

Chapter 16

Sam tried to think of a way this could mean something other than the obvious. Could it be a joke? It certainly didn't come across that way. He showed Lauren the text. She took his phone and held it up close, like she needed to be sure the words were real:

WE HAVE BAILLEY

Sam reached for her hand. 'I've been telling myself all this time that Chaz and Idham were exaggerating this stuff, you know, the likelihood of Brandis and his accomplices being corrupt. I knew it was a possibility, but I kept thinking there was another explanation. Something more plausible, given Brandis' position at the top of a highly respected global company.'

Lauren pulled her chair closer to Sam's and asked, 'What do we do?'

'Sweetheart, it's me who got us into this, and it's me who has to get us out of it.'

'I think we're past that, don't you? We're a team. Always.'

Sam put his arms around her. Lauren was right, of course, but these people might have seen Sam as part of their criminal game, and that placed those closest to him in real danger. He needed to be conscious of that. He had to protect her.

'I'm going to have to reply to them,' Sam said.

'Shouldn't you ring the police first?'

'Maybe. What's my number one priority? Getting Chaz out of harm's way. There may be a better way than going to the police.'

'What are you thinking?' Lauren asked.

'This criminal stuff, fraud, kidnapping…' Sam still wasn't sure what to do, but he needed to find out exactly what the kidnappers wanted. 'I'm going to text them back,' he said.

What do you want?

Within thirty seconds he had his answer:

We want the memo. The original
not a copy. If you speak to the
cops you will never see your
friend again. And that won't be
your only problem.

'I'd better respond,' Sam said. 'They might – do something terrible to Chaz.'

'If they haven't already,' said Lauren.

'I'm trying to stay positive,' said Sam, texting:

Okay. Where can we meet?

Again, the response came quickly:

Come alone. 9pm.
54 hatch street botany.
If you fuck with us
it won't just be your friend
who pays.

Lauren said, 'Can I see?'

Sam was about to hand her his mobile when it rang. Zoe.

'I've just got off the phone from Brie,' she said. 'She's in a complete panic. Seems Chaz told her a lot of shit last night.'

'Fuck.'

'When they were hammered. And screwing.'

'Oh, God. About Brandis? Zoe, they've taken Chaz hostage.'

'What?'

'I got a text. Someone claiming they're holding Chaz hostage. They're demanding the memo.'

'What the?'

'Look, I've got to get off the phone. Is Brie all right?'

'I don't know,' said Zoe. 'She's just the fucking receptionist.'

'Can you check on her?'

'Why don't *you* check on her?'

'Because they want me to come with the memo straight away. Or else. Understand?'

'What the hell have we got ourselves into?' Zoe muttered.

Chapter 17

The southerly had hit, the midday sunshine a distant memory. The Uber driver wished Brie well as she climbed out of his car in Bankstown, a stone's throw from the RSL. Brie stood still as she watched him drive off. It had been three months since she last saw her mother. The sky was grey and the wind howling, as if mocking her desire for colour and light. She walked slowly across the narrow strip of front lawn. One step at a time, she told herself.

She hoped her mum's partner, David, wouldn't be there. But even if he was, it wouldn't stop her saying what needed to be said. The house was a modern box of bricks, not to Brie's liking, but it had impressed her mum enough to make her want to move in with David. Fair enough. She wanted security, something Brie's dad had never offered her. His whereabouts were currently unknown, as they had been for the last three years.

Brie rang the bell. Her mum opened the door, but not the security grill. 'Can I come in?' Brie noticed her mother dressed for bed, and the look of disdain. 'I've been doing well, Mum. I swear. I've been clean for weeks. But something's happened. Something bad. Please, let me in.'

'You are joking, right?' her mum said. 'David will be home any minute. You know what he said last time. Get lost.'

'I understand that, Mum. And I don't blame him. I was a drunk and an addict, but I've sorted myself out.'

'No. I told you last time. Now go!' She slammed the door shut.

Brie stood there, unable to face the oppressive sky. Tears streamed down her face. Her mother was right; David would be mad as hell if he found her there. She didn't need that, but she didn't know where else to go.

She walked to the corner of the street, and then on to the next, until finally she thought she was far enough away to stop. She sat down on a metre-high front wall. There was no-one around. She used a little silver straw to do a quick line. She knew that escape was only temporary, but there was nothing else on offer.

***

Sam revealed his plan to Lauren, but there was just no way he could make it happen in the short window the kidnappers had given him. He desperately needed to buy time.

'Why not just go straight to the police?' Lauren asked. 'You're not a criminal. That's why we have a police force.'

'It's not that I don't think they're capable. But if there's a better option available…'

'Really?'

'People go missing all the time, so it's not the cops' first priority. My first and only priority is Chaz.'

'And?'

'And you, of course.' Sam sent the text:

> I don't have the memo with me.
> But I can get it in the morning. I
> can meet you at Hatch Street at
> 11am. Okay?

No response. Just dead silence. Sam emptied the bottle of white while they waited.

'They're not going to change the time of the meet,' said Lauren. 'Why would they?'

'If they want the memo enough, they might. Look, if we don't hear back from them in, say, twenty minutes, I will call the police.'

'Good.'

Ten minutes later, Sam said, 'Maybe I screwed up? Maybe I should go there now?'

Lauren was watching him as he moved squeamishly from side to side in his chair, staring at the empty glass in front of him. He thought he was doing the right thing, but he couldn't be sure. Twenty, and then thirty minutes passed.

Just as he was about to call the police, the notification came through:

> 11am. Remember, come alone.
> Or…

***

Darius sat on the steel table watching Viktor wander back and forth across the room, wondering when he would stop. The meeting had been confirmed for tomorrow, so there was no reason for them not to get some sleep. It would have been nice to go back to their five-star hotel by the park for a few hours, but Darius knew that wasn't going to happen. What could they do with Chaz Bailey? They couldn't leave him there. Or could they? He was still tied up and gagged, out cold.

One look at Viktor's face and Darius knew he wouldn't be open to any suggestion of creature comforts. 'No warm, soft beds tonight?'

'We stay where we are,' said Viktor. 'You can sleep. You have important job to do in the morning.'

'Sleep on this cold, hard floor?'

Viktor gave Darius a stare that said, *Enough*.

Step, step, step. Leather soles on concrete. Darius wanted to put the music back on. The speaker was right there. Would have been easy. But he didn't want to make Viktor mad.

'You know how, in the movies, they talk about loose ends?' he said at last. 'Which I guess, if you're in our caper, means you want to reduce your risk of things coming back to bite you?'

'You're asking,' said Viktor, nodding toward Chaz, 'what we do with *that* loose end?'

'Yes.'

Viktor smiled. 'We leave no loose ends.'

Darius was going to leave it at that, but then he had another thought. 'What about Roz and Idham from Pointer White?'

'They were too afraid to even hang on to the Memo. Their fear incapacitates them.'

'So, they are not a threat?'

'No.'

Not a threat, okay, but Darius thought they still seemed to fit the definition of a loose end. Just like Zoe Barnes, Sam Pride, and Lauren Pride. He wanted to learn as much as possible from Viktor, but if he wanted consistency, perhaps he'd have to look elsewhere.

***

Lauren threw Sam his jacket as he ran out the door. He was probably over the limit when he jumped into the car but, if ever there was a time to break the rules, this was it. Life and death. Lauren was safe for now. This next bit, he could only do alone. The clock on the dash told him he had eleven and a half hours.

He was doing eighty as he came out of the Harbour Tunnel and onto the freeway, rain lashing the windscreen. He wanted to put his foot down – he knew how fast this new car could go – but he resisted. If he crashed and was pulled over and breath-tested by the cops, he'd have no chance of rescuing his friend. Focus. He had to get to Ted Lansing's home in one piece.

Little Ted lived by himself in a comfortable full-brick house up a long driveway, nestled in between two larger properties. Sam had called earlier to discuss his plan, so he was not surprised to see the big guy waiting on the porch. Once inside, Sam said, 'You sure you're okay with this?'

'I got you, brother,' Little Ted said, and gave Sam a bear hug that squeezed the life out of him. Figuratively speaking. He wasn't actually dead yet.

Chapter 18

It was a little after 8am when Little Ted arrived at Bar Lucio in Victoria Street, Darlinghurst. Marco Bianchi, the flamboyant multi-millionaire said to have started without a cent to his name, was already commanding attention, surrounded by a bunch of good-looking young men hovering on wooden stools by the side of the road. Inside, the café was filled with a mix of people, early twenties to late fifties, chatting away beside the old boxing memorabilia that adorned the walls. As Little Ted approached, two of Bianchi's gym-junkie lads started to size him up. Little Ted didn't recognise them. Bianchi, physically distinguishable by his dark curly hair and thick beard, as well as his very ample torso, seemed to enjoy a high level of companion turnover.

'Hello Marco,' said Little Ted, standing before the hirsute figure.

Bianchi finished sipping his espresso before looking up. 'My friend,' he said. The warm tone was enough to make the hangers-on realise Little Ted had status. Bianchi motioned for one of them to give up his seat. 'Come, sit with me. Have a coffee.'

Little Ted sat between two young men, Soxy and Handy. Soxy was nearly as tall as Little Ted, though much thinner, with dark brown eyes. Handy, Ted soon learned, had been christened with the name Oliver Handwell, which turned into *Handsome* in his late teens because of his intense lapis-blue eyes. Apparently, the plan was for everyone to go out on Bianchi's yacht later in the day.

'You should come,' said Bianchi. He and Little Ted both knew that was about as likely as a manned flight to Jupiter.

Coffee arrived. Little Ted was about to raise the cup to his lips when he witnessed a middle-aged man with a grey goatee pulling over in a red Ferrari.

'That's what it's all about,' said Soxy, eyes glued to the sparkling sports car.

'What do you mean?' said Little Ted.

'A red Ferrari. It's what we all aspire to.'

'Really?'

'Car like that, you could have anyone you want. Male, female, animal, mineral…'

Bianchi leaned in towards Little Ted, the young guys realising that was their cue to pull back and talk among themselves. 'Now, what can I do for you?'

'I have a problem,' said Little Ted. He did not need to mention what he had done for Bianchi in the past. They both knew it had cost Little Ted two years of his life. It would not be spoken of, not today or any other day, but it would never be forgotten.

'You know me, my friend,' said Bianchi. 'If you have a problem, then I have a problem. How can I help?'

***

Lauren looked at the clock beside her bed, surprised by how long she'd slept. When Sam left for Little Ted's house last night, she wondered if she'd ever be able to get to sleep. Thoughts kept running around her head. She wanted to take the safe option, especially now that she had a baby on the way. As she lay in bed, hand on her stomach, she tried to rationally assess what the safe option was. Going to the police? Never in her life had she dealt with real-life criminals. She got out of bed and joined Sam in the kitchen.

'Coffee?' he said.

'Yes, please.'

She watched him adjusting the settings on their high-tech machine, another of the new toys that had landed post the agency sale.

'You know, I'm not very good with this whole – *criminal thing*,' she said.

'What do you mean?'

'My scene growing up was comfy kids from private schools, lush houses in nice suburbs. The biggest threat to my physical well-being was when a parent cheered a little too loudly at an inter-school sports game.'

'I know. You like the peace and quiet.'

Lauren thought about the baby, and the world in which he or she would grow up, she and Sam taking them to a school play or a musical performance. 'This stuff with Chaz, it's scary,' she said. 'Kidnappings and murder threats. My God, what's the world coming to?'

'Not sure I can answer that, sweetheart.'

'I want to get back to, well, you know…'

Sam sat down opposite her. 'You don't think I'm doing my best to…'

'I know you are. And I know you have an innate understanding of people. That's why you've done so well in the ad game. As weird and horrendous as this situation we're in might be, it is still all about people. How they think, how they behave. Maybe you're right not to go to the police. Not yet, at least. You seem so sure that Little Ted will be our saviour.'

'Little Ted is someone I know I can count on,' Sam said. 'Someone we can count on.'

Lauren didn't know exactly what Sam and Ted's history was. All she knew was that Little Ted felt he owed Sam, and someone else owed Little Ted. And they were all terribly loyal people, so debts, or acts of kindness, or whatever they were, they were repaid. No matter what. When Sam spoke about this stuff, the language seemed foreign. But she knew Sam loved her and she believed in him.

Lauren tried to think of the right words to tell Sam about the pregnancy. But would it be too much of a burden for him right now? Today's task was giving these terrible crooks their stupid rotten memo and getting back Chaz. Nothing should be a higher priority in Sam's mind. Until she told him the big news, at the end of the day.

Sam watched her taking a sip of her coffee, and then said, 'You're going to hang out with Janice today, right?'

'Yes, she's happy for me to go over there.'

'It's a pity your parents are in London.'

'They're better off, there. Don't worry about me. I'll be okay.'

'Janice loves you.'

'You don't think she's in any danger?'

'No. But I think it's good that you are going over there.'

Lauren thought about how her mother-in-law would react to the baby news. She surreptitiously touched her belly and began humming the theme from the Largo in Dvorak's *New World Symphony*. She didn't remember the rest of the symphony, but that longing in the melody of the Largo, the progression from A major to E major, the D major to C sharp minor section, and the gentle resolution back into A major, had always stayed with her. Maybe she would give Janice the good news today.

***

The first thing Chaz experienced when he awoke, before he'd even opened his eyes, was pain. Excruciating, all-consuming pain. His head hurt, his ribs hurt, but it was the stinging pain in his hand, where he was missing a finger, that most brought back the terror of the night before. He was now clothed, and he had a blood-soaked bandage wrapped around his hand, but none of it made any difference. He was defeated. Fully, one hundred per cent, defeated. He looked down at the grey concrete floor. The colour spoke of nothingness. As he raised his head, the man in the blue-patterned shirt came into view, perched upon the metal table against the wall. The other one, the older man, was nowhere to be seen. 'Please, mate,' Chaz begged. 'Some Nurofen. Panadol. Anything. You've got to get me something. I'm dying here.'

'You're not dying,' said Blue Shirt. 'Your friend will be here soon. With the memo. Then it will all be over.'

'You'll let me go home?'

'We will all go home. Everyone happy.'

Happy was not a word Chaz would have used. But if they let him go, the relief would be immeasurable. He would be able to get some real drugs for the pain. He looked at his bandaged hand again. He needed surgery. 'Where is my finger?' he asked.

Blue Shirt pointed to a scrunched-up cloth on the other end of the table.

Chaz had heard things about the progress surgeons had made in microsurgery. If the finger could be re-attached, even if it wasn't quite as good as it was before, that would be okay. He could live with that.

But the bigger question was the only one that really mattered. Would they let him live at all?

The fact that Blue Shirt never quite looked him in the eye when he addressed Chaz suggested he was lying. Chaz sensed that he was less comfortable – or at least less experienced – doing his job than the man in black. If the time came to pull the trigger, Chaz felt that Blue Shirt might hesitate. The man in black would not.

***

Viktor walked slowly around the driveway of 56 Hatch Street in front of the warehouse in which Chaz Bailley was captive. Haddad stood stock-still. Sam Pride would soon be coming to number 54, next door. If the police arrived, that's where they would look first for a supposed kidnap victim.

Viktor looked at his watch. 10.10am. Haddad's men were late. In Chicago, this would not have happened. The business they were in was unforgiving. Even his business partner, Robert Miller, knew that. Like many white, well-to-do Americans, he was a pussy. But not incompetent. And never late. Fucking Australian amateurs! Viktor lit a cigarette.

'You think Pride has called the cops?' Haddad asked.

'Maybe,' Viktor replied.

'Good that we're prepared for that.'

Viktor looked at Haddad like he was stupid. Of course, they were prepared. They had a camera watching the road between here and the cop station. It was being monitored by Haddad's men back in Riley Street. But Viktor had studied Sam Pride's file. He would be too worried about his friend being hurt to call the cops. He would back himself to fix this, to get Bailley out in one piece.

Just then, two men from Haddad's security company pulled up in a white Toyota Hilux. These were, fit, lean men, with military-style haircuts, dressed in dark track-suit pants and tight T-shirts.

Viktor looked at Haddad, clearly concerned. 'This is it?'

'We don't want to attract attention,' said Haddad. 'Best to keep it low key. In case the cops do come. *Nothing to see here.*'

'And what if there is trouble?'

'These guys know their stuff. Don't worry.'

'I do worry,' said Viktor. 'That's why I'm still alive. I don't take chances.'

'Look,' said Haddad. 'There's you, Darius, me, and my two guys. Five professionals.'

Viktor shook his head.

'What?' said Haddad. 'It's not like this advertising guy is going to turn up with an army, is it?'

***

Sam felt a complete mismatch for the vehicle he was climbing into. It was the most powerful, well equipped, and electronically sophisticated streetcar the famous German automobile manufacturer had ever produced. Then there was Sam: Tired; anxious; no experience in a situation like this; no weapon of any sort for protection. He tried not to let the fear overwhelm him. *Thank God for Little Ted!*

The clock on the dash told Sam he had thirty-three minutes. Better to be early, park a few streets away and simply hang out for a bit. Make himself as comfortable with the surroundings as possible.

***

Viktor left Haddad in the street and entered the warehouse. He locked eyes with Bailley, strapped into the chair but looking less vulnerable than he had been when he was naked. Was there still some fight left in this man?

'Gag him,' Viktor instructed Darius.

Viktor's phone rang. It was Milo from the Surry Hills control room. 'Pride's BMW has just passed the camera,' he said.

'Cops?'

'No sign of them,' said Milo, 'or anyone else you might need to worry about. Pride is alone.'

***

At ten fifty-seven, Sam parked opposite the designated meeting spot at 54 Hatch Street. Two men were standing in front of the house. He looked up and down the tree-lined street. It was a mixture of commercial and residential. No other human beings. No witnesses. The younger of the two men wore pale blue jeans and an overcoat, under which he appeared to be holding something. A shotgun? Sam looked back at the older one dressed in black and thought he could see a slight bulge under his leather jacket. Perhaps it was covering a revolver. There was no sign of Chaz. Sam couldn't be sure, but he had to assume his friend was still alive. If not, it would have been better to have just called the cops.

The free-standing house behind the men was freshly painted white, with grey window frames that matched the picket fence and roof tiles. There was a security gate for off-street parking on the side of the house next to a two-storey industrial warehouse.

Sam imagined Chaz behind the white walls of the house, sitting in the lounge room under guard, a couple of guys watching him, one with a gun at the ready. At the same time, part of him was saying this was all ridiculous. Some guy working for Brandis just wanted the memo back, and for Sam and Chaz to leave them alone. Brandis might have been a crook, but he was much more likely to be the typical white-collar kind who stayed well clear of violence, his only interest being the money. He would have the background and training to get his hands on his interest without ever getting them dirty. Brandis wasn't a drug lord; he was a high-level executive working for a global blue-chip.

Stepping out of the car, Sam felt a chill in the air. A cool south-westerly, blowing about twenty Ks. He picked up the envelope and crossed the road to where the two men were standing.

The older one gave Sam a hard look. 'This is it?' he said, motioning towards the envelope. Sam wondered about the accent. Croatian?

'It is,' Sam said.

The man held out his hand.

Sam didn't move. 'Where's Chaz?' he asked.

'Pocetnik,' the man said under his breath. Sam understood it to mean, *A beginner*, in Croatian. 'You give me the memo, I give you Bailley,' he said in a louder voice. Sam recognised the accent from the time he spent traveling around Croatia the year before he started TBA. A beautiful place. An ugly ex-patriot.

The younger guy pulled back his overcoat to reveal a shotgun. Sam didn't know much about guns, but it looked like the sort that could splatter him all over the driveway.

Despite this, Sam said, 'I want to see Chaz first.'

'Do you want to get your friend back or not?' said the Croatian. 'Just give me the damned memo.'

Sam felt like he was watching a cobra. 'I'll give it to you,' he said. 'But only after I see Chaz.'

The Croatian looked up and down the street. 'You call the police?'

'You asked me not to.'

'Anyone else?'

'You can see I'm on my own.'

The Croatian looked into Sam's eyes, no doubt trying to determine if his opponent could be trusted. He reached under his leather jacket, which scared Sam. But it was only to retrieve a phone and ring a number. 'Anything?' he said into the mobile. Sam couldn't hear the response, but the Croatian's look suggested he was satisfied. 'Get Bailley,' he told his younger colleague.

The subordinate went next door into the warehouse. Sam didn't know what they were up to. Maybe this would all end peacefully, after all. It seemed a bit weird to be so bothered about a signed original when Sam could have had a copy certified as true by his lawyers.

A few minutes passed, and then, to Sam's enormous relief, in the doorway to the warehouse, he saw Chaz's face come out of the shadows. He was accompanied by the younger man in the overcoat as well as three other men, all carrying revolvers. Chaz looked dirty and bloody, with a thick bandage on his hand. But he was alive.

They had bound his wrists together, and he appeared to be carrying some sort of scrunched up cloth in his left hand. He began to walk in Sam's direction. Slowly. But walking. That was surely a good sign. Two of the men followed, their revolvers on him.

'Stop!' yelled the Croatian, turning to Sam. 'Okay, you have your proof. Now give me the bloody memo.'

'My friend looks injured.'

'He is fine. You can give him some paracetamol and tuck him into bed when you get home. Now…'

Sam handed him the envelope, and he glanced through it. 'You see these men here,' the Croatian said. 'They all have guns. And yet, you don't seem to be afraid?'

'I'm not,' Sam said.

'Why is that?'

'It's those red dots all over your jacket.'

'What?'

'The red dots.'

The Croatian looked down at his jacket, perhaps suspecting some kind of trick. It wasn't. There were four laser targets reflecting off his chest – each belonging to their own sniper rifle. And Sam knew there were another four without red dot sights; eight total shooters, all with high precision weapons, targeting the Croatian from nearby vantage points. The best snipers money could buy. Courtesy of Marco Bianchi, who'd said to Little Ted a few hours earlier, 'I have one philosophy. Overwhelming force.'

Sam didn't know who Bianchi's men were, and he didn't understand how a stockbroker could also be so tightly connected to the underworld, or how anyone could get hold of eight pros in less than three hours, for that matter. All he cared about was getting his friend back. Alive.

The Croatian grimaced. 'What is this?' he said. 'You got some kind of army or something?'

'I have friends,' Sam said.

'Some friends.'

'You've got what you want. My friends are not here to hurt you. Just insurance.'

'Okay,' said the Croatian. 'We are done.' He turned to the other men. 'Let him go!'

Chaz held out his hands, and the man in the blue shirt removed a knife from his pocket to cut Chaz loose. Chaz walked towards Sam, who was about to give him a hug, when he suddenly turned to the Croatian and kicked him in the balls, yelling, 'That's for my finger, you fucking cunt!'

The Croatian's response was so fast, Sam could scarcely believe his eyes. Just as Chaz had turned to walk away, the Croatian pulled a knife from his ankle strap, reached out and pulled back on Chaz's hair, exposing his throat, and ripping the knife across it. In an instant, blood was spurting furiously from the severed artery.

Shots rang out from the snipers but only one of them grazed the Croatian. The two men wearing white T-shirts had both been hit and were lying on the ground bleeding out. The one in the overcoat lay motionless on the driveway, too slow to ever raise the barrel of his weapon into the air. The man in the blue shirt who, like the Croatian, had moved at lightning speed to avoid the sniper bullets, was unscathed, and, along with his injured comrade, was running helter-skelter for the warehouse doorway.

Sam dropped to the ground and tried to stop the bleeding from Chaz's neck, at first with his bare hands, and then with his sweatshirt. 'Chaz!' he yelled. 'Chaz, can you hear me? Come on, Chaz, hang in there!'

But Chaz was unconscious, and his loss of blood made Sam realise he was wasting his time. Little Ted, who had been directing the snipers from a nearby vantage point, arrived to help.

'We've got to call an ambulance!' Sam shouted.

'I'll do it,' said Little Ted.

Sam wanted to go after the man who had done this. But he couldn't bring himself to leave Chaz. 'Fuck. You go. I'll call.'

Little Ted didn't wait to be asked twice. He ran to the warehouse doorway and left Sam to extract his mobile from his pocket using his left hand, while desperately trying to maintain pressure on Chaz's neck wound with his right.

Chapter 19

Little Ted drew his weapon before entering the warehouse. He knew his heart rate was low, as it needed to be – genetics and training each playing their part – and he could feel that his breathing was steady, also a prerequisite for this game. He had only been to the shooting range twice since his time in jail, but he was confident his skills had not diminished.

The space inside the warehouse was vast, with very little furniture. A couple of chairs, a table or two, and a few large stacks of boxes. The two men Little Ted was after could have been hiding anywhere, or they could already have escaped through the rear door. The roof lights were switched off, and grills over the windows blocked out most of the natural light. Little Ted's eyes adjusted as he scanned the space, listening. Nothing but silence. If these guys were still in the warehouse, they were keeping very still.

'We don't have to do this,' Little Ted called out. 'We can just stop now. Nobody else needs to die.'

Nothing.

Little Ted crept forward in the direction of the largest of the piles of boxes. Moving into a crouching position, he held the peg-style grip of his Ruger Super Redhawk with both hands out in front of him. Some people didn't like the Redhawk because they thought it lacked subtlety. Little Ted chose it because it could put King Kong down with a single bullet. He edged around the left side of the boxes, his runners making next to no sound as he inched forward, gun still out in front.

Bang! The boxes crashed over, raining down on Little Ted's head as he clambered forward to find his prey. It was the gun, not the man, that he saw first. A black nine-millimetre Glock. The guy in the blue shirt took his shot before he had a clear line of sight, leaving him way off the mark. It was all Little Ted needed. A bullet exploded from his Ruger, blowing Blue Shirt's hand off at the wrist, hand and gun flailing into the air like a psychotic bird in flight.

Blue Shirt now lay on the grey cement floor, gasping for breath, his handless arm spilling blood interminably. Little Ted couldn't afford to worry about him now. It was the man in black that Little Ted wanted, Chaz's killer, and he might still be in the room.

Outside, sirens were closing in. Little Ted hoped it would be the ambulance that arrived first to take care of Chaz. He knew the cops would arrest him for what he'd already done to Blue Shirt, but he wasn't finished yet. Two stacks of boxes left standing. The man in black could have been behind either. Little Ted made his way around each, his Ruger at the ready.

Nothing. He was gone.

Little Ted moved quickly to the back of the room. An open door led to a bathroom, which had an open window sitting above the toilet; his target must have climbed through it and into the neighbouring driveway. From there, it was anyone's guess. The bird had flown. And now it was time for Little Ted to fly. The cops screeched to a halt right outside, and Little Ted was in the wind. Why give himself up if he didn't need to?

***

The cops had arrived before the ambulance, which upset Sam. Someone from the neighbourhood must have reported the gunfire, but he was pretty sure any combatants still alive had long since left the scene. It was a doctor, not a cop, that they needed now.

A young bloke in uniform held his police ID up to Sam's face and said, 'Your name?'

'Sam Pride.'

'What happened?'

This young guy was looking at Sam with suspicion and Sam had no idea where to begin. 'My friend, here – his throat's been cut,' he said, still holding the sweatshirt to Chaz's neck.

The cop felt for a pulse. A few moments later, he looked back up at Sam, solemnly shaking his head.

Sam looked at Chaz's bloodied face, eyes closed, then pulled his hands back and stared at them. They were shaking uncontrollably. Tears welled in his eyes. This was his fault! What had he done? Why didn't he just go to the police when he got that fateful text message?

He looked at the three other bodies lying nearby. One gone, for sure. Two others unconscious and probably dead, too. Maybe there were more bodies inside the warehouse. Was he responsible for all these deaths? How was he supposed to live with that? How does anyone live with that?

'Was it you?' the cop asked.

'No!' Sam yelled at him.

'I'm going to have to pat you down. To check for weapons.'

Without waiting for Sam to respond, he did it, which seemed to settle his nerves if not Sam's.

The paramedics arrived. They were about to move Chaz's body onto a stretcher but were stopped by the young constable. 'You need to wait for the Medical Examiner,' he said.

One of them, a slim guy with a pale complexion, asked Sam if he was okay.

'I'm fine,' Sam lied.

When Sam had done his army training after uni, he'd acted out battle scenarios, and contemplated scenes of carnage. Even killing another man. Perhaps it was the thought of having another human's blood on his hands that made him walk away from a military life. Now, here he was, carnage all around him.

He walked towards the doorway of the warehouse, but by then an older detective had arrived. She finished talking to the uniformed officer before turning her attention to Sam. She had a hard face; one that Sam guessed had seen a world of ugliness in its time. 'I'm Detective Inspector Reddy,' she said. 'You're Mr Pride?'

Sam nodded.

Reddy looked down at her notebook.

Sam noticed a couple more cop cars pull up, as well as the Medical Examiner and four more paramedics.

'What happened?' Reddy asked.

'I just explained to the other...' Sam looked over at the young constable who was now walking away from him.

Reddy was joined by another detective, male, early thirties. He showed Sam his ID: Detective Senior Constable Bolton.

'Can I see inside?' Sam asked.

'It's a crime scene,' said Reddy. 'Off limits, except for the forensics. You haven't been in there, have you?'

'No. I just wondered if—'

'I'll ask you again: what happened?'

'As I said to the other guy, my friend has obviously been killed.'

'And it wasn't you?'

'It was a man with a Croatian accent. Fortyish.'

Reddy crouched down on her knees to examine Chaz's neck wound. 'You saw it happen?'

Sam hesitated before answering. 'I did.'

'The knife?'

'What about it?'

'You get a good look at it?'

'No, it all happened in an instant.'

'Ever seen the man before? The one you say is Croatian?'

'He *sounded* Croatian. And he used the word, *pocetnik*. It means, *beginner*.' Sam felt like telling Reddy that he did not like her tone. 'And no, I've never seen him before.'

'And these other men?' Reddy looked over at the three corpses.

'I don't know who they are, either.'

Reddy walked over to them, squatting down to study the bullet wounds; there was a forensics officer taking photos at the same time, oblivious to the commotion going on around him. Reddy looked back at Sam quizzically before standing upright again and doing a slow three-sixty. Her eyes eventually settled on the location she guessed was that of the shooter, or shooters. Clear line of sight to the rooftop opposite. 'Do you own a gun, Mr Pride?'

'No, I don't.'

Reddy looked back up at the rooftop and asked Sam, 'If it wasn't you who shot them, then who did? Was that the Croatian, too?'

Sam wondered if she was trying to get a rise out of him. He recalled his army training and, for once, he wished he had done more of it. 'I don't know.'

'Were they already dead when you got here?'

'I guess so.'

Reddy looked mad. 'You arrive at a scene to discover three dead bodies. And then, how long after that was it you saw your friend being killed? What was his name again?'

'Chaz. I don't know. Not long.'

'Five minutes? Half an hour?'

'Minutes.'

'Five? Ten? Twenty?'

'Maybe five?'

Reddy looked around at the pretty white house with the picket fence. 'Is this where your friend lived?'

'No.'

'So, what was he doing here? What were *you* doing here?'

Sam knew if he told Reddy about the text message, she'd ask for his phone. And he needed time to think, to process. 'I don't know why he was here. He asked me to meet him, so I came. And I don't know why these other men were here.'

Sam thought about the texts again, the first from the kidnappers saying they had Chaz, and then the others arranging the meet. If the cops knew about those texts, they'd want to know why he hadn't rung triple zero immediately. Why would Sam take on a bunch of kidnappers by himself? They would assume he had something to hide.

Reddy went on. 'Your friend was – doing some sort of deal, was he?'

'Deal gone wrong?' threw in Bolton, apparently keen to get in on the act.

Of course, Sam thought. The cops are assuming it was a serious drug deal. That would explain the violence. But they were way off track. 'No,' he said. 'It wasn't anything like that. Look, I need to go and see my wife. She'll be worried.' Sam looked at his watch. It was twelve thirty. 'I was meant to be meeting her.'

'Never mind that,' said Reddy, 'you can ring her on your way to the station. At the very least, you're a witness to a homicide.'

Sam shook his head in disbelief. 'Can't I give you a statement later?'

'Best we do it now. While everything's fresh.'

'Okay,' Sam sighed. 'So long as I can call her.'

'Before we leave, forensics will photograph you.'

'What?'

'Your hands,' said Reddy. 'We'll also need to take some swabs, check for gunshot residue, or any evidence that you might have used a knife recently. We'll worry about a DNA sample later.'

'Is that really...' Sam couldn't argue anymore. Reddy was giving him a contemptuous look. He knew it would only dig him in deeper to fight off the photographer.

'Helps us eliminate you as a suspect,' said Reddy, 'as you *help us with our enquiries.*'

Sam tried to take a few deep breaths. The scene. The stench. It was all too much. He felt like he was drowning. He needed to get well away from here. He wanted someone to rescue him, and he knew it wasn't going to be DI Reddy.

Chapter 20

Sam called Lauren from the back of the squad car, anxious but determined not to let it show. He needed to be strong. 'Where are you?'

'I'm on my way to your mum's,' she said. 'You? What an ordeal.'

'Don't worry about me,' Sam said. 'I'll fill you in – later.'

He decided to ring an old friend, Kate Robinson, to ask if she'd meet him at the station. Kate was a barrister and, while homicide cases were not her stock and trade, she knew the law well enough to keep Sam from incriminating himself, or anyone else. Little Ted and Bianchi's guys had placed themselves in harm's way to help Sam, so he had to look after them. 'I'm hoping it won't take too long,' he said.

'Depends on the detective running the investigation,' said Kate, calm as ever. 'But don't stress. I'll be there for as long as you need me. See you out the front of the station.'

Kate arrived dressed in a dark designer suit. The look in her eye was enough to command respect. 'You look tired,' she said.

'You don't,' said Sam, 'thankfully.'

Kate had a reputation for being a warrior in court, but Sam had also seen her soft side. He'd been introduced to her in his first year at university, and he sensed at the time they'd be friends for life.

DI Reddy escorted them both to an interview room where they were joined by DSC Bolton. Reddy was stony-faced, her voice stern. Bolton took notes.

'Glass of water?' Reddy asked. 'I need to point out that the interview is being recorded.'

Sam knew Reddy had to treat him with suspicion, regardless of whether she thought he'd actually killed anyone. She was probably edgy with everyone she interviewed. Sam told himself to remain on guard.

The interview room was remarkably like the ones Sam's strategic planners held market research groups in for the ad agency: windowless, soundproof, grey walls, blue carpet, rectangular timber veneer table plum in the middle. The only real difference was the large one-way mirror to Sam's right, which he imagined concealed more police.

Reddy announced who was in the room and then, for the recording, said, 'Mr Pride, let me begin by thanking you for coming in to meet with us. You are not under arrest and are free to leave at any time.' The DI was in a relaxed position, chair slightly askew. She looked at Sam for acknowledgement.

'I understand,' he said. 'I'm here to help. If I can.'

'I'm sure you can,' said Reddy. 'Now, could you please confirm what you do for a living?'

'I run an ad agency named TBA.'

'Thank you. Now, if you could tell us, from the beginning, exactly what happened today.'

Sam thought about his words carefully. 'My friend, Chaz Bailley, was murdered. That's what happened.'

'Yes. Though, clearly, he was not the only one. But let's start with Mr Bailley. He worked with you at TBA?'

'That's right.'

'And why were you at the warehouse in Botany?'

Sam wasn't really at the warehouse; he was at the house next door with the picket fence. But he didn't want to say that. 'To see Chaz. Like I told you earlier.'

'So, you went to see Chaz Bailley at this place in Botany, and there you discovered three dead bodies, and then witnessed your friend getting murdered?'

'Yes.'

'You said it was a Croatian man who murdered him? Can you describe him in any more detail?'

'I'd say he was in his forties.' Reddy squared up, now with her left elbow on the table, a pen held lightly in her right hand. 'He spoke with an accent,' Sam added.

'Yes. And what exactly did he say?'

'I can't remember. Honestly. It was only a few words. Didn't mean anything to me.'

Reddy narrowed her eyes. 'But he said enough for you to detect an accent? And he used the Croatian word for, *beginner*?'

'That's right.'

'Then he cut your friend's throat with a knife. What sort of knife?'

'It wasn't a huge Crocodile Dundee-type of thing. I suppose it was the size of a vegetable knife.'

Reddy looked down at the file in front of her. 'Just like that?'

'Just like that,' Sam repeated.

'Did your friend say or do anything that might have prompted the attack?'

Sam hesitated, a bit too long for Bolton.

'Well?' Bolton demanded. 'Your friend must have done *something*.'

Sam bit his lip. 'I can't honestly say.'

Reddy leaned across the table, her eyes flaring. 'This is a murder enquiry. You do realise there are serious consequences for withholding evidence?'

Sam's head was spinning. Kate intervened, 'My client knows exactly what this is.'

'I'm not,' Sam said, pausing to rethink, 'I mean, no comment.'

'In no way does this look like an unprovoked attack,' said Reddy.

'Is that a question?' asked Kate.

'Your friend's finger had been sliced off,' Reddy went on. 'Did that have something to do with it? The Croatian bloke decided to finish him off?'

'No comment.'

'And then he did what?'

'Ran inside the warehouse,' said Sam. 'I guess it was around the time I heard the first of the sirens.'

'And you chose not to pursue him?'

'I stayed with Chaz, holding my sweatshirt to his wound, trying to save his life.'

Bolton took more notes.

Reddy continued, 'Okay, now, apart from sounding Croatian, the man you say was the killer, was he short? Tall?'

'Hundred and eighty centimetres,' Sam said. 'About ninety kilos.'

'Hair?'

'Dark.'

'Would you mind spending some time with one of our sketch artists?'

'I thought with all that new technology you wouldn't need me to.'

'We don't need sketch artists if we can pull the suspect's image off surveillance equipment, or a smart phone. Or if they can be identified by forensic evidence. But right now, all we've got is your memory.'

Sam again looked to Kate. 'My client's happy to help you,' she said. 'We'll get back to you with a time.'

'You can't do it now?'

'Sam is here of his own free will,' said Kate, 'as you've kindly pointed out, but he's also shaken by the events of this morning.

We'd appreciate it if you allowed him to see his wife now. It's been one hell of a day for him.'

Reddy glanced over at Bolton's notes. 'Why were you meeting Mr Bailley, the man you describe as a friend, at this location?'

'Because he asked me to.'

'You agreed to meet him without knowing what the meeting was about?'

'I meet with – met with – Chaz all the time, in all sorts of locations. He was my CFO. I am the CEO. Meeting up and talking is what we – did.'

'Have you had any run-ins with him recently? Any disagreements?'

'No.'

'Was he in any sort of financial trouble?'

'No, not at all.'

'Might anyone have seen or heard the two of you arguing in recent days?'

'No, we don't argue. We're friends and colleagues. Or we were.'

Kate stood up. 'Unless there's something else you need to ask right now, something specific, DI Reddy, I think it's time my client was allowed to leave.'

But Reddy wasn't done. 'The three other men who died today, and the fourth whose hand was blown off, do you know who they were?'

'Sorry,' Sam said. 'I don't.'

'And you also have no idea how they were killed? Or by whom?'

A part of Sam wanted to tell Reddy everything he knew but he had to let Kate do the talking. 'My client has told you what he knows,' she said, 'and he's happy to speak to you again tomorrow. But, unless you are charging him?'

'Ms Robinson, we have four murders and one attempted murder we have to get to the bottom of. We are far from done here. The two men in the white shirts...' Reddy looked down at the folder in front of her, then back up at Sam. 'Mr Charles Tanenbaum and Mr Connor Glaser. Did you know they worked for a company called Triple S Security?'

'No, I did not.'

'As did the other deceased man, a Mr Michael Haddad.' Reddy stared intently at Sam. 'Did you see who shot these men?'

Kate was having none of it. 'Detective Inspector, that question has been asked and answered. I appreciate your desire to bring whoever is guilty of these crimes to justice, but you and I both know that isn't my client.

He is as law abiding as they come, and as you've made patently clear, he is not under arrest. If you have any pertinent questions you'd like to follow up with, please let me know.' Kate handed Reddy her business card. The DI also stood up and stepped forward to block their exit.

'Ms Robinson, you know very well that for a crime of this nature, given the circumstances we found your client in and the vagueness of some of his answers regarding what exactly he was doing at the crime scene, I could hold him for a lot longer than this. However, there is a way we might be able to speed things up. Would your client be willing to give us a DNA sample?'

Kate leaned over to Sam. He knew that he could not be forced to give them his DNA because he hadn't been charged, but he figured he had nothing to hide, and it would help him get out of the station faster if he played ball. 'I don't mind,' he whispered in her ear.

Kate nodded at the DI.

'Thank you,' Reddy said, looking at Sam. 'Detective Bolton will do a buccal swab. That means he'll take a sample of saliva from your mouth. Quick and easy. Soon as that's done, you can be on your way – for now.' Reddy turned to Kate. 'But, tomorrow, I'd like your client's passport. Mr Pride should be available to speak to us on a daily basis. Until his DNA or any of the crime scene evidence rules him out, he will remain a suspect in a multiple homicide.'

Kate looked displeased, but she agreed that Sam would hand over his passport within twenty-four hours. Sam just wanted to get out of there. He had not seen who shot those three men, but he knew where they had come from, and he didn't want to tell the police. He certainly didn't want to lie to them in a recorded interview.

Once outside the station, he gave Kate a hug. 'Thank you so much.'

'It's my pleasure,' she said. 'And you're paying me.'

Sam knew that Kate was on his side and would remain so, no matter what. He smiled in appreciation as he watched her walk back to her car.

Driving away from the station, he called Lauren. 'I'm on my way, now.'

'How did you go?' she asked.

'Fine. I think. I was glad to have Kate by my side.'

'Of course.'

'There was a company that the detective mentioned. Triple S Security. Have you ever heard of them?'

'No,' answered Lauren.

'I'll do an internet search on them later. Anyway, I'll see you shortly.'

'Love you.'

'Love you, too!'

Sam wondered if the Croatian might also work for Triple S. Perhaps they had a link to YRG, perhaps not. Sam certainly thought it likely they had a link to Brandis.

***

Sam turned left off Old South Head Road and found a park right in front of his mum's place, a boutique block of apartments for people aged over fifty-five. His mum's had a view over the greens of Royal Sydney Golf Club, so she wasn't complaining.

'We were just having a cuppa,' she said, welcoming Sam in. 'Would you like one? Lauren told me—'

Lauren sang out, 'Janice and I have been having a wonderful time.'

'Sure, Mum,' Sam said, looking over her shoulder to see how Lauren was doing. He didn't want to scare his mother by rushing past her, but he was desperate to give his wife a big hug. His mum moved to one side, and Lauren threw her arms around him, silent tears of relief in her eyes.

Lauren pulled back to look at Sam's face. 'You're okay,' she said. 'Thank god.' Then she looked down at his hands and noticed the blood.

'Don't worry,' he said. 'I'm fine. Just give me a moment.' He went to the bathroom and cleaned himself up.

Sam's mum, the only calm one in the room, having not noticed his bloody hands or at least acting like she hadn't, poured him a cup of tea and said, 'Well, go on, sit down. Tell us everything.'

'Yes, Mum,' he said, finding solace in her quiet commands. He had a sip of Earl Grey, his mind still spinning, but the key was to manage the situation. He needed to prioritise. His wife and mother were safe. He wanted to keep it that way. His mum took the seat next to him, Lauren directly opposite.

'Lauren told me you had some serious business to attend to,' his mum said.

'You know the company I sold my agency to?'

'Yes. YRG.'

Sam leaned in over the table. 'Seems there's a guy working for them who is, well, I think he's a criminal. Anyway, I had to meet someone connected to this guy – at least I think they're connected – in Botany.

Just now. And things got – out of hand.'

'What happened?' asked Lauren, looking more concerned than his mother.

Sam thought about how it was going to look on the nightly news. His mum was an avid news watcher. 'My friend, Chaz.'

'Something's happened to Chaz?' said Lauren.

'He's – dead,' Sam said, almost crumbling.

'Jesus Christ, darling! What the hell?' Lauren stood up and walked over to kneel beside him. She squeezed his hand.

Sam tried to focus. 'The police are doing their job, and I'm sure they'll arrest the people responsible.'

'So, they know who did it?'

'They soon will, I'm sure. But look, what this means is, we're going to have to be careful. Just for the next little while. I don't think any of us are in danger, but…'

'But what?'

'We just need to play it safe. Mum, I'm sure they wouldn't come after you. But for the next few days, please be extra cautious. Don't answer the door. And make sure you've got someone with you if you need to go out. Okay?'

His mum looked frazzled. 'No, that's not okay.'

'Mum. Please.'

'Who are these people?'

'The YRG man is probably in Chicago or London. Not in Australia. I don't know who the other guys are.'

'These other men. The ones who killed Chaz. They could come after you?'

'Mum, I'm sure it's fine. I just want to play it safe.'

'Do they think you're a threat to them?'

'Maybe. As a witness.' Sam shook his head. It was time to get moving. 'I don't know. I just need you to trust me on this.' Sam's mum looked unconvinced. 'Please?'

'I guess I don't have a choice.'

'Thank you.'

Sam and Lauren said their goodbyes, Janice protesting. 'But, if your life is in danger…'

'Mum, we'll be fine. Just keep the door deadlocked and answer to no-one.'

Chapter 21

It was early afternoon, three hours before the winter sunset. There were a few tradies on the road, some parents soon to be doing school pick-ups, but not a lot of traffic compared to peak hour. Sam made his way back to Old South Head Road, steady as she goes. The plan was to drive home, get settled, and then touch base with anyone who might be able to help them. He took his left hand off the steering wheel and reached for Lauren.

Lauren said timidly, 'Sweetheart, this might seem like really odd timing, but there is something *else* I've been wanting to talk to you about. In fact, your mum and I...'

They were heading west in slow traffic, when Sam noticed a white Hilux behind them. There were two men in it, both in white T-shirts. Not again! For a second, he wondered if he was imagining it. He kept looking in the rear-view mirror to make sure they were still there. 'Sorry, darling, what was that?'

As the traffic stopped, Lauren turned around to see what Sam was looking at in the mirror. 'You recognise them?'

Sam took his foot off the brake and nudged forward a few metres. 'This is weird. They look like two of the men who were at the house in Botany.'

'Maybe it *is* them?'

'No, they were shot dead.'

'I thought it was just Chaz who was killed.'

'There were – at least three others,' Sam admitted.

'Is there anything *else* you haven't told me?'

Sam looked in the mirror again. They were approaching the big five-way intersection at the bottom of the hill leading up to Bondi Junction. 'Darling, I'm going to swing right and head towards the harbour. If these guys follow us, we can't go home.'

'Where can we go?' Lauren asked anxiously.

'I don't know, but hold on tight!'

The traffic opened up long enough for Sam to accelerate and weave his way through a handful of cars. Just as he sped up, so did the Hilux. He hadn't indicated that he was going to turn into O'Sullivan Road yet. He waited until the last moment. Every second now was going to count.

'Why are they following us?' asked Lauren. 'Didn't you give them the bloody memo?'

'Yes, but now there's another problem.'

'What?'

'I witnessed Chaz's murder. His killer will consider me a problem needing to be fixed.'

'Oh, God,' said Lauren. 'When will this nightmare end?'

The light turned green. Sam slammed on the accelerator and turned hard right. He could hear a screech of tyres on the road behind him as the Hilux tried to cut across the traffic to follow them. The BMW's powerful engine felt incredible, like they were about to take off. Sam had never driven a car at speeds like this: over 80 km; over 100 km; over 120 km! They were putting some distance between them and their pursuers as they passed the local rugby club. If he kept going straight and onto New South Head Road, he'd be too easy to follow. So, at the next roundabout, Sam swung a hard left, and the car handled it with ease.

'Careful, sweetheart!' yelled Lauren.

'How far back are they?' Sam asked.

'Not far enough!'

Sam glanced again at the rear-vision mirror. He wasn't rid of them yet, but he had a plan. He hugged the left kerb, hoping they wouldn't encounter any oncoming traffic. Latimer Road was super narrow when cars were parked on either side of the street. Hard enough not to scrape one when you're the only car on the road!

If the guys in the Hilux were more than a hundred metres behind them when they got to the corner of Boronia, they wouldn't be able to see whether they'd turned left or kept heading up the hill towards Victoria Road. Sam figured he had a fifty-fifty chance of escaping them. He stuck with Latimer, then hit the brakes hard as they screeched around the Balfour Road intersection and then swung to the left along the relatively flat stretch of Bunyula heading south. He took his foot off the pedal and slowed down as they approached the dip in the road, just before the ninety-degree bend to the left.

Lauren turned around. 'No sign of them,' she said.

Sam brought the car to a complete stand still. 'Let's listen for a moment,' he said. He couldn't hear anything. He reached out to take hold of Lauren's hand for a moment. Like him, she seemed comforted by the absence of any loud car noises.

It appeared they'd lost the Hilux boys. Part of Sam said it would be good to just hang right where they were. It was a wider stretch of road than the previous one, with large trees sheltering stately homes. It could have been called peaceful, even serene. The other guys must have taken the wrong turn and there was no reason to think they'd want to turn back to search every nook and cranny of Bellevue Hill. There were a lot of windy roads in this suburb, and they could have finished up anywhere.

'What do you think?' he asked Lauren.

'Don't ask me. You're the driver!'

Sam drove forward slowly. He had right of way as he approached the next intersection, so he sped up a little. By the time he saw the Hilux, almost airborne as it flew out of Boronia Street on the left, it was too late. They missed the main body of the car but just clipping the rear was enough to send Sam and Lauren into a shuddering tailspin. Lauren screamed as they were hit; Sam just tried to hang on, hoping they wouldn't flip. He somehow managed to regain control of the car and point them back towards O'Sullivan. The crash didn't seem to have affected the engine or the steering. He didn't look to see what had happened to the other guys, instead keeping his eyes glued to the road ahead. He braked and swerved, just enough to avoid hitting a passing car as he swung a hard right, back towards the five-way intersection.

'They're still behind us!' yelled Lauren. 'And one of them has a gun!'

The light at the intersection was green so Sam was able to quickly veer to the left, whipping past two slow-moving sedans and grilling the car's suspension as their rapid pace made even the smallest of bumps seem like mountains.

Lauren turned around again. 'Still there,' she said. 'Front of their car's smashed in, but it doesn't seem to have slowed them down.'

Sam remembered the Hilux marketing slogan. *Unbreakable.* He hoped it was false advertising. 'Hold on tight,' he said, as he turned sharply into a side road. It felt like they were about to roll, but, again, the car managed to stay upright. There were two cars in front of them going too slowly for them to stay ahead of the Hilux.

'Fuck it!' Sam yelled, as he pulled out to overtake them, giving himself a few seconds to get back onto the right side of the road to miss the oncoming traffic.

'Shit!' yelled Lauren and braced herself for an impact. But luckily there wasn't any, because the cars coming the other way had slowed down.

Sam could see an old lady up ahead about to cross the road. Would she look both ways?

'Oh, God, he's leaning out the window,' shouted Lauren. 'I think he's going to fire!'

Sam heard the shot ring out, but they weren't hit.

'Maybe he was aiming for a tyre,' said Lauren. 'And missed.'

'Small mercies,' Sam muttered.

The old lady froze on the footpath.

'Phew!' thought Sam.

They gained a little distance as they picked up speed and raced towards North Bondi. A gap in the traffic allowed Sam to kick straight out into Campbell Parade.

'Do you hear that?' asked Lauren.

Sirens. Yes, he heard them, but he had no idea which direction they were coming from. He swung to the right to do a U-turn in front of some Mexican joint and almost ran into the two motorcycle cops coming south down the hill on Campbell Parade. The Hilux guys obviously saw the cops, too, and drove away towards the waste-water treatment plant.

With the boys in blue right behind them, Sam and Lauren pulled over on the left, about fifty metres from the Bondi parking station. One cop stayed on his bike while the other dismounted and walked up to the car window. 'Licence?'

Sam handed it to him, his hand trembling.

'Where are you off to in such a hurry?' he asked, looking down at Sam's licence like he was having trouble reading it.

'A meeting at my office in Darlinghurst. Really important client.'

The cop had world-weary eyes. 'The back of your car. You've got some serious roadworthiness issues there, mate.'

'It just happened. We'll obviously want to get it fixed right away.'

The officer walked around to the rear of the BMW to note the broken taillights, deformed boot and dysfunctional bumper bar. He shook his head.

The other cop, still perched on his motorbike, yelled out, 'Briggsy, crime in progress!'

Briggsy gave up. 'Just keep to the speed limit, okay?'

'Yes, sir,' Sam said.

It took a few minutes, but eventually Sam started to feel normal again. He looked at his hands on the steering wheel and told himself to stop squeezing.

'Did you just lie to a police officer?' Lauren asked.

The traffic came to a halt at the Watson Street lights. Sam looked at his wife, pleadingly. 'I didn't know what else to say.'

'You're not a very good liar.'

'Is that a good thing or a bad thing?'

'I just don't want you getting arrested. Perverting the course of justice, or something. Now, I'd better tell you what I wanted to say earlier.'

The light turned green.

'Something you were chatting to Mum about?'

'I'm pregnant.'

***

'Oh, wow!' Sam managed to hold in his excitement until he'd pulled over and hugged Lauren. 'I feel terrible,' he said. 'I wouldn't have driven like that if I'd known. Do you think the baby's okay?'

'It wasn't just the baby you nearly killed,' she said. Then she smiled. 'Lucky I love you! By the way, I think it's a boy.'

'Isn't it too early…?'

'Just a feeling.'

'You know I'd be equally thrilled if it were a girl? Maybe we should go to the hospital. Check that everything's okay?'

Lauren put her hand on her belly, then she took Sam's hand and placed it there. 'I suppose a quick check-up would be wise,' she said. 'To the Prince of Wales?'

After he'd spent most of the day feeling like death was knocking at his door, Sam was excited to learn of a precious new life coming into the world. 'I can't tell you how much pride I feel, knowing you're going to be the mother of my…'

'Our.'

'Our child.'

'I'm glad to hear it.'

'You know I think you're the most beautiful woman in the world?'

'Don't let that stop you from telling me. Often!'

Lauren's words were accompanied by her gorgeous dimple-laden smile. Sam kissed her and walked back round to the driver's side of the car.

They took off towards the hospital. They had a few minutes of silence before Lauren asked if Sam felt like listening to music. He put on the radio. Then she asked him, 'Are you going to tell me the truth – what really happened to Chaz?'

Back to the darkness. 'He was an idiot,' Sam said. 'I mean, he was my friend and everything, a super impressive guy, but he was an idiot. I'd handed over the memo, they'd let him go, and then he kicked the bloody Croatian in the balls.'

'What?'

'So, the Croatian slit his throat.'

'Oh my god. Poor man. He was always a bit crazy. But I can't believe he's been killed.'

'I'm going to miss him,' Sam said. 'Zoe's my creative partner but it's Chaz I've spent so much of my time hanging out with. It was Chaz who really shaped the deal.'

'That bloody deal,' said Lauren.

Sam remembered the night the YRG guys confirmed their number, seventy-four million, over the phone. He and Chaz were in the office, but Zoe had gone home. Sam didn't know what time it was, but it was late, and the office was empty. Even the cleaners were done for the night. He said he ought to leave, given the time, but Chaz insisted they pop a bottle of Dom Perignon that he just happened to have in the fridge. Then he cranked up the music and they laughed, talked about the completely over-the-top things they would spend the money on, and carried on drinking until three or four in the morning. Sam probably should have been at home with Lauren at the time, but this was one occasion when he couldn't resist Chaz's enthusiasm. He'd worked so hard to pull off the sale and Sam was a major beneficiary. Maybe he felt like he owed Chaz.

'We're having a toast,' Sam remembered his buddy saying. 'To sucking the juice out of every day. Not letting a second of life go to waste.'

A part of Sam had died with Chaz today. If the Croatian was still alive – and Sam had a feeling he was, even though he never got to see inside the warehouse – he had to make sure the bastard was caught.

Sam reached for Lauren. 'You alright?' he asked.

'I will be,' she said. 'You thinking about Chaz again?'

'Even more than the Croatian, I want the man most responsible for Chaz's death brought to justice.'

'Do you mean…?'

'A man I've never met. But one whose hands I know, instinctively, are well and truly blood-soaked.'

'Don't do anything – you know…'

'At least Little Ted is okay,' Sam said. 'Or, I assume he is.'

'How can you be sure?'

'After Chaz was killed, he ran into this warehouse, chasing the Croatian and some other guy. I heard gunshots, and then what sounded like a scream. But I don't know if anyone was killed in there. The police wouldn't tell me.'

Sam pulled up at a red light. He shook his head and said, 'I got a text from his phone just before I arrived at Mum's place. It said, *Sorry I had to run*. Presumably that means he didn't cop a bullet.'

'Well, that's *some* good news.'

Chapter 22

Robert Miller left his Chicago home for a breakfast meeting with Jean Koziol, one of YRG's largest shareholders. Robert had known Jean since she first started dating Tony, the man who later became her husband. Robert and Tony were the two stand-out tennis players in their year at school and had remained friends until Tony's death from brain cancer twelve months earlier.

Jean chose the usual venue, the Margeaux Brasserie on the third floor of the Waldorf Astoria. Robert considered it a fine blend of modern and vintage, much like Jean herself. He greeted her with a warm embrace. 'You're looking great,' he said.

'And you're a liar,' she said. 'But I love you for it.'

They made their way past the wood-framed mirrors and the leather-clad booths to a table near the large windows where the curtains were pulled back tightly to welcome in the morning light.

Jean ordered coffee and a juice, Robert the same. As the waiter turned to walk away, she called him back to add a serving of quiche to the order. Robert did the same.

'So,' she said, with a wide-open smile. 'What can I do for you, my darling?'

'You're still on the Board of YRG, aren't you?'

'I am. Why?'

'Have you heard about what's been happening in Australia?'

'I can't imagine anything much happening down there. For YRG, I mean. It's a relatively small market.'

'I get it. Australia doesn't figure...'

'We've got to have a presence there, but the board doesn't spend time worrying about it. So, what's this about?'

'Do you remember my business partner?'

'Viktor Tomic. Hard man to forget.'

'He's in Sydney. Has been since May 23. Apparently, there were some issues, some problems, with YRG's takeover of a local ad agency. TBA. So, Viktor took Darius, one of our young up-and-comers with him to sort things out.'

'And?'

'They linked up with a man by the name of Haddad, who runs Triple S Security in Australia. They're an affiliate of ours.'

The waiter arrived with the food, which provided a moment for Robert to catch his breath. He continued, 'I haven't heard from Viktor in three days. Nobody has heard from him, or Darius.'

'And what about this Haddad character?'

'Nothing.'

Jean bit her lip and looked down at her half-drained coffee cup.

'There's something else,' said Robert.

'Yes?'

'Just before I came here, I read a news story online about a shooting. Three men from an Australian security company have been killed. And the police are looking for another man, possibly of Croatian background, aged in his forties, to help them with their inquiries.'

'Surely there are lots of other security companies in Australia,' said Jean.

'And lots of other men who could be from a Croatian background aged in their forties,' Robert smiled. 'But Viktor was up to something with these guys from Triple S, something he wasn't prepared to talk about to anyone back here in the Chicago office.'

'And you think...?'

'Honestly, Jean, I don't know what to think. That's why I wanted to talk to you. I read this note in Viktor's files. It mentioned a memo. A memo that I believe may have been on YRG letterhead. I've got a feeling – I may be completely wrong – but I've got a feeling the memo...'

'You think it's somehow linked to the killings?'

Robert nodded. 'And I'm worried about what it may mean for our companies.'

'I'm still not clear on what the connection is to YRG. Do you think the killer or one of the victims was connected to the agency?'

'I do.'

'It's hard to imagine someone from YRG would... Three men killed? Our business is in advertising and market research. This sounds more like the goings on of a drug cartel.'

Robert didn't know what else to say, so he simply took another sip of water while he collected his thoughts.

'Do you think Margaret Whitfield is involved?' Jean asked.

'If not, then she's pretty loose with the reins.'

'Let me speak to my people. I'll get back to you very soon.'

'Thank you, Jean. I didn't know who else to turn to.'

'It was brave of you. If Viktor is in the thick of it, as you suspect, then your business will be impacted. It doesn't matter how clean you are personally. He still has fifty per cent equity in your company, right?'

Robert nodded and lapsed into silence. If Viktor was *the* Croatian the Australian police wanted to speak to, there could be no doubting the trouble he was in.

Chapter 23

Sam felt like he had been asleep for days, though the clock on the bedside table told him he'd barely managed five hours. Memories of yesterday flooded his brain. After learning that Lauren and the baby were both fine, he drove them from the hospital to a city hotel he thought would be safe. He would deal with getting the car fixed another day.

They ordered room service and tried to watch TV, telling each other they needed to de-stress. They settled on a couple of classic movies from the fifties. Sam's eyes gazed at the screen, but he wasn't taking anything in. Peter O'Toole might as well have been Peter Dinklage for all the sense it was making to him. He was still stuck in Hatch Street, Botany. He kept seeing the Croatian cutting Chaz's throat, the bodies of those men from Triple S just lying there, blood everywhere, hearing the shots fired by Marco Bianchi's men. What was Sam's part in this? What was his level of guilt? Just two of the questions he was struggling to avoid.

Eventually, he and Lauren passed out. He woke up a handful of times, flashes of the mayhem forcing their way back into his head. But somehow, he drifted off again. He was so physically and mentally drained he didn't think his body had any choice but to sleep.

And now a new morning, but one frighteningly tethered to the events of the day before. Sam took a deep breath and looked at his wife curled up on her side. He wanted to kiss her. But knowing she needed her sleep, Sam slipped out of bed and pulled back the curtains just enough to catch a glimpse of the western harbour. The Langham was in The Rocks, a historic part of the city once rough and tumble but these days, at least in pockets like this, distinctly upmarket. The sky was overcast, mostly obscured by clouds. He felt much the same, hoping the sun would poke its way through.

He looked at Lauren again, lying so peacefully on the bed. What an idiot he'd been. As long as Sam had her, he had all the sunshine he needed.

The volume was switched off, but Sam could see his mobile was ringing. Undisclosed number. Sam ignored it. No voicemail.

He sat down at the desk to check the multitude of apps on his phone. Lots of work emails that could wait, but a couple of messages caught his eye. The first was from Brie Allinson:

> I saw a story online. A thing in Botany. Just wondering if one of the men killed might have been Chaz? They didn't say the names. Hope you don't mind me asking. Be great to talk.
>
> Brie
> x

Sam guessed she signed off all her emails and messages with a kiss, regardless of whom she was talking to. He put off his reply, thinking he needed to read the news coverage himself, if for no other reason than to be sure he wasn't part of the story. Could the police leak his name to a journalist to try and put pressure on him? Not likely, but maybe it was something to be checked with Kate.

The other message was from Kitty Zhang:

> Could we meet for a drink? I'd like to discuss the Zoe situation.
>
> KZ

Meet for a drink? What planet was she on? If Kitty had spoken to a lawyer about making a claim, no way would they have allowed her to send something like that!

Calm down, he told himself. Focus.

He replied:

> Thanks for your note, Kitty. I'm afraid I can't meet up today, but I'll get back to you asap.
>
> Best regards,
> Sam

Now, back to Brie. He felt sorry for her. She obviously cared for Chaz and was looking for support. Sam could not leave her out on her own. He emailed her back:

> I've got some things I have to do this morning, but I promise I'll get back to you very soon. Hope you are well.
>
> Sam

He walked back to the window and saw an elderly man walking a dog. Rax! Oh, no. He really needed to be fed. Taken for a walk, too, if possible. How was he going to do that if the house was being watched? *Was* it being watched? This cloak and dagger routine was so alien to Sam that he was now questioning everything.

He tried to think of someone who could feed the lovable black Lab for them. They knew the neighbours, but Sam didn't have their phone numbers or email addresses. He certainly couldn't ask his mum to do it. Likewise, his sister. In fact, he couldn't really ask anyone else. The Triple S guys had shown their intent, and Sam couldn't know what harm might come to some unsuspecting person going out of their way to feed his pet dog.

'I'm desperate for a coffee,' said Lauren, finally coming to life.

'Five-star hotel. They should be able to manage that.'

When the doorbell rang half an hour later, Sam registered how irresponsible he was being. When they'd had room service last night, it hadn't occurred to Sam that it could be one of the *bad guys* at the door. When checking in, he'd used the name John Teague (a random name he'd made up on the spot). The front desk had asked him for ID, and Sam said he'd left his wallet in the car but would show them his driver's licence when he grabbed it a little later. They'd insisted on a credit card for the guarantee, and Lauren had given them hers. Sam was hopeful the hotel staff wouldn't give the game away if someone phoned or dropped by asking if Sam or Lauren Pride were guests, but, of course, he couldn't be sure.

'Who is it?' Sam asked through the door.

'Room service,' sang a high-pitched cheery voice. 'Your breakfast?' If that was the voice of a killer, then Sam had no hope of surviving the day; he opened the door. A beaming smile greeted him. The woman couldn't have been more than nineteen years old. 'Where would you like it?' She wheeled in the breakfast order and left them to it.

Sam and Lauren grabbed a tray each and sat down on the bed. They were wearing the hotel dressing gowns. 'Two lots of room service and we're both still breathing,' Sam said.

'I was about to name that girl Nikita,' Lauren said.

'The assassin?'

She nodded and took a large sip of juice. 'Maybe we shouldn't joke.'

'I think we need to,' said Sam. 'That or freak out. Humour gets cops through their bad days. Doctors, too.'

Lauren reached for her coffee cup. 'What are we going to do?'

'I suppose I'd better deal with the car. Can't keep driving it around the way it is.'

'Then what do we use for transport?'

'Your car is back at the house, isn't it?'

'No, I left it at the office. You think we should pick it up?'

'I wonder if they'll have anyone watching your building.'

'Seriously? It's a Saturday. Even if they were trying to track me down to get to you, they wouldn't expect me to be at the bank. Not now.'

Sam wondered what lengths these Triple S guys would go to. There was just no way of knowing. And how many of them were there? Three were dead, the ones killed in Botany. Then there were the two in the Hilux who chased after them. Were they just the tip of the iceberg? Maybe there were another twenty or thirty of the buggers, all connected to the Croatian, searching for him and Lauren right this minute? How paranoid did he need to be? He didn't want Lauren to panic but he also knew they had to be on guard.

He said, 'Before we get to the car, I want to bounce something off you. Do you mind?'

'Go on.'

'If you were the Croatian guy, what would you do?'

'I really don't think I...' She paused and asked, 'Do you think he works for Triple S?'

'I'd have thought so. If it wasn't for something the detective said. She gave me the impression that the dead guys worked for Triple S, but maybe the Croatian didn't.'

'You think the whole thing is being run by Brandis, don't you?'

'Possibly.'

'And where do you think Brandis is? I know he's overseas, but where exactly?'

'Chicago, I guess. But I'm not sure.'

'Let's say he is in Chicago. It's where YRG's head office is, so it makes sense. If the Croatian was in charge of the kidnapping, then there's a good chance he's also from Chicago. If so, maybe he'll try and head back there.'

'After killing me?'

'You *are* their loose end, my darling.'

'You say that – like a loose end is something to be craved.'

'The important thing is, you're *my* loose end, not the bloody Croatian's.

I need you right here, in good working order, and so does this little one.' Lauren pulled her robe aside and pointed at her belly. She was barely showing but Sam was now very aware of the baby inside.

Sam ate the fruit salad and yoghurt he'd been gawking at for some time. When that was done, he raised the matter of Rax to Lauren. 'Someone's got to feed him.'

'Well, it certainly won't be you!'

'I could get into the house unseen. We can't leave him with no food or water.'

'Of course, we can't. And there's the small matter of your passport. You've got to hand that into the police, don't you?'

Sam nodded.

'Today?'

'That's what they said.'

'For all we know, your Croatian friend is waiting there. And not to feed Rax.' A short time later, Lauren said, 'You could tell the police, you know? Get them to accompany you to the house. If they thought whoever murdered Chaz was going to be there.'

'One small problem,' Sam said.

'You'd have to give up Little Ted?'

'Exactly. I can't tell them the full story. Not yet. I need to know that Little Ted is safe. Physically and legally.' Sam's mobile rang; an undisclosed number again. He intended to ignore all such calls for as long as he and Lauren were on the run. He finished his coffee and said to her, 'I'm nervous about getting your car. If they are as well organised as I think they might be, it could be too much of a risk.'

'If we go now, I think we'll be fine,' Lauren said. 'Sam, seriously, if they are looking for where we're hiding then they won't expect us to be at the bank. And we have to do something about your car. It's a magnet in the state it's in.'

'You think it would be safe to drop it at a panel beaters?'

'The bad guys are not going to be staking out all of Sydney's panel beaters. So, yes.'

'What if I asked Little Ted to come with me to the house?'

'Ha-ha, you really don't like Little Ted much, do you?'

'I'm just not sure what else to do. We've got to do something about Rax. And look, maybe the Croatian has left town, to save his own arse. He'd know the cops were on his tail. Too dangerous for him to hang around and to try to knock me off.'

'And the other guys from Triple S?'

'They're a danger. But they haven't tracked us down yet, and if they aren't hiding in the garage at your office, then I like our chances. If Little Ted hid somewhere as a lookout, and I snuck in…'

Lauren was shaking her head.

'It is our house,' Sam continued. 'I do know the place better than any security guy coming from God knows where.'

The look on Lauren's face made it clear she was not buying it. 'What are you expecting me to do while you put your life on the line to give our black rascal a bowl of Prime Chicken Fillet Dog Treats?'

'Hang out here in the hotel room? Watch a good movie?'

Sam ducked for cover as Lauren flung a blueberry from her fruit salad bowl at his head. He avoided it but was a soft target for the strawberry that followed.

***

Joseph Khoury had been perfectly content to occupy the number two position at Triple S Security, assuming Michael Haddad, the boss, would always be around. Financially, Joseph had no right to complain. He was a director and a shareholder, so he received cash dividends when the company had a good year. And the last couple of years had been very good ones. Now life had taken a turn. Michael was gone and fate had thrown Joseph a bone. He could have let one of their senior staff take on the role of Managing Director, or recruited externally, but why would he? He was forty-two years old with a wife and two kids to look after. He felt an ambition deep in his gut bubbling to the surface. He wanted the money and control that went with the top job, and he no longer wanted to be bossed around by someone else. The other company director, Ben Misty, was the finance manager and clearly not cut out for the top job. Ben knew nothing about operations and client service. It was Joseph's time, and that was all there was to it.

Until today, Joseph had never met Viktor Tomic. He'd heard about him (*a hard man*, were the words Michael used) as had many of the Triple S staff, but Michael had chosen to keep Joseph at arm's length from the Chicago connection. Now Joseph was in the thick of it. He vowed to himself that he would do whatever it took to keep the USA-sourced rivers of gold flowing.

When Viktor arrived at the Riley Street property, Joseph was not surprised by the coldness in his eyes. No smiles, just business. The dark red stain on the bandage around his arm made it look like he was still bleeding from the bullet wound.

'I could call someone to take a look at that for you?' said Joseph.

'No,' said Viktor.

Joseph took an uneasy breath.

'I want to be in the control room,' Viktor explained. 'I want to see those screens. I want to find Sam Pride.'

Joseph was not sure if Viktor wanted Pride alive or dead. 'Is there anything I can get you?' he asked the Croatian.

'Vodka,' said Viktor.

'Give me one minute.' Joseph went to a fridge upstairs and retrieved a bottle of ice-cold Russian vodka. He returned and poured a glass for Viktor.

'What is wrong with you?' said Viktor.

Joseph did not normally drink vodka, especially not on its own, but he knew what Viktor was saying. He poured himself a glass and, when given the nod, joined Viktor in throwing down a shot.

'This is good,' said Viktor.

Joseph didn't know if he was talking about the vodka, or the fact that they were drinking together, or the circumstances in which they found themselves in the YRG case. The YRG business was, as far as Joseph could tell, a complete disaster. Three colleagues murdered and a very important client unlikely to be happy. As far as Joseph knew, nobody from Triple S had ever spoken directly to anyone at YRG. They worked as subcontractors to Viktor and his firm, Alliance, but they all knew it was YRG who paid the bills. So, it was important for them to be happy. Unhappy clients don't pay their invoices, and that's a problem that swims all the way downstream.

'The police contacted you?'

'I haven't spoken to them,' said Joseph. 'A detective from Surry Hills phoned our office in Greenacre, asking to speak to whoever was in charge. Julie, our office girl, said that would be Michael. The detective asked if Charlie and Connor worked for us. She confirmed they did. And that was it. Julie said the copper told her to get someone in management to call them back. I haven't.'

'And this building is not owned by Triple S?'

'No, it's owned by me, Michael's estate, and Ben, our finance guy. We always thought it would be handy to have a less conspicuous address we could do our surveillance from. Everyone knows the Triple S office at Greenacre. It's publicly listed in the company records. But very few people know about this place.'

'When I leave this room,' said Viktor, 'I want one of your men watching these screens every minute of the day. If they see Sam Pride, they need to let me know immediately. You understand?'

'I do,' said Joseph. 'Do you want me to also look out for Zoe Barnes, his partner?'

'I'm not so concerned about her. She's the creative one. Doesn't get involved in business matters.'

'Okay. Understood.'

'For now, I watch the screens.'

Joseph wanted to better understand what was going on in Viktor's head. 'Where do you think he is?'

'I think he will visit his office. Maybe not today, but soon. The large number of staff will make him feel safe there.'

Looking at the surveillance feed from Bondi, Joseph said, 'He's not going to be stupid enough to visit his home.'

Chapter 24

They picked up Lauren's car from the bank with no signs of trouble and dropped Sam's at the smash repair joint in Alexandria. Driving back to The Rocks, Sam thought some more about poor Rax, all alone in their house at Bondi. The Croatian knew Sam's face; a goofy disguise probably wasn't going to fool him or his mates.

They drove Lauren's 3 Series into the hotel guests' lot and caught the lift to the fifth floor. Lauren had just opened the door to their room when Sam's mobile rang. 'Darling, I think I have to take this,' he said.

'Do what you need to.'

'Hey Brie,' Sam said. 'I got your message. Sorry, I haven't had a chance to call you back.'

'That's okay. I want to know what's happened to Chaz. Is he okay?'

'Brie, I'm really sorry to have to tell you this…'

'He's dead, isn't he?'

'I'm afraid so. He was killed in Botany yesterday.'

The phone was silent for a torturous five seconds, before Brie came back with, 'I know you're probably busy, and it's a Saturday and everything, but is there any way I could see you? I'd just really like to talk. You knew Chaz better than anyone. Would you mind? I could meet you anywhere.'

'Well,' he said, suddenly realising that Brie could be of help. 'There *is* something you could do for me.'

'Anything. Just name it.'

'It's our dog, Rax. He needs feeding.'

'I'd be happy to feed him. But, um, are you and your wife away or something?'

'Yes. And I'm a little worried there could be someone watching it.'

'You don't mean – whoever it was who killed Chaz?'

'There's a chance there could be someone there looking for me. They'd have no interest in you. If you can do this, I'd be nearby, keeping an eye out. But I really don't think you'd be in any danger.'

'Wow,' said Brie. 'Sounds kinda heavy but, if you think it's safe, then okay. I trust you.'

Those last three words made Sam feel terrible, dragging Brie into the mire, but it wasn't enough to make him change course – and he'd just thought of a new way to lessen her endangerment. 'Brie, you are a lifesaver. Rax means the world to me.'

'Glad to help. Then afterwards we can go for a drink?'

'Um, not sure about that,' Sam said, thinking not only of Lauren but also Kitty and that whole nightmare with Zoe. Brie was attractive and in need of comfort, but he was the older person in a far more powerful position. 'But I'd be happy to talk. Maybe in the next few days we could grab a coffee.'

'Fair enough,' she said. 'I just want to talk.'

'One more thing. I'm going to need my passport. It's on my bedside table.'

'Okay,' said Brie hesitantly.

***

When Sam explained to Lauren what his new plan was, she suggested it was foolish. 'Why would you involve Brie?'

'She asked me for something, and I thought, why not? She'll be alright. I'm going to ask Little Ted to join me.'

'Isn't he…?'

'The cops probably don't have anything to tie him to Botany – yet. They'd need more than twenty-four hours to do all the DNA analysis, and Little Ted probably didn't leave any trace evidence behind, anyway.' They could be analysing the bullet or bullets he fired, Sam thought, but they didn't have his gun. 'Even if they find something,' he said, 'I don't think they'll rush to charge him. And I need him for this.'

Lauren looked unhappy, but there was little Sam could do to change that, at least for now.

Little Ted replied to Sam's text, confirming he'd be there. Sam knew there were only so many favours he could ask of his friend, and this was likely the last.

He stood at the door, holding Lauren in his arms, struggling to say goodbye.

'You know, I'm not comfortable with this,' she said.

'I know.'

'I don't think you do!'

'Darling, I promise you, it's all going to be over soon. I'll see you in a few hours.'

She squeezed him tight. 'Come back safe!'

Sam met Little Ted in Bronte Road where he'd left his car. His was a Nissan Patrol and, most importantly, not something the bad guys would be looking out for. Sam explained where things were up to with the police. Little Ted did not seem too worried. If he was, he hid it well.

'You're not hurt?' Sam said, checking his friend's leather-clad torso for any obvious signs of damage.

'Nah, I'm good,' Little Ted said in his usual deadpan voice.

'Did the Croatian get a good look at you?'

'I don't think so. Bastard was gone from the warehouse before I came in. Left the other poor bloke behind to try to take care of me.'

'The bloke with one less hand?'

'Yeah, I didn't like to do that. But he's alive, isn't he?'

'Apparently so,' Sam said. 'So, if they don't know what you look like, we could do a drive-by.'

'To see if there's anyone watching the house from the outside?'

'Just in case the Croatian is there,' Sam nodded. 'More likely it'll be the Triple S guys. That's the security company those white T-shirts were from. I want to do that before we pick up Brie.'

'What if someone's inside the house?' said Little Ted.

'I think this will give us a feel for what's going on. If they're not outside, then, yes, they could be inside. We'll deal with that if it eventuates. Okay?'

'Of course.'

Sam's mobile rang. It was DI Reddy. 'Are you alright?' she asked.

'I'm fine.'

'I wanted to check what time you're coming by the station – with your passport?'

'Yeah, yeah, no problem.'

'So, what time will that be?'

'Couple of hours or so.'

'As long as it's *today*. Please call me if you're not going to make it, for whatever reason.'

The only reason Sam believed he might not make it there did not bear thinking about.

Little Ted turned into Tamarama Street, and then took his foot off the accelerator as he approached Imperial Avenue.

'Don't go too slow,' Sam said, from the back seat. 'We want to look like we're driving past, not casing the joint. Got it?'

'Yep.'

Sam slid down in his seat to avoid being seen. 'Tell me what you can see.'

'Nothing. Wait…'

'What is it?'

'We just passed a white Hilux with two blokes in it. Just this side of your house.'

Sam let out a nervous laugh. 'These Triple S boys aren't exactly the crème de la crème of covert ops, are they? They all seem to drive bloody Hilux utes.'

Little Ted drove on to the end of the road, past the appliance store and turned right. From there they headed down to a café in Hall Street to pick up Brie. Sam climbed out of the car to greet her.

'Hey, Sam,' she said.

'Hey, yourself,' he replied.

From a distance, Brie's smile was reassuring. But up close, not so much. Sam thought she looked wired. Maybe because she'd been up all night worrying about Chaz, or maybe there was another reason; her pupils were dilated, and her jaw tightly clenched.

'You know Little Ted?' Sam said, motioning back at the car.

'Yes, of course. I *am* the receptionist. And he's always got a nice word to say.' She ducked down to the car window. 'How are you?'

'Couldn't be better,' Ted responded. 'Your chariot awaits. Jump in!'

Brie settled herself in the back seat.

'You sure you don't mind?' Sam asked, getting in after her.

'I am a little nervous. But I'll be all right.'

As they took off back towards Sam and Lauren's home, Sam asked Little Ted to loop around to Birrell Street so they could enter Imperial Avenue from the south again. Sam had kept the next part of the plan to himself. It involved improvisation.

Once they got to the corner, instead of slipping down like last time, so that he wouldn't be spotted, Sam asked Little Ted to pull over. They knew the white Hilux was three or four hundred metres away, and there was a small amount of traffic, so the Triple S boys were unlikely to notice them at this distance. There were also five pedestrians walking along the street between them and the Hilux.

'Is this your house?' asked Brie, pointing across the road.

'No,' Sam said. 'It's just up there.' He pulled out the pre-paid mobile, a burner, that he'd purchased with cash on the way, rang triple zero and got put through to the police. 'Hello, I'd like to report a crime in progress,' he said. Then, after going through the usual police Q&A, Sam added the details. 'Two men in a white Hilux ute hit a pedestrian in Bondi Road, left the scene, and are now parked in Imperial Avenue in Bondi. Licence plate CYM99G.'

Declining to give his name, Sam hung up the phone, wiped it with his shirt sleeve, and threw it out the window. 'The fuse is lit,' he said.

Within a few minutes, they could hear the sirens. 'All right!' said Brie. 'Here come the good guys!'

The first of two cop cars screeched into Imperial Avenue from the Bondi Road end, red and blue lights flashing, sirens blaring. They cornered the white Hilux and the first two cops had their weapons at the ready as they approached the beefcakes.

'Hope your dog is grateful,' quipped Little Ted.

'He's part of the family,' Sam said. 'I couldn't let him starve.'

***

The vodka glass smashed into a thousand pieces as it hit the wall. 'Fucking idiots!' Viktor yelled. 'These are your people. What are you doing?'

Joseph was stunned. He and Viktor had watched the monitor, witnessing Sam Pride and the other two enter the Imperial Avenue house like they owned the place. Well, Pride did own the place. But he seemed to be singing? There was no audio coming from the camera, but, yes, he looked like he was singing!

'Where the fuck are they?'

'I spoke to them only ten minutes ago,' Joseph said. 'They were in position. But they're not answering their phones. I'll try again.'

Joseph and Viktor stared at the feed from the internal surveillance camera, where Pride, his big black dog, and two others could be seen walking towards the front door like one happy family.

'The bastard's got something in his hand,' grumbled Viktor.

Joseph tried to zoom in, but the angle was bad. 'Do you want me to go there? If I—'

'Too late!' yelled Viktor. 'The horse has well and truly bolted.'

Joseph's mobile rang. It was one of his guys, Milo, talking fast, hyperventilating; Joseph quickly made out that they had the cops all over them. 'Delete your call history,' he shouted, 'before they confiscate your phone.'

Viktor was shaking his head. 'You bunch of fucking amateurs.'

'I'm sorry, sir,' Joseph mumbled. 'What do you want me to do now?'

'Fill up my bloody glass!'

Chapter 25

Sam felt good about how things had gone. Back in Little Ted's car, he thanked Brie for her time and knocked back her fervid invitation to go to the nearby pub for a game of pool and a drink. 'Much as I'd love it,' he said, 'my wife is stuck in a hotel room, and I don't think she'd forgive me if I didn't get back to her pronto. I also have to pop into the police station.'

'Hope it's a nice hotel,' Brie said. 'One of those fancy ones in the city?'

'It is,' he assured her. 'In The Rocks.'

They dropped Brie back at the café, and then drove to Lauren's car.

Before climbing out of Little Ted's Nissan, Sam patted him on the shoulder. 'You okay – really?'

'Couldn't be better.'

'What about Marco?' Sam asked.

'Yeah, he's good. His boys did well, hey?'

'They saved my life,' Sam said. 'I wish they could have saved Chaz's, too. But that's on the Croatian.'

'I wasn't fast enough,' said Little Ted. 'And I wasn't counting on Chaz to...'

'Mate, you were plenty fast. And don't worry, we'll get that mob. One way or another, we'll get justice for Chaz.'

'I hope so.'

'Oh, there is just one other thing,' said Sam. 'I can't believe I'm asking you for another favour!'

'What is it?'

Sam told Little Ted about a concern he had regarding his mother. Little Ted responded in his usual way, saying he'd take care of it. 'I don't know what I'd do without you,' Sam said.

Little Ted nodded and was on his way.

Sam drove off with Rax to Charlotte and Jacob's house in Banksmeadow. It took them a little over twenty minutes to get there. He told Charlotte just enough about what was happening to convince her to look after the dog till things were sorted. He didn't want to scare her, but he did ask her to act with extreme caution over the next few days. Just in case. 'These guys play rough,' he said.

'Lucky I've got that stash of automatic weapons out the back,' she smirked.

Sam kissed her on the cheek and bade farewell to Rax. 'Keep 'em safe, mate,' he said.

At Surry Hills station, Reddy came out to meet Sam at the front desk. 'Passport?' she said.

He handed it to her. 'When do I get it back?'

'In good time. Would you mind if I asked you a few more questions?'

'Do I need to call my barrister?'

'Just a few quick questions?'

'I'm trying to be co-operative. You wanted the passport. I don't know if I was legally obliged to give it to you, but now you have it. If you want something more, I'll call Kate Robinson and tell her we need her here urgently.'

Reddy raised her hands and said, 'Don't worry, it doesn't have to be today.' She opened his passport and examined the photo. 'Just make sure you stay local and that you answer the phone when I call. And don't forget about the sketch artist. She's lined up for tomorrow morning at eleven.'

***

When Sam got back to the Langham, Lauren drilled him for details, before asking if they could go for a walk.

'That would be lovely,' he said. 'Down by the harbour?'

'You're being facetious?'

'We should stay inside the hotel for now,' Sam said. 'I haven't given the police enough info for them to think we're in obvious danger, so they're not protecting us. And until the truth comes out about whoever is really behind all this, we want to lay low.'

'I guess we've got a comfy room here,' said Lauren. 'We could order room service for days if we want to.'

Sam rang the front desk to check out their options. The clerk explained that the hotel restaurant, Kitchens on Kent, was doing tea, and in fact their timing was perfect because he and Lauren could come down right now to enjoy their very special, *Afternoon Tea with Wedgewood*. When Sam told Lauren, she laughed. 'Just your kind of thing,' she mocked.

He took the lift down and picked up two coffees. Back in the room, he said, 'Darling, do you mind if I do a bit of desk research? I need to find out a bit more about those security guys.'

'I've already watched one movie on my own. I suppose I can watch another.'

Sam opened his laptop and checked out the Triple S website. No revelations about whether YRG was a client of theirs. Ad agencies often bragged about their client list, but security companies were clearly more discreet. He struggled to work out if they were global or just Aussie-based. If they weren't global, could they be affiliated with a global firm? If so, was YRG a client of that company? These relationships between Aussie independent firms and affiliated global companies were something Sam had come to understand intimately when selling TBA to YRG. It was a tangled web these big companies managed to weave.

Eventually, using the Australian Securities and Investments Commission website, he established that Triple S was an Australian company with Australian directors, but key questions remained unanswered. So, he rang the number of the Triple S Greenacre office. 'Hi there,' he said. 'My name is Peter Buchanan and I'm interested in procuring a firm to do some work for us in New York. Do you operate in the States, by any chance?'

'No, I'm sorry, Mr Buchanan, just Australia,' said the receptionist. 'But our sister firm, Alliance Security, operates in the US. Can I put you through to one of their managers? I'm sure they'll be able to help you.'

'Thanks, but no, that's not necessary. Alliance? Okay, I can have our New York office contact them directly.'

He hung up and immediately typed Alliance Security into the search engine. Lo and behold, their base was in Chicago along with YRG. 'Two directors,' he mumbled. Robert Miller and Viktor Tomic. Bingo!

'Hey, sweetheart,' he said with a note of triumph.

Lauren was lying on the bed, reading a book, latte within reach. 'I'm still here,' she said.

'Does the name Viktor Tomic sound Croatian to you?' She looked at him like the question didn't justify the interruption from her book. 'He's a director of Alliance Security,' Sam added. 'Could be Chaz's killer.'

Lauren gave up on her book. 'How many company directors are there?'

'Only two.'

'So, there's a Chicago-based security company with a connection to Triple S that has a director with a Croatian sounding name?'

'Yes.'

'But even if Alliance was involved, they could have a hundred different Croatian employees.'

'You don't believe…?'

'I'm saying you're clasping at straws,' said Lauren. 'Why would a company director from a firm in Chicago fly to Australia just to murder someone? If he wanted someone murdered, wouldn't he have some local lackey do it for him?'

'Murder is often personal. Maybe not the sort of task you delegate to an office junior?'

'Now you're being ridiculous!'

'Maybe,' Sam said.

'All this for, how much was it, eight million dollars?'

'It's not just the eight million. I think the guy behind this has done it before. Confidence in fraud comes from experience. Maybe he's done it loads of times. In bigger markets, the amounts have probably been much larger. All up, he could have stolen fifty or a hundred million. But it's the Sydney fraud that he's been caught out on. So that's the one he has to go to great lengths to cover up.'

'So, he doesn't get done for the rest?'

'That's my thinking,' said Sam. He resumed his internet searching, looking for links with Alliance as well as mentions of a security firm of any name in posts or sites relating to YRG.

Lauren had returned to her novel for a moment before saying, 'Now I can't read, Sam.'

'Sorry.'

'If you really think this director – what was his name?'

'Viktor Tomic.'

'If you really think he might be your guy, his photo should exist somewhere on the internet. If it's not on the Alliance website, it will be in some directors' listing or on Linked In, or on some other social media platform.'

'You're probably right,' Sam said. 'As always.'

This time Lauren threw a pillow at him. It missed.

For the next half hour, Sam searched high and low, following every internet thread he could. Turns out, there are more Viktor Tomics in the world than one might think. He clicked and typed, and clicked and typed, until he figured he'd pretty much exhausted all options. The guy's photo was nowhere to be found or Sam lacked the requisite skill as a researcher to find it.

The landline rang. He looked at Lauren, as if she might know who it was. She shrugged her shoulders.

'Hello?' Sam said.

'Mr Pride?' said a deep voice. 'I believe you ordered room service?'

'No, I…You must have the wrong number. There's nobody by that name here.'

'Oh, I'm sorry, sir. Our mistake.'

Sam quickly hung up and shouted at Lauren, 'We've got to get out of here!'

'What? What is it?'

'They called me Mr Pride. Grab your handbag. We've got to run. Now!'

'Jesus Christ,' she said, jumping off the bed and slipping on her shoes.

Sam opened the door to check if the coast was clear. 'Okay,' he said. They ran down the corridor to the lift.

'Maybe we should take the stairs?' said Lauren, already flustered.

Sam nodded and they bolted for the fire exit.

'If they were here,' said Lauren, trying to keep up with Sam as he leapt down the stairs, 'they would have come to the door, wouldn't they? Rather than phoning?'

'Who knows? Maybe it was one of a hundred calls.'

'How would they have known we're in a hotel?'

'They knew we weren't staying at our house, or with any of our friends, so there's a reasonable chance we'd be at a hotel. Ring enough of them, try lots of different names, make up some bullshit about how you're looking for a married couple our age…'

'You like getting inside their heads, don't you?'

'Just trying to keep us safe, sweetheart.'

***

Sam was anxious about these guys catching up with him while Lauren was around, but he told himself that he was one step ahead. Three of their people had been killed at the Botany shoot-out so the cops must have been putting pressure on them as an organisation to try to find out what happened. If Triple S had skeletons in their closet, surely DI Reddy and her colleagues would be all over them. From what Sam had observed, Triple S was the sort of company that must have had brushes with the law in the past.

He drove from The Rocks to the Harbour Bridge, and then pushed north on the A8, past the Oaks Hotel, and onto the old Hayden Orpheum Picture Palace.

'Where are you taking us?' asked Lauren.

'I thought Manly might be an option. Well away from the eastern suburbs and the CBD. Hopefully we'll be a bit harder to find there.'

He slowed down as they drove down the hill past the two speed cameras and onto The Spit Bridge. He really didn't want to be pulled up by the cops just now.

He had been to a function once at The Sebel on South Steyne, down the southern end of Manly Beach, so he thought he'd give that a try. It might not be five stars, but that didn't matter, as long as they were safe there. It had private indoor parking, which was a good start.

Climbing out of the car, Lauren said, 'A spa and two swimming pools. You're such a hedonist.'

'Just trying to look after my wife.'

'I appreciate that.'

Checking in at reception, Sam wondered if the thirty-something woman scanning Lauren's credit card would say anything about them having no luggage. She didn't seem to care. Coincidentally, Lauren then encouraged Sam to check out a middle-aged man dressed in jeans and a black shirt, who had followed them through the front door to sit in the lounge area. It was possible he worked for Triple S and had pursued them to Manly, but it seemed unlikely. The guys Sam had seen in the white utes were much younger and seriously buffed. If this guy had ever spent time working out in a gym, it wasn't this century.

Once up in their room, Lauren asked if Sam thought it safe to venture out onto the balcony. She could not be seen there from the street, but the room did have a view of the South Pacific Ocean.

'If you're worried about the surfers,' he said.

'Yes. The Triple S guys have gone out to sea on boards to secretly observe us.' Lauren retrieved the novel from her handbag. 'I just thought I'd ask.'

Sam was trying to stay calm, but he couldn't relax. He grabbed out his laptop and headed for a small table by the lounge. Free of any immediate threat, and with time to kill, he wanted to get back to his digging. He was never going to be able to rest until the Croatian was behind bars – or dead.

Chapter 26

Sam slipped out of bed to a blurry Sunday morning. His head was throbbing from the wine he polished off late in the evening. He remembered that awful stage of lying in bed, eyes closing, turning his pillow over, shifting irritably, images of the Croatian threatening him with the knife he'd used to kill Chaz forcing their way into his head.

Lauren's eyes were shut as she lay peacefully on her side. Was she enjoying a dream about what life would be like when the baby was born? The happy threesome building sandcastles on the beach, or something cheesy like that?

Sam walked out onto the balcony. There wasn't much surf but there were still twenty or thirty devotees having a go, kept warm by their full-length wetsuits. He sighed while watching them ride the waves.

When he came back inside, Lauren was awake. He asked if she'd mind him popping over to the police station and helping the sketch artist, like he'd promised. Before he went, though, he wanted to make one phone call. 'It's a long shot,' he said. 'But I've got to give it a try.'

He used his mobile to ring the number of Alliance Security in Chicago. It was Saturday their time, but they claimed to be open seven days a week anyway.

A chirpy woman answered. Sam asked for Viktor Tomic.

'I'm sorry, sir, but he's out of the country. May I put you through to someone else?'

'Of course, he's in Australia, isn't he?'

'Why, yes, sir, he is indeed.'

'Can you tell me when he'll be back?'

'The day after tomorrow. Now can I—'

'Thank you, ma'am. That's all I needed to know.'

Sam told Lauren what he'd heard. 'Sure you're not jumping to conclusions?' she asked.

'No, I'm not sure,' Sam admitted. 'But if Viktor Tomic's in Australia, it makes it all the more likely that he's the killer.'

'Maybe.'

What to do next? Should he go to Chicago? Would the police even allow that? 'I might ask Kate what she thinks I should do,' said Sam.

'I think you should tell the police everything,' said Lauren emphatically.

'And what about Little Ted and Bianchi? I can't sell them out.'

'I'll bet Kate will agree with me.'

'She may well.'

'You're seeing the sketch artist, anyway. Reddy will be there. Make her your friend, rather than your enemy.'

Sam was about to leave when Lauren grabbed his arm. 'Wait,' she insisted, taking two Nurofen tabs from her bag and placing them in his hand. 'You might need these.'

He took them. A hangover and a visit to the police station were not a good combination.

***

Lauren was surprised to see Noah's name pop up on her call screen. She probably should have deleted him from her contacts. At first, she thought not to answer him. But what if he kept calling? What if Sam answered one day? It couldn't hurt to answer him just this once.

'Lauren. Hi. How are you?'

'I'm fine,' she lied. 'I thought we agreed not to contact each other?'

'I know. I know. We did, but, well, you don't come to the gym anymore. I guess I just wanted to hear your voice.'

Lauren wanted to be polite, but she didn't want the complication of any sort of relationship – even a friendship – with Noah. 'Okay, well, I've really got to go.'

'I miss you,' he said.

'Look, Noah, what happened was a mistake. I'm sorry, but can we just leave it at that?'

'If that's what you really want.'

'It is. Goodbye, Noah.'

Lauren felt her cruel words weighing heavy in her heart. What if Noah turned out to be the father of her child? It wasn't a thought she could contemplate right now. Moments later, he rang again. This time there was no hesitation in letting it go through to voicemail. Shortly after, she listened to the first part of the message – some sweet sentimental rubbish – then deleted it without suffering through the rest. She hoped he wasn't the type to turn into a stalker. That was all she needed!

***

Kate met Sam in the front of the Surry Hills station and insisted he say nothing in response to any questioning without her prior approval.

'Have you seen the news?' she asked.

'No, what?'

'When the story of the shootings first came out, the journos were asking the cops if it was terror-related. They said it wasn't, so the story suggested it could be drug-related. So, now, it's become a law-and-order issue. Drugs and guns on the streets mean we need more money for law enforcement and harsher penalties, mandatory sentencing, for any and all offenders. Zero tolerance. All that rubbish.'

'What will they say when they discover the truth?'

'The media? So long as the story helps their ratings, they couldn't care less about the truth.'

Sam did his best with the digital sketch artist. 'That's pretty close,' they said.

What he didn't say to DI Reddy, who seemed to be running the show, was that he might have known the suspect's name. But he was still trying to keep Little Ted and Marco Bianchi out of trouble. He also wasn't sure he wanted his agency to be in the headlines over this (though how could it not be when Chaz was the CFO). Part of him wanted the Croatian caught and the other part just wanted this to disappear like Botany had never happened. He hadn't even told Reddy about Chaz being kidnapped and the text messages he'd been sent beforehand.

The DI motioned to the interview room. 'We just have a few more questions.'

Kate interjected, 'My client's wife—'

'Not a request, counsellor.' said Reddy. 'Come with me. Now.'

Once the recording device was switched on, Reddy was less snappy than she had been on Friday, but still direct. 'I want you to tell me about Triple S Security,' she said.

'I don't know anything about them,' Sam replied, perhaps too quickly.

'That would seem to suggest your CFO, Chaz Bailley, was acting on his own. He must have had a reason for meeting these people.'

'I am sure he did, but like I said, I don't know what it was.'

'Has your company ever done business with Triple S Security or any affiliate of Triple S Security?'

'No.'

'Which security company do you use?'

'Force Security. They do the building we are in. Always have, even before we were there.'

'And they're not connected to Triple S?'

'Not that I know of.'

'During his time with TBA, has Bailley ever given you cause to believe he might sympathise with any extremist groups? Right wing, left wing, whatever?'

'Absolutely not.'

'Has he ever had a problem with drugs?'

'No,' Sam said, perhaps too slowly.

Reddy narrowed her eyes. But she must have known Chaz did not have a police record; he might have committed a misdemeanour or two in his time, but he'd certainly never been caught on a serious charge. Sam watched Reddy tap her pencil on the table.

'Are we finished here?' asked Kate. 'My client has answered—'

'Yes,' snapped Reddy. 'For the moment.'

'I really do hope you catch whoever did this,' Sam said, standing up.

'Oh, we will,' said the DI. 'We always do.'

Except when you don't, thought Sam, hopeful.

As Sam drove back to Manly, the clouds turned dark, and a few minutes later, the rain began pelting down. He watched the windscreen wipers go like he was in a trance, his mind once again drifting back to that moment when the Croatian cut Chaz's throat. He turned up the radio. It was a classic hits station, and the Stones song Tumbling Dice was on. There was a lot of tumblin' going on inside Sam's head. He wondered what he could to make sure the dice rolled in his favour.

When he entered the parking area, he thought about ducking out to grab some takeaway – but that was probably too reckless. Lauren would certainly think so. They could manage with whatever was in the room, or order *genuine* room service.

He caught the lift up to their floor and observed a young couple exiting a room a few doors from theirs. Any strangers in their midst were a cause for concern, but when Sam saw these two holding hands, he breathed out, nice and slow.

Lauren was sitting on the sofa chair with a cup of tea by her side, reading her novel. 'How did you go?' she asked.

'They've got their sketch.' Sam went to the fridge and pulled out a bottle of white wine. 'You feel like a glass?'

'I'd better not,' sniffed Lauren. 'But you can have a drink for both of us.'

He poured himself a hefty glass. 'If Viktor Tomic is on a flight back to Chicago, and he's not left any DNA at the crime scene, maybe he's home free?' He thought about it for a minute longer and then said, 'Actually, they wouldn't have his DNA on file, would they? So, it wouldn't matter even if he had left DNA at the scene.'

'What about the witness?'

'Me? If I told the cops everything and agreed to testify, it would still be my word against Tomic's.'

'You're believable.'

'Only if I tell the whole truth. But how can I? I either withhold vital information by saying nothing about Little Ted and Bianchi – and am therefore guilty of obstructing justice – or I tell all and become guilty of betraying my friends, as well as being an accessory before and after the fact to three murders and one attempted murder.'

Lauren sat upright and said, 'So, what's the answer?'

'I wish I knew.'

They hung about in the hotel room, occasionally reading, occasionally chatting, Sam drinking his wine, and Lauren sipping her soda. Just killing time. Sam walked over to the balcony and looked out at the rain splashing down on the ocean. No surfers out there now. He wanted to know what was going on. 'Do you mind if I put on the news?'

'Go for your life.'

He flicked on the TV, watching story after story, waiting for them to say something about Chaz and the other killings. But there was nothing. Maybe it was old news until the police released some new information or the journos could find a witness with a first-hand account of what had gone down. He kept thinking the sketch he'd helped create would suddenly appear on screen, but it didn't.

'The guy I really want brought down isn't the Croatian,' he said.

'The guy from YRG?'

'Brandis. That's who is paying Viktor Tomic.'

'You can't be sure of that.'

'Maybe I should let the murder go for now, and instead follow the money trail? If I can prove Brandis stole the eight million dollars, then it's obvious he'd want that covered up. Prove Brandis was paying Tomic, let it slip that Chaz had found this out, then we have a motive for murder. And maybe then I don't have to explain who killed the Triple S guys in Botany.'

'Should *you* let the murder go?' Lauren asked cautiously. 'Sam, it's not you who has to prosecute the Croatian or this Brandis guy. You need to let the police do their job. And you need to look after me and our baby.'

'Of course,' Sam said. Lauren and the baby were indeed his first priority. But if the police could not get to Tomic and Brandis, then he could not sit back and do nothing. Chaz's family and loved ones deserved more than that.

Chapter 27

Jean Koziol looked out the second storey window to see her daughter, Bella, running along the path beside the tennis court, carrying the flowers she'd picked from the sprawling garden out back. The summer holidays had not yet commenced but the exams and all other serious scholastic activity was over for the term, so Jean had allowed Bella to stay home with her on this bright sunny day. She suspected she'd been too soft on the child since her father had died, but she didn't care. Jean missed her husband terribly and was certain her daughter did too. They had been a close-knit family when Tony was around, and Jean would have done anything to fill the painful void left by her best friend and lover. There were times when their six-bedroom, nine-bathroom mansion in Barrington Hills, forty-five minutes north-west of Chicago, felt as desolate as a barren island.

She sat back down in front of the computer and reviewed the monthly finance report from YRG. There was no denying that the business was making a lot of money. Margaret Whitfield must have been doing something right.

A question popped up on the screen asking Jean if she wanted to save the document. This seemed to happen all the time, nowadays, but she had no idea why. Infernal technology!

When Jean decided to give up her crowded, white-walled office space in the city to work from home, she'd used the IT consultants contracted to YRG. Margaret had told her the company would cover the cost, but Jean would have none of it. She paid the consultants personally the moment the work was done. She did not want to owe anyone any favours and, as a company director, she needed to be at arm's length from transactions between YRG and their clients or suppliers.

After she'd electronically signed off on the profit and loss report, Jean felt like joining Bella outside. They'd had fun earlier that morning throwing large plastic objects in the pool. But it was time to address an issue that had been weighing on her mind for several days. She had a Microsoft Teams meeting scheduled with the Chief Executive for 1pm. That only left a short amount of time to check over the email she'd received from Robert Miller. She wanted to be sure she'd not misunderstood the gravity of its contents.

The meeting with Margaret began promptly. After the usual pleasantries, Jean got right to it. 'I'm worried about Don Brandis,' she declared. 'From what my friend tells me, he's not a man to be trusted.'

'I'm not sure where you're getting your information,' said Margaret.

Jean's concern deepened. Challenging her sources was not the way to go if Margaret wanted peace with the Board.

'Don's not a bad man,' Margaret continued.

'You're sure of that, sure that he'd never do anything fraudulent?'

'Fraudulent? Heavens, no! He's not a criminal. And he has played a very valuable role for our company, for quite a few years now. Even if he were guilty of some minor indiscretion, and I doubt that he is, we'd want to handle that sensitively.'

'What do you mean?'

'We certainly wouldn't want it going public. As you know, YRG does an incredible amount of good in the world. There's no need to do anything drastic. We don't want to ruin the brand's reputation.'

'You're one of those people who likes to – avoid mess, aren't you, Margaret? Hide or even bury the truth if it doesn't match your story? If it is, say, unflattering?'

'The way I see it,' said Margaret, ignoring those remarks, 'YRG matters. We employ eighty-nine thousand people in 102 countries. Two hundred and three of the Fortune Global 500 are clients of ours. Why is that? Because we do what we do better than anyone else. We're more innovative than our rivals, more progressive. Smarter. We give brands purpose. We help clients build sustainability into the core of their businesses. Our creativity has saved one of the world's most important rainforests from destruction and is now inspiring people to clean up our oceans. And you want to throw all that away? Well, I say, no. If Don has taken a misstep of some sort, taken a short cut on some paperwork or something of that nature – and I say it again, I really don't think he has – then you wouldn't want to undo all the wonderful work being done by our eighty-nine thousand staff to satisfy some misdirected need for righteousness you've only just discovered within yourself.'

'Margaret, I really don't like your tone.'

'I'm sorry, Jean, but...'

'What do you think we should do?'

'Let it go.'

'Really?'

'For the greater good. You fix the problem, make sure it never happens again, and then you move on. You get back to making the world a better place.'

'And our shareholders richer.'

'You're one of our largest.'

'Yes, I'm aware of that,' said Jean, ready to end the meeting. Jean felt it was time to discuss the future of the company's current leader with some of the other board directors. As far as she could tell, YRG's culture needed a thorough investigation – clearly the company's official values as stated in its constitution played no part in it – and there was not a moment to lose.

***

'Is everything alright, sir?' A stewardess had been wheeling the drinks cart by and noticed Viktor drag his arm from the aisle.

'It's nothing,' he said.

'Would you like some water?' She reminded him of a girl at his favourite strip club.

Viktor forced a smile. 'Sure. Thank you.'

The stewardess couldn't have seen the four-day-old bullet wound under his jacket, but Viktor was annoyed at himself for showing any signs of pain at all. He wouldn't have minded something stronger than a couple of walk-on paracetamol tablets. Once back in Chicago, he knew exactly who to call. But for now, he had one objective, and that was getting home without being arrested. That meant drawing zero attention to himself.

'Wine? Champagne, perhaps?'

Viktor felt like a vodka but settled on wine. With glass in hand, he said to the stewardess, 'To beauty'. The stewardess blushed, which pleased him.

The last time he'd uttered such a phrase was with Darius, his comrade now lying in a Sydney hospital bed with something far more serious than a flesh-wound. The surgeons had tried to stitch his hand back together, but metal and plastic were no substitute for the cartilage and bone he'd lost.

Viktor looked at his watch. Twenty hours to go. He wanted a cigarette, but it would be a long wait before he could disembark and legally light up. He removed the packet of sleeping pills from his jacket pocket and breathed a sigh of relief. Very shortly, he would be converting his seat to its flat-bed configuration and, some minutes after that, he would be dead to the world. When he next regained consciousness, he would be in 'the land of the free', never to return to this God-forsaken country. There was only one more thing he ever wanted to hear about Australia, that the men at Triple S, with whom he'd left a very large sum of money, had carried out his instructions and finally disposed of that maddening thorn in his side.

Chapter 28

Sam knew Lauren was sick of being stuck in the hotel room. 'I don't know when it will be safe for you to leave,' he said.

'When I leave is up to me,' Lauren responded. 'I'm not some pathetic damsel in distress, you know? I did a lot of boxing classes at the gym. Five years' worth. I'd be at least as fit as a lot of those blokes from Triple S. I'm pretty sure I could take you out if I had to. Maybe not Little Ted, but certainly an averaged sized guy.'

'Now you're calling me, average? Darling, I'm sorry if I ever doubted you.'

'No, you're not. I'm going to make a cup of tea. Do you want one?'

Sam sent Kate an email asking if she'd heard from the police, but he didn't have to wait for her reply to know what the answer would be. She would have let him know if she had news.

He felt like he was being too passive. The police obviously hadn't arrested the Croatian, and Sam started to believe it more and more likely that the killer and Brandis would get away with their horrendous crimes. That was not something he could allow to happen.

He was sitting at the desk and going through his emails when he saw one from Brie. She was not at the office, but she said everyone there was talking about Chaz's murder. 'I think you need to say something,' she wrote.

She was right. Sam thought about calling an all-staff meeting but knew Lauren wouldn't like him going into the office, and he didn't want to talk about Chaz via a giant Zoom extravaganza. He was going to do it by email. He felt like that was the way to control the narrative. Before sending it, he let Brie know what he was going to say about her.

> Dear all,
>
> I have some terribly sad news to report. On Friday, our beloved CFO, Chaz Bailley, our colleague, was killed. The police are currently investigating what happened and I don't think me or anyone else speculating at this point

would be helpful. Please join me in sending our condolences and very best wishes to Chaz's family at this extremely difficult time. I have already sent flowers on our behalf and will let you know as soon as a time has been set for the funeral.

If the news about Chaz raises issues for your personally, and you would like to talk to a counsellor, please contact Brie Allinson, who will give you the contact details of someone who is standing by, ready to take your calls.

Thanks,
Sam

The moment he hit send, his mobile rang. It was a landline number. He hesitated but then decided to answer.

'Hello, Sam?' said a well-spoken woman's voice he didn't recognise.

'Speaking.'

'Sam, hi, it's Eva Halliwell from *Advertising Week*. I wanted to let you know we're planning to run a story on sexual harassment in Australian agencies, and we're going to feature TBA. I think you can guess why. Would you like to comment?'

'I have no idea what you are talking about,' he said.

'We know about the case being investigated there.'

'And which case would that be, Eva?'

'One involving a young woman in a relatively junior position and an older person in a very senior position.'

'You run what you feel comfortable with, Eva. I know what our policies on harassment are, and I know that our approach to dealing with any concerns raised by our employees is second to none.'

'Sam, I wouldn't have called you if I didn't have a source. Someone happy to go on record.'

Sam felt certain she didn't know that Zoe was the woman being accused, otherwise she'd have been more specific; and she'd probably have tried Zoe first. This was a fishing expedition.

'Eva,' he said calmly, 'if you had a credible source, you wouldn't have called. As a company, we have nothing to hide. You, on the other hand, should know that TBA have a passion for litigation. If you were to indulge in baseless speculation, in any manner which might potentially impugn our reputation, then we'll litigate against Adweek and against you personally.'

'So that's a denial?'

'Eva, I think my language was pretty clear. Have a great day.'

Sam hung up and looked at Lauren, who'd started paying attention to the call after the first sentence. 'What I really wanted to tell her,' he said, 'was that there's a much bigger story about our agency. One that involves global fraud and multiple homicides. Her parent company would have liked that one.'

'If you'd offered that up, I think she'd have been willing to drop the harassment story. By the way, *is* there a harassment case being investigated at TBA?'

'You don't want to know.'

'Just tell me it's not you.'

'It's not. But as I said, darling, you don't want to know. The only thing that matters is that the complaint is a work of fiction.'

He regretted having not told Lauren about the Kitty matter sooner. He had just hoped it would disappear, given how baseless it was. Now he needed to know if this journo from *Adweek* really had anything or not.

He sent Marilyn Banks an email asking her if she'd heard anything more about the matter. He mentioned the security camera in the lift, suggesting that any recording from the night in question would prove Zoe's version of events. He was confident she'd already have thought of that but since she hadn't mentioned it, a reminder couldn't hurt. But before he'd had a response from Marilyn, an email popped up from Kitty:

> I am sure you wish I'd just disappear but I'm not going to. Not if you refuse to make amends. Zoe really did hurt me you know. I think $250,000 would be fair compensation for everything. Then I could leave TBA and start afresh. I am sorry that it has come to this.
>
> Thanks,
> Kitty

Sam wasn't shocked by the fact that she wanted money, but he was by the way in which she was demanding it. No HR investigations, no lawyers, just an old-fashioned extortion demand. Dressed up with some pretend pathos. Curious that she was sending the email to him rather than to Zoe.

An email followed from Marilyn. She said she'd approached Kitty on May 20 after speaking with the other account exec, but Kitty insisted the incident not be pursued. With no complainant, no witness, and no evidence of any wrongdoing (other than the hearsay of the exec who refused to go on record), Marilyn had no basis on which to conduct a proper investigation. And since then, nothing more had come of it; the account exec had not made further contact and there had been no word from Kitty herself. But with Sam's mention of the call from the journo, and now what was clearly a blackmail demand for money, Marilyn wrote back that she would follow up with Zoe for a formal interview and pursue the matter 'relentlessly'.

None of that eased Sam's mind. It was just one more thing to worry about, as if Brandis and the Croatian were not enough. He phoned her. 'Am I right in thinking Kitty did some time at McKenzie & Roberts before she joined us?' he asked. 'I know there were no red flags in her references, but could you give their HR manager a buzz and poke around a bit? It's hard to believe there were absolutely no signs of this kind of form before Kitty joined TBA. It's pretty extreme.'

'I'll make the call right away,' said Marilyn.

'If you don't get anywhere, let me know and I'll call Cressida Roberts, their CEO.'

***

Viktor entered the Alliance Security boardroom first, with Robert following close behind. They had not spoken since Viktor returned from Australia.

Viktor began. 'You don't need to know all the details, but we had some problems in Sydney.'

'No kidding,' said Robert.

'Don't start with any of that self-righteous shit. You know what I do. It's made both of us rich. Just 'cause you don't get your hands dirty...'

'What is it you want to say, Viktor?'

'If you are contacted by anyone from YRG, simply refer them to me.'

'That's what I normally do.'

'And, if I am not around, do not speak to anyone but Don Brandis.'

'Don Brandis?'

'He's the man who approves our invoices.'

'And what do you want me to say to Brandis until you can be contacted?'

'Nothing. Just listen.'

'What if he asks about those events in Australia?'

'As far as you know, everything went perfectly.'

'But that's not true, is it?'

Viktor stared a moment at Robert, for effect, and then answered with a finality that wouldn't be challenged. 'What's true is what we say is true.'

***

It was late. Sam could see that it was Marilyn calling from her mobile. 'I've got to take this,' he said to Lauren.

'Okay,' Lauren said, barely awake.

Sam put the phone to his ear. 'Any news?'

'You were right about Kitty,' said Marilyn. 'Well, half right, at least. I spent quite a bit of time talking to the HR Manager from McKenzie & Roberts and, while Kitty didn't try to extort money from them, she did leave with a cloud hanging over her head. Apparently, she claimed to have had a one-night stand with one of their Group Account Directors. He denied it and said he could prove he was home alone at the time she claimed it happened. She had no evidence for her version of the story but that didn't stop her trying it on. She said if she wasn't given a major promotion, the whole world would find out. He was senior, she was junior, clear case of sexual harassment in the workplace. M&R said they'd call in a professional investigator to deal with the matter but before that could happen, Kitty resigned. She never went public with the story and M&R certainly didn't want to talk about it. So, that was it.'

'Thanks for letting me know,' said Sam. On the one hand, he was relieved, because it supported Zoe's version of what had happened, but on the other hand, it distressed Sam to recognise how easily the people who chose to rort the system could get away with it. 'If only it was a little easier for the truth to get out,' he said.

'Oh, and I've also completed my formal interview with Zoe,' said Marilyn.

'How was she?'

'Upset at having to go through the process, but she gave me a full account of the night and everything she said rings true. She also suspected Kitty might have had some history of this kind of thing.'

'Did you tell her?'

'I said we are looking into it. She wanted to do something herself, make some calls, but I told her not to. A thing like this, we have to be impartial, and we have to be seen to be impartial.'

'It will be driving Zoe crazy, but you are right, of course.'

***

He might not have been born there, but Joseph Khoury knew Rose Bay. Triple S had over half a dozen clients in the affluent, sleepy suburb where families go to bed early and the bright lights and loud noises of the city's bars and clubs seem as distant as a dust storm on Mars. People living in the area pay well for the privilege and, once asleep, don't expect to be woken until their smartphones or alarm clocks tell them it's time for another day's toil.

Joseph slid down in his seat to avoid being seen by the Mercedes SUV as it turned into the residents' parking area of the apartment block. It was late and he guessed this was the last of them. They weren't exactly spring chickens living in this particular complex. It probably had special conditions where only pensioners could buy in. Wheelchair access, lots of handrails, that kind of thing. He pulled out his mobile and checked the photo again. This was a woman who wouldn't be putting up much of a fight. Maybe he should have given the job to a subordinate but after what Viktor had said to him, he didn't want to risk it. He believed in the saying, 'If you want a job done right...'

He waited another half hour before getting out of the car. He stood completely still. A handful of parked cars either side of the road but no occupants. Another quick glance up and down the street, and over at the golf course. Not a peep.

The apartment block sat between two single-storey residences, each with their lights out. He heard a dog bark, but it must have been at least five hundred metres away. He crossed the road; thankful the streetlamp was a safe distance away. Even if someone saw him enter the building (which was unlikely because of all the trees along the pathway) he was dressed in black with a black beanie, and it was dark. At best, a witness might recall seeing a person, possibly male, about medium height, possibly Middle Eastern (but hard to be sure), with no distinguishing features. Joseph liked that about himself, that he had no distinguishing features.

A barely audible squeak from the front gate as he pushed it open. Then a short walk up to the front door, next to which sat an empty bottle of Fat Yak Pale Ale; he was careful not to knock that little bugger over. A quick, twenty-second pick on the lock, and he was inside the building.

This was going like a charm. He'd be in and out in no time.

He reached her apartment's front door on the third floor; everything was going perfectly. He began picking its lock when he suddenly heard a grunt from behind. He turned around. 'Who the fuck?'

He saw a man, hunched down, his legs slightly bent, his left foot forward, as if ready to spring into action. He was enormous, but tucked together like a trained fighter, elbows tight against his ribs, hips square to shoulders, evenly balanced, his chin down and his eyes unblinking as they stared down their target.

Joseph was in a state of shock but still managed to scramble for his pocketknife.

The big guy drove forward off the ball of his back foot, opening his stance with his right and then closing with his left. As he repeated opening and closing, opening and closing, Joseph saw his right hand become rigid, the knuckles raising slightly, his thumb tucking behind its fingers. Suddenly, the man's left hand was on Joseph's arm, spinning him into a rigid right that chopped into his solar plexus. The punch had an audible *snap* to it that completely knocked the wind out of him, the pain of it all making him wonder if he'd ever recover. His last thought before passing out was the same as his first had been.

Who the fuck...

Chapter 29

Sam was still half asleep when he saw the text from Little Ted. It had been sent at 3.15am:

> Don't worry, everything's fine. I've moved your mum to a friend's place. She'll be 100% safe there. She doesn't know about what happened. Sometime soon a bloke will be waking up in the bunker of a Rose Bay golf course. He'll be pretty sore. Maybe he'll think twice about going after an elderly lady next time.

'Fuck!' Sam cried out.

'What?'

Sam showed Lauren the text. 'What do you think happened?' she asked.

'They obviously tried to get to Mum.'

'What was Little Ted doing there?'

'I asked him if he could get someone to keep an eye on her. Just in case. He decided not to delegate.'

'Little Ted to the rescue once again.'

'I just can't believe it.'

'You've got to go the police, now,' said Lauren. 'These people are out of control. Going after Janice like that!'

'I hear you,' said Sam. But he still didn't think he could be entirely open with DI Reddy. He knew Lauren was anxious, even angry, but he had to deal with the situation his way. Maybe he'd seek forgiveness later rather than permission now.

He got up to take a shower and was wearing only a towel when the mobile rang. It was Jenny Graham, the Melbourne GM. Sam was surprised. 'Sorry to bother you,' she said. 'I confess, it's a strange one.'

'Okay,' Sam said slowly.

'Margaret called and, well, she told me not to say anything, but fuck her. I work for you, Sam. Anyway, she asked me if I could run the show if you got hit by a bus.'

'What?'

'I'm not joking. Those were the words she used. Seems ridiculous, but it was as though she was planning to fire you, which would make no sense since they just bought an agency which, we all know, has your blood running through its veins.'

Sam thanked Jenny for the call, but he had no idea what to make of the news. It struck him as truly bizarre after all the conversations he'd had with Margaret prior to YRG purchasing the agency.

He told Lauren.

'First the thing with your mum, and now this,' she said.

'I know. It's incredible.'

'You thought Margaret was – on your side?'

'Over and over again, she and the rest of them told me how important I was to the business. How incredibly rosy my future was. How we were a partnership, a family, and that over the next decade my star would rise and rise within the YRG world. Does that suddenly count for nothing?'

Sam didn't expect Lauren to have the answer, but she came back with, 'They're all a bunch of untrustworthy fuckers!'

Sam and Lauren hung around the hotel room for another couple of hours, stressing over all the unknowns that they were now drowning in. Eventually Sam said, 'I just can't sit here and do nothing.'

'I'm not exactly loving being stuck here, either, you know.'

'I'm going to suggest something,' he said, 'and you probably won't like it.'

'You want to go to Chicago?'

'I have to go above Margaret's head. If she wants me gone, whether it's because she's in cahoots with Brandis or simply because she thinks I'm too much trouble, the result is the same. I want justice for Chaz, and I want to end this thing. I want my mum, you, all of us to be safe. That means bringing down Brandis. And I want to have a future for myself, and that means taking on Margaret. If she later says she fired me because I was shit at my job, or implies I did something sinister, then how can I, an unemployed nobody in some remote corner of Sydney, ever counter that. It will be her word, that of a Global CEO, not mine, that is written into history.'

'And your mum?'

'If Little Ted says she is somewhere safe, I believe him.'

Later that afternoon, Brie called to ask when the funeral for Chaz would be taking place. Sam explained to her that there would be a delay in the police releasing the body. Chaz was, of course, the subject of an open homicide investigation.

If he was going to leave the country, Sam decided he needed to know what could be done about his passport. He sent Kate an email, and she invited him to attend her chambers in the city.

'You're going to leave me here, alone?' said Lauren. 'Just like you're going to leave me alone when you fly off to Chicago?'

'I'm sorry, I know you don't agree with me. But I can't just be some passive wimp in a conspiracy that's being controlled by people who have committed crimes that – well – they can't go unanswered.'

He left the hotel room and walked down the corridor. While he was waiting for the lift, another email notification came in:

> Hi Sam,
>
> I hope you are as well as can be, despite the tumultuous events of the past week. I am so sorry to hear the news about Chaz. Would you be able to come over to Chicago? I think it's important we meet face-to-face. I'd like you here as soon as possible.
>
> Many thanks,
> Margaret

***

Marilyn Banks took a seat directly opposite Ian Caldwell in the small meeting room. 'You've got your coffee?' she said. 'You're all good?'

'Yes, thank you,' said Caldwell.

Marilyn opened a note pad and wrote down the date and time. 'Do you know why I've asked you here, today?'

'I think so.'

'I don't normally meet with consultants, and I've never met with anyone from NetGen before. But today, I need your help.'

'Okay,' said Caldwell.

'You're familiar with the lift in our building?'

'Yes.'

'And you know there's a security camera in that lift?'

'Yes.'

'And you know where we keep the footage taken from that security camera? NetGen manages that, right?'

Caldwell nodded sheepishly.

'Do you know where the footage from that camera is for the night of Thursday, May 14?' Marilyn gave him some time before adding, 'I ask because it appears to be missing.'

Caldwell shifted in his chair. 'No, why would I?'

Marilyn put down the pen she'd been holding and looked Caldwell in the eye. 'Ian, I can't overstate the importance of what you say next. Do you want to tell me about Kitty Zhang?'

'Tell you what?'

'Ian, I know you didn't think you were doing anything wrong. Just a favour for a friend. The problem is, Kitty is demanding a large amount of money for what happened to her in the lift that night. There may be a crime involved. If so, it becomes a police matter. That could mean one or more people being charged. You understand?'

He shifted nervously in his chair, blinking and twitching, seemingly hesitant to speak until he'd asked, 'A large amount?'

'A quarter of a million dollars.'

'Oh, my…'

'Did she offer to give you any of that money?'

'No,' said Caldwell. 'I didn't know anything happened in – in the lift.'

'I believe you,' said Marilyn smiling. 'I do. But that doesn't resolve this issue.'

Ian sat himself upright. 'What if I could find the file?'

'Could you?'

'Would that be enough?' Ian swallowed and said, 'Enough to resolve it?'

'That would show you were intent on doing the right thing. It would make you one of the good guys.'

'And that would be everything?'

'Ian. The footage is all I'm after right now.'

'Okay, leave it with me.'

Marilyn nodded. 'Thanks, Ian. This means a lot. Really.'

Chapter 30

The car park entrance to Kate's office in Philip Street was tenant-only, but she had allowed Sam access to drive in. Her chambers were on Level 31, where she resided along with twenty-seven other barristers who, between them, offered a wide range of advocacy and advisory expertise. At reception, Sam was offered a cup of coffee, which he declined, before being escorted to a small meeting room. Grey carpet, predominantly white walls, and lots of glass, just in case a client wanted to take in the view. It was a very different vibe to the TBA offices. Sam could see the Opera House, the Harbour Bridge, North Sydney and beyond.

Kate walked in carrying a folder full of documents. As far as Sam was concerned, he was only in here for a quick chat about flying to Chicago, but he was also wondering if he should bring up the Kitty situation and the call from the *Adweek* journo. After all, Kate was also his friend, not some random lawyer working for BHP.

He and Kate hugged. 'You're not looking too bad,' she said. 'All things considered. How's Lauren doing?'

'Worried. And sick of being stuck in a hotel room.'

'I can imagine. Now, how can I help?'

'I need to go to Chicago.'

For a split-second Kate looked at him like he was delusional. 'Okay. Putting to one side the fact that the police are holding your passport, why would you want to go to Chicago?'

'Two reasons. First, my boss sent me an email saying she wants me there. As in, *right away*. And second, I'm worried that if I don't go, Chaz's killer will never be brought to justice. And that the guy I believe to be behind it all, Don Brandis, will get away scot-free.'

'Okay, but...'

While Kate seemed to be searching for her opening arguments, Sam thought to double down on his own. 'I now believe that Margaret, my boss, wants to fire me. That could mean I don't get the rest of the money that's owed to me. And it would put a black mark against my name for the rest of my career.'

'So, you want to know if the police can stop you leaving the country?'

'That's right.'

'The answer is, yes, they can. You're still a suspect in a homicide case.'

'But if I explain that I *have* to go. For my work?'

'Reddy cares about solving murders, not protecting your job. Look at it from her point of view. The media's watching and that means the politicians are watching. The Minister for Police will be on the Commissioner's case every waking hour until an arrest is made.'

'Could we at least try? Surely there's no harm in asking?'

'But if Chicago is where the man who killed Chaz, and the one who gave the order are hanging out, I would imagine your life would be in grave danger there.'

'You're sounding like Lauren.'

'Is that such a bad thing?'

'I get it. And I obviously feel conflicted. Lauren is pregnant, and me going to Chicago could rob her and the baby of a husband and a father. But I'm not stupid, and I'm not going to take unnecessary risks. I know you doubt me, but I feel confident I'll come home safely. And, frankly, if I never stood up to do the right thing – and I am certain that trying to get justice for Chaz is the right thing – then what sort of a father would I be, anyway?'

Sam was just about to mention Kitty when Kate's phone rang. She blocked the call and apologised, but Sam sensed it was time to go. He simply thanked Kate and drove back to Manly.

***

Lauren was watching the news on TV when Sam walked in. She turned the volume down to ask him how he went with Kate. He made them tea while he explained what had happened, starting with the email from Margaret.

'You really want to go?' she said.

'No, I don't. But now, with Margaret's demand for a face-to-face... Look, I think it's the right thing to do. We're all in danger if I do nothing. Yes, there's a risk, obviously, but I think it's manageable. If Reddy will give me back my passport.'

'I feel like a drink.'

'Me, too!'

'Yes, but you're allowed to have one. Me, on the other hand...'
Lauren put her hand on her belly. 'It's all *his* fault.'

'Now you're sure it's a boy, are you?'

'I wouldn't be blaming him, otherwise.'

'Yes, let's blame him,' Sam said, patting Lauren's belly. 'Great start
to his life. All our problems are his fault and we're happy to let him
know it.'

They both let out a nervous laugh.

***

Kate rang Sam on his mobile and sounded excited. 'What is it?' he
asked.

'I phoned Reddy and pushed her on the prelim forensics. They've
done the analysis of the swabs they took on the day of Chaz's murder,
and there were no traces of gun residue on you. That's a big deal. And
there's now evidence that suggests Chaz's killer was left-handed. We
all know you are not.'

'And so?'

'I argued that there simply wasn't any basis on which Reddy could
refuse to give you back your passport. And she reluctantly agreed.'

'Wow! Kate, you are the best!'

Sam tried to think back to that moment at Botany when the
Croatian cut Chaz's throat. The whole thing happened so fast it was a
blur in his mind. He was looking at Chaz's face – the fear in his eyes,
the sudden realisation that his life was being taken away from him
– not which hand the Croatian held the knife in. It was a moment
Sam had tried to erase from his memory, a moment too heavy, too
overwhelming for him to willingly revisit. But placing himself there
now, he did picture it. And yes, it was the left hand.

Kate said, 'It also helped that it was you who made the triple
zero call. Your concern for Chaz was pretty obvious to anyone who
listened to that recording.' Sam remembered the moment when he
told Little Ted that he would call the ambulance so Ted could go after
the Croatian. It was good they did not have Little Ted on tape. 'They
still regard you as a material witness, so you can't just do whatever you
want.'

'I understand.'

'But if you need to go to Chicago for pressing work reasons, and
you commit to keeping in touch at all times, then you're free to go.'

'That's so good.'

'I should add, just because you are allowed to go doesn't mean you should.'

'I know. But I don't feel like I have a choice.'

Sam's mind began to wander. 'If they've already done some forensic analysis, maybe that means they have a lead on who killed Chaz?' As well as what happened with Little Ted and the Triple S guys, he thought to himself.

'Reddy gave nothing away,' Kate said.

'Maybe she wants to wait until she has proof that I'm withholding information from her, particularly in terms of who shot the security guys, before she tries to press me again?'

'Don't stress about what's going on in Reddy's head,' Kate said. 'I think you've got enough on your plate, just now.'

***

The news from Kate meant Sam had a lot to talk to Lauren about. He knew she wasn't going to agree with his thinking. What he hoped was that he could convince her to accept it. 'It's absurd to say that I can't go for a walk down the street,' she protested, 'when you're deliberately flying into the hometown of two men who want you dead.'

'You know what happened to Mum,' said Sam. 'It's not safe for you.'

'That's not the point. It's one rule for you and a different one for me.'

'I know it might sound like that—'

'Because it is like that!'

Sam tried to collect his thoughts. 'If the Triple S guys were to find you, they'd try and use you to get to me. That could mean kidnapping you. Lauren, that would make me completely impotent because, if they had you, I'd give up instantly to try to protect you. They'd kill me, and there'd be no more witnesses to Chaz's murder. Game over!'

Lauren took a deep breath. 'I'll stay in the damn hotel. But only because of the baby. If it was just me, I'd go and stay at Mia's place. But if you're not back in one week, that's what I'll do regardless.'

'Good plan. Mia and Otto would look after you well – if it comes to that.' Sam had always liked Mia, and her husband, Otto, seemed the sensible type. 'So, seven days,' he said.

'Seven days.' There was a finality to the way she repeated his words.

He kissed her and lifted her T-shirt to kiss her belly. Then he held her in a long embrace, allowing himself to float in a bubble of harmony. No more words needed to be said, or so he felt.

Lauren pulled back from him and said in a trembling voice, 'Sam, there's something else I've got to tell you.'

His smile faded. 'What is it?'

Lauren looked down at the ground, and then back up at her husband, now with a tear in her eye. 'I cheated on you.'

Sam stared at her for a moment. He'd heard her perfectly. 'What?'

Lauren burst into tears. 'It was just one night. Totally stupid. Totally meaningless. But – I was unfaithful.'

'Fucking hell,' he said. This was the last thing he expected to hear. He simply could not fathom it. 'When? Why are you telling me this now?'

'I've wanted – to tell you for so long but – there was just never a time.' Lauren was struggling to speak over her own crying. Sam was shocked into silence. 'I'd understand if – if you could never – forgive me.' Lauren's tears did not subside.

Sam was angry and hurt but he didn't know what to do with those feelings. How could he scream obscenities at the mother of his unborn child?

'Who was it?' he asked.

'Noah Campbell.'

'Who is he?'

'He goes to the same gym as me. Though I've stopped going there, now.'

'When did it happen?'

'Just before the baby was conceived.'

'You don't mean…?'

'It's very unlikely…but possible.'

Sam wanted to smash glasses and break furniture. He was not violent by nature, but this felt like a test. 'So, what if the baby is his?'

'That depends on you. I have no interest in Noah. I don't know why I did what I did. It was one night of madness, and I can promise you, it will never happen again.'

Isn't that what they all say? Sam thought. 'Are you sure?'

Lauren nodded, still sobbing, still struggling to speak. 'If you could bring yourself to forgive me…'

Sam felt his eyes tearing up. He was lost for words. Lost in so many ways. How could he move forward? How could they move forward? 'You're absolutely sure that it won't happen again? Ever?'

'I've never been so sure about anything.'

'I don't know,' said Sam. 'Just be honest with me. Is that too much to ask?'

'No, it's not.'

Sam didn't know what to think. He was upset, and felt he should be expressing that more strongly, but he still loved her. Given the timing and what was about to happen, there was only so much he could say. He might feel differently on that long flight to and from Chicago, but for now...

Lauren wrapped her arms around him. 'You're amazing,' she said. 'I love you so much.'

Sam pulled back. 'Don't think for a second that I am okay with this,' he said. 'I am not. But if it's only this once...' Lauren reached for his hand. Sam said, 'I hate that this has happened. I thought that we were...Well, it doesn't really matter what I thought, does it?'

'Yes, it does. I just screwed up.'

Sam didn't want to lose what they had, and he didn't think Lauren did either. If the baby wasn't Sam's, that would be complicated. A complete nightmare, actually. But Lauren sounded like she mostly believed he was the father. He'd just have to run with that, especially in the present circumstances.

Chapter 31

Sam walked out of the police station clutching his passport firmly in his hand. He climbed into the taxi and decided to check his itinerary one more time. He'd have a two-hour-fifteen stop-over in Dallas-Fort Worth before going on to Chicago. He'd have the space to comfortably lean forward and remove his shoes. If things went pear-shaped with Margaret, he probably wouldn't be flying business class again. And if things went *really* badly, he wouldn't be flying again, period.

He thought about how the next forty-eight hours might play out. He remembered at school being told about the fight-or-flight or 'acute stress' response, the adrenal medulla producing a hormonal cascade and the secretion of catecholamines. He obviously wasn't running away, so it wasn't a flight response. But he probably *should* be running away. Was he completely mad? Maybe.

***

Marilyn Banks knew she could be intimidating to some people, but she tried hard not to be. She thought she was quite average looking, medium height, medium weight, dark brown hair in a conservative bob. She was not aggressive, but one young guy she'd given notice to last year told her she had a very hard face, and that he feared her. When she sat down opposite Kitty in the meeting room, she offered a broad smile and poured the young account executive a glass of water. 'Can I get you anything else?' she said.

'No, I'm fine, thank you,' said Kitty.

Marilyn placed a thick blue folder down in front of her on the table but did not open it. 'Now, Kitty, I know we've touched on this before, following the conversation you had with Chaz, but I just need to check a few things. You said it was in the lift, on the night of the party, that Zoe assaulted you. Is that right?'

'Yes, in the lift.'

'Right. And there weren't any other people in the lift at the time?'

'No.'

'Could anyone else have seen what happened, say, when you got in the lift and the doors were open, or when you arrived at the third floor?'

'No, I don't think so.'

'Okay, I need to make something clear. My starting point is always to believe the complainant in a matter like this. That's because I understand it's so difficult, often traumatic, to come forward and make a complaint of this sort. Very few people would choose to go through the investigation, relive the event, and deal with all the consequences – if what they were saying was not true.'

'Quite right,' said Kitty.

'So, I'm here to support you in any way I can. To make this case as simple as possible and remove any sort of argument about what happened – you know, we don't want a *he said she said* situation if we can avoid it – we just need the security footage from the lift.'

'Yes, that's what we want.'

'The problem is, Kitty, that's missing from the files.'

'Who took it?'

'We don't know if someone took it, or if it was never there in the first place, or if it was accidentally deleted.'

'Is someone's trying to cover this up?'

'We don't want to go jumping to conclusions but, I have to ask, do you have any idea how the video footage came to be missing?'

Kitty shrugged her shoulders.

'Have you discussed this case with anyone else?' asked Marilyn. 'Anyone who could have—'

'No!' insisted Kitty. 'I was traumatised by it. No way would I have talked to anyone about it.'

'You haven't spoken to a lawyer? Or anyone from the press?'

Kitty's expression changed from anger to suspicion of the investigator. 'No.'

'Not even a counsellor?'

Kitty shook her head.

'Would you like us to arrange one for you?'

'No.'

'What would you like us to do? I mean, how do you see this playing out? In an ideal world? Putting aside the issue of the missing security footage.'

'I just want compensation.'

'Two hundred and fifty thousand dollars?'

'Yes.'

'Okay, Kitty.' Marilyn nodded and smiled. 'Thank you for your time. We're hoping to finish our investigation very soon. I'll get back to you, shortly.'

Kitty stood up, smiled, and left the room.

***

Sitting on a plane by yourself forces you to reflect, Sam thought. He should have been focussed on what he had to accomplish in Chicago but, instead, his mind was tied up with Lauren. Feelings of guilt for leaving her vulnerable in Sydney.

All the time he'd been engaged to Lauren he'd thought about how wonderful it would be to live with her. The small intimacies, the Sunday mornings she might wake up and choose to pop on an old T-shirt of his, the evenings they might fall asleep together on the sofa, the choices they'd make jointly on how to decorate the place, so that it wasn't his or hers, but theirs. They had spent plenty of time sleeping over at each other's places – in the months leading up to the wedding they'd probably spent fifty per cent of their nights in the same bed – but prior to getting married, they'd kept their two separate flats. Only after they tied the knot did they move into the house in Bondi together. The real thing was better than Sam had imagined.

Each new item of furniture in their home spoke to the development of their professional careers. And there was the magical day they found a little black puppy who had completely failed as a guide dog and would become the centre of their attention as he took them for walks and trained them as carers (foolish Sam, thinking it would be the other way around). The only thing Sam looked back on now with regret was that as TBA had grown he'd found himself working more late nights and traveling too frequently, often to Melbourne, and occasionally overseas, which meant he had not been around for Lauren as much. This was something he was determined to change, for both Lauren and the baby. He'd put his wife through hell in recent days, especially by choosing to go to Chicago, and he needed to make up for that now. It was the very least she deserved. Yes, there was the affair, but despite how hurtful that was, he still loved her. The complexion of that love had changed, but it was still love.

***

Sam's flight landed in Chicago on June 11, the same date he had left Sydney, only a few minutes late. He'd managed to get some sleep on the leg to Dallas-Fort Worth, so he was feeling okay. Sam thought about whether he should meet anyone or do anything before he was scheduled to see Margaret the next day. After what he'd been told by Jenny Graham, he no longer felt he could trust his boss. But there was one person he knew he could trust: Jono Swift, the guy who'd been on the jury when Zoe won her first Cannes Gold.

Jono was a great creative, and had won loads of Cannes Lions himself, but he also knew how to play the game. And he could talk business with the best of the suits. The thing Sam loved about him was that he had the classic Aussie absence of bullshit. He never said an idea was strong if it wasn't, and when he saw potential in a piece of work, he supported it, just as he supported the person. If a copywriter needed a hand to get an idea over the line, Jono would roll up his sleeves and use his magic to turn the good into the great.

Sam texted Jono and asked him if he was free for dinner. Jono replied to say they should meet at seven and insisted he was paying. That may have meant his employer, also Sam's employer, was paying, but this was no time to be cynical. Jono messaged:

> So looking forward to seeing you,
> mate. Chicago's a great town.
> You'll love it!

Sam just hoped he could *survive* it.

He checked in at the Paragon Hotel and was unpacking his clothes when a text message came through on his mobile. Sam thought it would be a reply from Lauren after texting her about his safe landing five minutes earlier, but it was from Brie:

> Hey Sam – you ok? can I see
> you? would love to catch up for
> a drink. still can't stop thinking
> about chaz. be great to talk. x

He felt sorry for Brie. She was such a sweet kid, and he could hardly blame her for being caught up in the middle of this unholy mess. But he did want her to find someone else to focus her attention on. Any request to meet up with him without Lauren made him uncomfortable. He texted back:

Hi Brie,
Yeah, I think we're all having
trouble dealing with Chaz
no longer being around. I'm
overseas now but maybe there's
a friend or family member
you could chat to? It is really
important to talk to someone
if you are feeling down. If you
don't want to talk to the agency's
counsellor, do give Lifeline or
Beyond Blue a buzz. They are
brilliant.
Best wishes,
Sam

He hit send and hoped that would be the end of the matter. He certainly didn't want to be getting into a text frenzy with Brie for the next hour.

He lay down on the bed and considered whether or not it was too dangerous for him to go out that night. Margaret knew he was in Chicago. He hadn't told her what hotel he was staying at, but she could easily have found out. The booking was made in his name; the bill being picked up by TBA (a mistake, in hindsight, but too late now). As its CEO, Margaret was paying for him to be there. One could say she had every right to know which hotel she was paying for. If she passed that information on to Brandis, he would no doubt pass it on to Viktor Tomic. And that might mean a bullet in Sam's head.

For now, Sam would just run with the theory that Margaret was neither evil nor in a conspiracy with Brandis, and had no desire to see Sam killed. The glass half-full approach. And Sam wanted to see Jono. Without the help of someone like Jono, he had no chance of achieving his objective. Justice for Chaz, that was what this was all about. Sam kept that thought front and centre.

At 6pm he called Jono and asked, 'Where are we off to?'

'Oriole. It's in what they call the West Loop. Pretty fancy.'

'A full plate and a glass of vino and I'll be happy as Larry,' Sam said.

'You'll love the food, and I don't think you'll complain when you see their wine list.'

Sam figured he could take Jono's word for it.

***

Sam asked the concierge to help him out with a taxi. The concierge was a short man with a neat round belly and thin grey hair, and only too happy to be of service.

The yellow cab took Sam down North Michigan Avenue and right into East Wacker Drive. He enjoyed watching the people in the street, just as he did for the first few days in most cities. Did they look happy or sad, dress up or down, seem frantic or relaxed? It was summer here so he thought the locals would be bouncing around more than they were; most looked serious and concerned. Maybe that was because he was in the centre of the city where work lives were most intense. He suspected the mood would change as the night wore on.

A hostess greeted him, tall and slim, dressed in black trousers and a white blouse done up to the neck. 'Welcome to Oriole,' she said, handing him a pink cocktail. Sam was escorted through what the hostess explained was once the freight elevator, and then into the modestly sized dining room.

Jono stood to greet him, immaculately groomed as always, wearing a dark designer suit and pale blue shirt. He was older than Sam, but his face looked youthful. He had a radiant smile.

'Good to see you, mate,' he said as they shook hands.

They chatted about what it was like to live in Chicago. Jono said he missed Australia – particularly in the cold of winter – and his old friends. But he was on a good wicket, earning a small fortune, and he had made plenty of new buddies. He thought there was good talent in his creative team here and that made it a pleasure to go into work each day.

They were half-way through their main courses, having just knocked off a second glass of an exquisite French red, when Sam explained what was really going on. He'd hinted at it earlier, but now he had to be frank. 'I may want your help,' he said. 'If Brandis is a crook, and he had this Croatian guy kidnap and then kill Chaz, then – I guess I'm in a bit of danger. And I'm not sure I can trust Margaret. What are your feelings about her?'

'I've known her for quite a while,' said Jono. 'She's not my favourite person, but she doesn't seem bent. I'm probably biased though. She's the boss, and she's paying me a lot of money.'

'But she might be in with…?'

'Anything's possible.'

'And Brandis?'

'I've never actually met him. One of those faceless behind-the-scenes dudes. Doesn't have anything to do with me or my section. I really don't know what he does.'

'I wonder if anyone knows.'

Jono's face became more serious. 'Can I just ask, why are you pursuing this? Why not just let it go? Keep you and your family safe?'

'Do you know why I started the agency?' Sam said.

'Not really. Why did you?'

'Because – I know this is going to sound, well – I wanted to be someone who made a difference to people's lives. I'm not talking Nobel Peace Prize difference. I mean daily existence difference. I wanted to make existing better. Even if I only ever employed one person, I wanted that person's life to be more enjoyable, more satisfying, more fulfilling than it would have been if the company didn't exist.'

'And, mate, you wound up with a lot more than one person working for you!'

'But having built TBA into a decent sized agency, it really mattered to me who we sold it to. I needed to know they'd look after our staff in the same way. TBA had to continue to be an agency where people could come and live up to their potential, without fear of being abused or mistreated. I wanted it to be a place run by good people. Not the bastards we know run some companies, right?'

'I hear you,' said Jono.

Sam told him about the lunch he and Chaz had at Nour with Roz and Idham. 'I was shocked when I found out Brandis had stolen money from Pointer White, and probably other YRG agencies, too. Stealing from the company's clients. Chaz was even more shocked than me. Angry. We couldn't just let it go.'

'And fraud turned to…'

Sam shook his head. 'It never occurred to me that Brandis' pilfering would lead to kidnap and – murder.'

'It's incredible! You think it goes well beyond just the money he stole from Pointer White?'

'I do. And now – I've got to keep going. I have to do the right thing by Chaz. And I want those men and women who put their faith in me, all the TBA staff I've hired over the years, to be treated like human beings. Not trodden on like cockroaches.'

'But I can't believe Margaret would…'

'Yeah, I have to get to the bottom of that. If she is crooked then I'm going to bring her down, or die trying.'

'Don't die, mate,' said Jono. 'I think we've had enough of that!'

Chapter 32

Phil Sinclair and Yves Martin were nicknamed Starsky and Hutch the moment they started working together three years ago. Phil was Starsky, dark and compact, Yves was Hutch, blond and lanky. Yves firmly believed he was the better looking of the two, though Phil had a habit of punching him uncomfortably hard anytime he suggested it, which was becoming less often. They'd earned Viktor's respect by instilling fear in those that caused the company problems. Fear that led to compliance. Their methods were simple but effective, unexpected, and occasionally brutal. Yves called it their trademark, but Phil said it was SOP (Standard Operating Procedure). They were on an upward trajectory at Alliance.

Phil approached the concierge at the Paragon and handed him a thick yellow envelope. No need to look inside. The recipient knew it was more than double his monthly salary. In return, Phil was handed a swipe key with a room number on it. This was not the first time the pair had done business together.

Phil turned around and noticed two young women sweeping through the lobby, looking at nobody on their way to the Paris bar. He wondered if they were hookers. Even if they weren't, he reckoned they could be bought. If maybe he wasn't busy on a job himself.

Up in Sam Pride's hotel room, Phil checked the bathroom and the cupboards. Nothing. No cause for concern. The Australian probably didn't even have a weapon. This was all looking too easy. He sat down on the sofa chair and removed a gold lighter from his pocket. He wasn't going to smoke here, not now, but he enjoyed flicking the lid. He tried to give it a bit of rhythm, the way Eric Clapton did in that song with Sting for *Lethal Weapon 3*. He hummed the tune. *I hate to say it. But it's probably me.*

'That real gold?' asked Yves.

Phil nodded.

'I like gold. I wouldn't mind one of those lighters.'

'You don't smoke.'

'So?'

Phil dropped his head in despair.

Yves stood up and walked over to the minibar, made a quick inspection of the contents, and removed a small bottle of whiskey.

Phil's mobile was on silent, but he felt it vibrating in his pocket. It was the boss.

'Where are you?' asked Viktor.

'In his room.'

'He's leaving the restaurant now. Sit tight.'

***

Jono asked the restaurant to organise a cab and promptly dropped Sam back at the hotel. 'You want me to come in with you? Just to check it's safe?'

'No, I'm good,' Sam said. 'But thanks. Hotel security should be able to look after me from here.'

Sam stumbled out of the cab, but managed to catch himself before causing any real embarrassment. Passing the grey-haired concierge he'd spoken to earlier, he tried to look confident, in control. He was suddenly mindful of all the wine he'd drunk. Not a huge amount by Aussie standards. Just enough to make him a little tipsy. Bad idea in the present circumstances, but for now he felt safe enough. He just needed to get to bed.

He made his way into the empty lift and pressed the button for his floor. No response. He reached into his trouser pocket for his security swipe. Success. Lift now in motion.

He got out at Level 14 and wandered along to his room. He didn't know if it was jet lag or the booze, but he felt like he could have gone to sleep right there in the hallway. He pressed the key into the lock. Green light. Success again. He was so on top of this modern technology. He kept the door open for a moment while he worked out how to insert the swipe key into the slot to get the power working. Lights on, he walked towards the bed.

Smash!

Despite his attempt to be on the ready, the attack still took Sam by surprise. There were two men, though he only saw the face of the one who came at him low from his right-hand side. The assailant went for his knee with whatever was in their hand; Sam thought it was a baseball bat. The pain was instant and excruciating. As he went down, helpless, the other man grabbed him and put him in a chokehold. He tried to scream but nothing came out. He felt a needle prick his arm, and a cold sensation flowed through his body.

***

Sam woke with his head full of Chaz. Seeing him at Botany and thinking the deal was done, only to watch him mercilessly lose his life. From there, Sam's mind drifted to the moment he was attacked in his hotel room. It made him paranoid. How did those guys know he'd be there? How did they get the timing so right? Was he being followed? Had someone leaked information to Brandis and his cronies?

Snap to it, he said to himself. He was lying in the back of a dark van with his hands tied in front of him. By his side was the tall blond man who had smashed his knee in the hotel room. It hurt badly. Sam gave his eyes a minute to adjust to the light and then asked where he was being taken.

'You'll see,' the man said. His accent was American, which somehow gave Sam comfort. At least he wasn't Croatian.

'Is it far?' Sam asked. 'I am in a lot of pain.'

'You want to complain? I'll do your other knee, you fuck.'

Sam could have tried to sit up, but he didn't want to upset the guy. So, he just lay still, biting his tongue anytime they hit a small bump and his knee silently cried out in pain. He leaned slightly to one side and snuck a glance at his watch. Two-thirty. He couldn't see outside but he assumed it was two-thirty in the morning, not the afternoon. Which meant he must have been out for about three and a half hours. The dinner with Jono, the luscious red wine, seemed like a lifetime ago now. Sam had no idea if the throbbing in his head was a result of the booze or the drug they'd injected into him, but whatever the cause, his brain felt as if it was in as bad a shape as his knee.

The van slowed down. He felt them go over a little speed hump and then down a slope that might have been the entrance to a car park. The sound of traffic disappeared, and he was pretty sure they were inside a building.

'When we get out of the van, you're going to walk beside me,' said the blond man. His voice was deep, and he spoke with authority. Sam wasn't about to challenge him. 'Nice and calm, no sudden moves, and you're not to say a word to anyone we pass. You can lean on me if your knee buckles. But see this gun?' He brandished it like Sam might not have known prior to this moment just what its true purpose was. 'It's a Glock 19. Fifteen nine-millimetre cartridges in the mag and one in the chamber. Why's that relevant to you? 'Cause if you open your mouth when you're not supposed to, I'll start unloading 'em into you.

One after another. You won't get shot once; you'll get shot over and over. Not so quickly that you die instantly. No, we'll let you bleed out. I'm just making the point that there'll be no gettin' away and there'll be no recovery.'

Sam wondered if the guy had mistaken him for someone with a death wish. 'Easy, mate. I'll do whatever you tell me to.'

The van stopped. Its rear door was opened by a short and stocky man with dark hair. 'Come on,' he said in a gruff voice.

The blond guy untied Sam's hands and pushed him out of the door. They were in an underground garage; there was a handful of parked cars but no other people around. Sam tried to walk but his knee hurt terribly. The best he could do was a pathetic hobble.

'I'm going to have to hold onto your arm,' Sam said to the blond man, who nodded in agreement.

They got into a lift and went all the way to the top floor. When the doors opened, Sam couldn't believe his eyes. Soft lighting, pale pink décor, and women wearing, well, very little! It was a strip club. Of all the places they could have taken him...

He was led past a platform on which a topless girl was dancing for a handful of seedy looking men in suits. He couldn't walk properly and had a gun pointed at him, but neither the dancer nor her fans nor the two buxom ladies in underwear serving drinks had any interest.

'Can you slow down a bit?' he said to his blond captor as they climbed up a handful of stairs. The man complied and they slowly moved into an upper-level hallway, out of sight from the customers. The stocky guy tapped a closed door, it opened, and there he was: Viktor Tomic, in person. He wore a black leather jacket and jeans and obviously wasn't surprised to see Sam. He didn't speak, he simply directed the blond guy to sit Sam down on the far side of an office table. There was an enormous bloke in a dark suit standing in the corner of the room. The bright gold of his watch was hard to miss, despite the dimmed lighting. Perhaps he was Viktor's personal bodyguard, Sam thought. As if the Croatian needed one.

'Leave us now,' Viktor told Sam's handlers.

It may have been survival instinct, but Sam started to consider possibilities other than Viktor simply killing him. The Croatian had used kidnap as a means of getting information he wanted from Chaz, so maybe he was trying that approach again. If so, Sam really hoped it wasn't going to involve torture. He didn't consider himself soft, but he didn't want to lose any of his appendages.

Viktor sat down opposite him. 'Why couldn't you just walk away?' he said. 'Why keep pushing? By coming to Chicago, you must have known we'd find you.'

'If I'd stayed in Sydney, you wouldn't have let me walk away,' Sam said. 'I saw you kill Chaz.'

'If you'd kept your mouth shut, maybe we could have let you – walk away.'

Sam wasn't sure who it was Viktor believed he'd been talking to, but it didn't matter. 'Men like you…' Sam took a long breath before continuing. 'You cover your tracks.'

'I try to,' said Viktor. 'But sometimes I have to be practical. Compromise.'

'What do you want from me?'

'Very little. You just need to tell me who else knows about the memo. Who have you told since you saw me last week in Sydney?'

'Everyone.'

'We both know that is a lie. If you lie again, you will be dead before you can say another word. Who?'

Sam felt his stomach churning. He said, 'You think you're in control, but you're not. Go ahead. Kill me. You've done it before. No doubt you'll do it again. People know about the memo. My lawyers have a copy of it. People know about Brandis. The police know. You're finished.'

'Do I look finished?' Viktor smirked. 'I don't think so. But you – you have said your last words. And now you die.'

Sam watched Viktor remove a knife from his pocket. As he did so, Sam's mind left the scene he was in. Lauren and the baby! How would they manage without him? This was not fair. It was not right. He had to find a way out of this, for them, if not for himself. In the starkness of the room, his eyes told him there was no way out. He was finished.

But, as Viktor took his first step around the desk towards Sam, from out of the shadows stepped an enormous guy with a shiny gold watch. He had a piece of razor wire, small handles at either end. With remarkable speed for a man so large, he lifted the wire over Viktor's head to his neck and pulled back, cutting straight through the flesh. Blood spurted everywhere, including on Sam, as Viktor fell to the ground. There was a moment, just when the wire hit his neck, when Viktor's eyes seemed to bulge out of his head to reveal his shock at what had just happened. Viktor was semi-decapitated.

Sam looked at the big man in the fancy suit and gold watch, wondering if he was next. He had no idea why the man had killed Viktor, whom Sam had assumed was a colleague, perhaps even a friend of his, and he couldn't imagine a reason for the bloke to spare him. The big guy had simply replaced Viktor as a man who needed Sam out of the way. But his demeanour shifted entirely, and he suddenly looked at Sam with – what was it – understanding?

'The two men who brought you here,' he said in a thick Russian accent, 'they will take you back to your hotel. You will never speak of what happened here. If you do, I will find you. It doesn't matter where you are: Australia, New Zealand, Greenland, wherever. I can reach you.'

And then he left the room, Sam still seated at the desk with his dodgy knee, damp with sweat, blood spatter on his clothes. A few minutes ago, he was certain he was going to die. And now – being driven back to his hotel? It was so hard to believe. Was he being fooled the way Viktor had been fooled? Lured into a trap?

***

Boris Federova gave Phil Sinclair and Yves Martin their instructions in his usual no-nonsense fashion and then walked down the hallway to his private office. He went to the drinks cabinet and poured himself a Russo-Baltique vodka. Next, he used the basin to wash the blood from his hands and face. His approach to life was methodical. He looked at the marks on his suit. They disturbed him but they could wait. He extracted the mobile phone from the pocket of his jacket and called the number of the man he had been talking to only half an hour earlier.

'Is it done?' the man asked.

'It is,' said Boris.

'The body?'

'Will never be found.'

'The money will be in your account by mid-morning.'

Boris hung up. If the money didn't land in his bank account within twenty-four hours, Viktor Tomic's blood would not be the last to spill over this matter.

Chapter 33

Brie looked down at her phone, not because she needed to but because she didn't know where else to look. She felt pathetic. What was she doing here? Relax, she told herself. You'll soon feel better. She was trying to stay inconspicuous.

She'd walked up Crown Street and, desperate not to be seen by anyone from the office, turned into Little Bloomfield. Then, she'd waited, and waited, becoming more anxious as every minute went by.

Now she was pacing. Stop it, she told herself. Her lunch break was nearly over, and she had to get back to reception. Finally, he arrived in a silver convertible BMW. Brie didn't think a dealer should drive a car like that, a beacon for the cops. She approached the driver. A woman she didn't recognise was in the passenger seat. Maybe that was supposed to be his cover, presenting as a respectable husband and wife and not a shifty fucking meth dispenser.

'Hey,' she said.

'Hey, yourself,' the driver replied. He handed her a white envelope. 'It's a gift. My man in Chicago says thank you.'

Brie placed the envelope in her handbag and hurried back to the office. Without speaking to anyone, she went straight for the bathroom. Locked inside the cubicle, she opened the envelope and was thrilled to discover two grams instead of one. She felt terrible about what she'd done, but for now, she just needed to survive. She'd barely left the bathroom when she began to feel her spirits lifting. The pain was gone, and she was ready to kiss guilt goodbye.

She took her place behind reception and would be the smiley welcoming face everyone loved to see when they entered the offices of Sydney's best ad agency. The world's best ad agency. The universe's best ever ad agency.

***

Sam woke up with no idea where he was. Fancy hotel room. Got it. He shut his eyes again for a minute before giving in to the day's obligations. After the two goons who worked for Viktor, or rather the

179

big guy with the fancy gold watch and slicked back hair, had dropped Sam back at the hotel, he threw down a little bottle of tequila from the minibar to dull the pain of his knee injury, and passed out at about 3.30am.

The clock by the bed said he'd slept for six hours. He felt jet-lagged, hungover, and his knee ached. He rang room service to ask for some breakfast. The main thing he needed was coffee. He also asked them to bring some ibuprofen.

He walked over to the table where he'd put down his laptop, flipped it open and carried it back to the bed. He began looking at emails but got sick of it after a few minutes. Ninety-nine per cent of them were related to work in Sydney and could wait.

He checked his phone. There was a text from Lauren asking if he was all right. He reassured her that he was. However, a text didn't seem like it was enough, so he intended to ring her as well. But, before he could, Jono called.

'There's a woman named Jean Koziol,' he said. 'A Board Director. You need to meet her.'

'My meeting with Margaret's not until three,' said Sam. 'I've got time.'

'Great! I'll pick you up in half an hour and drive you to Jean's house. It's just outside the city.'

'There's something I need to tell you – about last night.'

'After you left me? Didn't you just go to bed?'

'If only.' Sam gave Jono an abridged version of what had happened.

'Shouldn't I be taking you to the hospital?' Jono asked. 'By the sounds of it, we should really be getting your leg looked at.'

'No, I'll be fine,' insisted Sam. 'We'll see your friend, Jean, and—'

'Only if you're sure.'

Sitting on the edge of the bed, Sam rang Lauren and chatted for about twenty minutes, updating her on what had happened, most notably the death of Viktor Tomic. 'Hopefully that makes me a little safer around here!' he said, unsure of whether it was true but hoping it might be a reason to feel more positive.

'Darling, as long as people are getting murdered around you, I'm hardly going to relax. Who do you think ordered the killing of Tomic? Could that have been Brandis?'

'Possibly.'

'Why wouldn't he have wanted you killed, too?'

'Maybe he thinks I'm easier to control than Tomic.'

'He might have the original of that Memo, but you know what's in it. You know what he's done. At least, the fraud.'

'Yes, but I'm guessing he thinks that if I'm foolhardy enough to speak up, then it's just my word against his. And he's a powerful man.'

'One in a position to cover his tracks.'

'Or at least make them very muddy.'

'Now, when are you coming home?'

'Soon. Very soon.'

'You know I refuse to stay in this bloody hotel room for much longer.'

'I know. But honestly, I'll be back before you know it. And it means everything to me, knowing that you and the baby are safe there. Hidden from the world.'

'The clock's ticking.'

And didn't Sam know it! He had a shower and took some ibuprofen to ease the pain in his knee. He needed something stronger but now was not the time to worry about that.

As he wandered through the hotel lobby on his way to meet Jono, Sam thought about how the thugs might have broken into his hotel room. He guessed they had picked the lock, or whatever the digital expression for getting through a modern hotel security system is these days. Maybe they'd pinched a swipe key from a maid or cleaner, like you see in the movies.

Jono was waiting out the front in his sporty black Mercedes. 'How's your leg?' he asked.

'I don't think I'm going to be running in any marathons for a while, but I'll live.'

'You're clearly not an easy bloke to get rid of!'

'Having been in Chicago less then twenty-four hours, I'd suggest it's early days.'

'Hey, it's not usually that bad here.'

'I just hope my luck continues long enough for me to make it back to see the birth of my baby.'

'You didn't tell me you guys were expecting. Congrats!'

'Thanks, Jono. You'll have to do a trip to Sydney and meet the little girl or guy.'

'For sure!'

They drove down North Michigan Avenue and then turned west along Ontario Street. Jono said it would take them just under an hour to get to Barrington Hills. 'I've not been to her house before, but I'm told it's spectacular.'

'How do you know this lady?'

'By chance,' said Jono. 'She's into art. We met at an exhibition. I was looking at a painting and she asked me what I liked about it. I told her and then she said, if I wasn't going to buy it, she would. And she did. Anyway, I bumped into her again at a charity function two weeks later. We got chatting. I told her what I do. She said she's a major shareholder in YRG. We've bumped into each other a couple more times since then, and she always asks me how I'm going. Seems genuinely interested in our creative work; that makes me genuinely interested in her. And I figured it was better to have the company's major shareholder as a friend rather than an enemy.'

When they arrived at the security gate, Jono pressed the buzzer on the intercom, and they were allowed in. 'Looks more like a resort than a home,' Sam said.

A gravel road weaved past clusters of sturdy old trees set among the carefully manicured lawns, up to the main house and its neighbouring guest quarters. The tennis court and swimming pool were partially obscured by a row of tall trees. The garage doors were shut but, by Sam's calculations, there was room for at least eight or nine cars.

'Where do you think I should park?' asked Jono.

Sam suggested they leave the Merc out the front. 'Someone will let us know if we need to move it.'

Jono led them in the direction of the entrance way but before they arrived, the large walnut doors opened to reveal a diminutive but powerful-looking lady in her late forties, dark hair pulled back tight, and steely grey-blue eyes. She stood beside a blond waspy-looking man about ten years her junior who appeared to have stepped out of a Ralph Lauren ad.

'Jono,' said the woman. 'Very good to see you. And you must be Sam.' She reached out her hand to greet him. 'Please allow me to introduce you to Robert Miller.'

Miller shook hands with them both. Sam gave Jono a sideways glance to try and ascertain whether he'd been expecting this other man. A raised eyebrow suggested not.

They walked through a stark hallway into a vast sunlit space, with a glass-sided turret at its centre, and floor-to-ceiling windows allowing one to see straight out to the rose garden.

'You have a beautiful home, Mrs Koziol,' Sam said. 'I love the garden. We have a few Crepuscule roses trained against a trellis at home, but nothing like yours.'

'Our rose garden was only very small at first. A couple of old varieties, like the Crepuscule and the Lamarque. Every year or two we'd add another variety. And please, call me Jean. I'm far too young to be Mrs Koziol!'

Sam and Jono were taken to the library, a site that would have been striking for the number of books it contained in any era, so for their modern day, when so many people Sam knew did their reading on digital devices, it seemed other-worldly. They were invited to sit at a large antique table that occupied the middle of the room.

'Tea? Coffee?' said Jean. 'Something harder?'

Sam and Jono both opted for coffees.

'Is your leg all right?' asked Jean. 'I noticed you were limping.'

'I'm fine,' Sam said. 'But thank you for asking.'

Jean left the library for a minute to pass on their requests. When she returned, they quickly got down to business. She said, 'You're probably wondering why Robert is here. He runs a company called Alliance Security. His partner, Viktor Tomic, who was recently in Australia, is now missing.'

Jean looked at Sam like he might have something to say on the matter. Sam knew Viktor was dead, but he didn't know where the body was. He would have shared what he knew immediately if he was sure he could trust Robert, but he needed to take a minute to study the man. From what he'd read, Robert's background seemed like that of a straightshooter's. But then why was he in business with a murderer?

Robert looked Sam directly in the eye and spoke gravely, 'I don't like saying this, but I have evidence that suggests Viktor might have been involved in some serious criminal behaviour.'

Sam decided to go out on a limb. 'I saw a man I believe was Viktor murder my colleague and friend, Chaz Bailley.' There it was; he'd said it, and immediately felt a sense of relief.

'The Botany incident?' asked Robert.

'That's right,' said Sam. 'And last night he was murdered by another man here in Chicago. I have no idea where that was but—'

'Sam was knocked out cold by two thugs,' said Jono, 'and taken to a strip club.'

Jean looked shocked by what she was hearing but remained attentive. 'Go on,' she said.

'I don't know the name of the killer,' continued Sam. 'Some enormous guy dressed in a silk suit. He wore a distinctive gold watch.

I wish I could say where we were. I guess there are only so many strip clubs in Chicago.'

'Why would…?' began Jean. 'Did it seem spontaneous? I mean, do you think the man with the gold watch made the decision himself? Or was he just following orders?'

'I can't be sure,' said Sam, 'but my instincts say the man pulling the strings was Don Brandis.'

Jean looked at Robert, gesturing for him to speak up.

'That's also my working theory,' said Robert. 'It was certainly Brandis who sent Viktor to Australia. And, for quite some time, Brandis has been Viktor's key contact at YRG.'

'I don't know how we track down the big guy from the strip club,' said Jean, 'but we can certainly track down Don Brandis. He works for YRG, and I'm a director of the company. We can compel him to answer our questions.'

'There's one other person we need to consider,' said Sam.

'Margaret?'

Sam nodded. 'Do you think she's a part of it?'

'I have my suspicions. She defended Brandis quite vigorously in a recent conversation, but that doesn't necessarily mean she's part of a conspiracy. It's hard to be sure.'

'What if we assume she is crooked?'

'Wouldn't it be great if there was a way to catch two fish with one hook?'

Sam said, 'I think I might know a way.'

Chapter 34

'The YRG building's been a prominent Chicago landmark since it was built in 1991,' explained Jono. 'Fifty-eight storeys of granite, glass, and steel.'

'The guys up there must get a pretty grand view,' said Sam, squinting upwards.

'Right over West Wacker Drive to the river. There are obviously famous agencies in London and New York, but YRG has always been the standout in Chicago.'

Jono led Sam into the building and showed him where to catch the lift up to Level 20. 'Now you're on your own,' he said with a wink. 'But you know where I'll be.'

Sam exited the lift and approached the extremely long desk – with three different receptionists – and was directed to take a seat in a booth on the far side of the room. He pulled out his phone and started checking emails from home.

***

Don Brandis didn't want any confusion. 'Are we good?' he asked, gripping the phone a little too tightly.

'Yes, we're good.'

'You're sure?'

'I got the money. We are good.'

'Because I may need to call on you again.'

There was a pause on the other end of the line. Brandis could hear Federova's heavy breathing.

'You can call,' the big man said.

Brandis hung up. He felt satisfied. After the disaster in Australia, the mess was now being cleaned up. In Viktor's absence, he needed Federova. It annoyed him that there were so few people in this world he could rely on. Viktor had seemed like a man who knew his business, but he'd screwed up and become a massive liability. He could have brought the whole show crashing down. In the end, the only person you can rely on is yourself; Brandis' father had told him that when he was just a teenager. Trust nobody. At the time, those words seemed harsh. Not now. Now they seemed obvious.

He texted Margaret to say she could re-join him.

She entered the room, took a seat, and said to Brandis, 'There's something I've got to talk to you about.'

'Yes?'

'It's our relationship with Alliance Security.'

'There's no need,' said Brandis. 'We'll no longer be working with them.'

Margaret looked perplexed. 'What exactly is it that they've been doing for us all these years?'

'You honestly don't know?'

'Don, I've relied on your advice. You've always said they were important in keeping the company secure, whether that be cyber security or physical real-world security. I took you at your word.'

'Whatever, Margaret. You signed off the payments, and they did what they needed to do. You don't need to know any more than that.'

'You're sure there's nothing that's going to come back to haunt us?'

'I don't know what might haunt you, but I'll be sleeping fine.'

Margaret stood up, looking ready to walk out of the room, when she suddenly turned back. 'What about Sam Pride,' she said. 'Is he harmless?'

'No, Pride is a concern. For you *and* me.'

'So, should I get rid of him?'

Brandis gave her a doubtful look. 'When you say, get rid of him…'

'I don't mean that!' said Margaret. 'I meant fire him. Or make him redundant.'

'Well, let me try to talk some sense into him. He might play ball if he understands the rules of the game.'

'And you're the man for the job?'

'I dare say I am.'

***

A smartly dressed woman in her mid-twenties accompanied Sam to Level 56, where he was taken to a large, very empty meeting room. 'Ms Whitfield will be with you shortly,' he was told.

He sat down at the far end of the table, on the river side, and began to ponder. It was strange to think that such a short time ago, he was worried Margaret was going to fire him. That was still a real possibility, but it was no longer a cause for concern. He had left the home of Jean Koziol with a mission, and it was one he would carry out.

He looked up as the door opened. He could hardly believe his eyes. Standing just behind Margaret was a man in a tailored grey suit, one whom, judging by his features, Sam knew to be Don Brandis. The glasses, the bald patch, the weak chin. Sam was finally face to face with the one person he believed could answer his questions about Chaz and everything else that had happened.

Margaret came over and shook his hand. 'Sam, I don't believe you have met Don Brandis. Now, you two have some important matters – differences, shall we say – to discuss. And I think it in the best interest of the company, as well as you both, that we resolve those differences. So, I'm leaving the two of you to sort this out – today.'

Margaret left the room.

Brandis stood by the window, looking down at the river.

'Was that you?' Sam asked. 'Last night? Viktor?'

'I don't know what you're talking about.'

'You knew I saw him kill Chaz. And if he was charged with the murder, what, you thought he might give you up for a plea deal, to save himself?'

'Son, you are so far out of your depth. Forget what you think you know and start all over again. Go with the flow. You can still have a career, and a happy life, if you just keep your mouth shut and go back to Sydney, and—'

'You remember that memo you wrote?' interrupted Sam. 'The one about moving the eight million dollars to a British bank account?'

Brandis didn't flinch. 'Even if I did write such a thing,' he said, 'I can tell you it doesn't exist now.'

'How do you know that?'

'Because I know the man who took possession of it from you.' Brandis let out a half laugh. 'And he destroyed it!'

'Is that right?'

'You think you can bluff me? I have video footage on my phone of the memo being burnt.'

'Do you know the one thing I am best known for? I have a photographic memory. I know some people say that, when all they have is a good memory, but mine is scientifically verifiable. And then, of course, there's the copy of the memo I gave to my lawyers.'

Brandis was looking at Sam, like one of those judges allowing a lawyer's argument only so much latitude before it would expire their patience, but he hadn't interrupted.

'There's nothing about that memo I can't recall,' Sam went on. 'From the number, 20219873, to the placement of the commas, seven of them, occurring throughout. And, who could forget the signature; your signature, that is, with its overly inflated capital B, even the arrogant upward whip at the end of its flourish.'

'Son, I'm a lawyer. You might be able to bullshit an Australian court with your tall tales about this magic memory of yours, but no US court's going to buy it. You've got nothing. And you never gave a copy to your lawyers. You didn't have time.'

'Is that right? I've got the bank records, the UK company records, the emails to and from Idham – even a legally certified copy of the memo.' The last bit was untrue but that didn't matter. 'You're right,' said Sam, looking Brandis in the eye. 'I didn't have time, not enough to satisfy my own expectations, but more than enough time to bury you three times over.' Sam raised his hands. 'Figuratively speaking, of course.'

The expression on Brandis' face hardened. 'What do you want?'

'I've even got Viktor's business partner, Robert—'

'Miller?' Brandis scoffed. 'What does he know? Come on, son. This is the point at which you tell me what your number is. What else are you going to do? Get me prosecuted for a breach of ethics? You'll never be able to prove anything.'

'You want to know my number?'

Brandis raised his hands up in the air as if to say, *Hallelujah*. Sam finally got it.

'Just to be absolutely clear,' Sam said, 'You're willing to pay me to keep my mouth shut about the money you instructed Idham Halim to take from Pointer White and put into a private company, Premier Enterprises, owned and controlled by you?'

'You're obsessed with details, son. When you get to my age, you'll understand that details like that don't matter. What does matter is who's in control. The person with the power controls the narrative. Sure, Premier Enterprises is my company. Maybe the money was a payment for services rendered. So what? If I say that was a legitimate expense, then it is. Because, in this company, I have the power to make my truth *the* truth. End of story.' Brandis shook his head. 'Now, shall we get on with it? Everyone's got a number.'

'What are you saying?'

'It's not complicated. Everyone's got a price. Even you, with your smug attitude and your Australian swagger. I'll give you six million dollars cash. Today. Think what that would mean to your lovely wife. What's her name? Lauren?'

'That's a lot of money.'

'Yes, it is. But do you know what? I'm going to give you another million. So, seven in total. Go buy some incredible gift for your wife. What's she into? Diamond necklaces? Enormous yacht? A Ferrari?'

'You'll give me seven million dollars to bury the fact that you stole money from Pointer White?'

'Yes. Give me your bank account details, and the money will be in there before five.'

'One last thing. Was Margaret in on the act? I mean, did you split the money with her, or was it all for you?'

'You've got no idea, do you? Margaret would never steal from the company. The funny thing is, she thinks she's been protecting me. Not because she likes me, not because she wants to support any kind of nefarious activity, but because she *loves* the company. She's such a believer in the YRG brand that she's unwilling to believe someone as senior as me might be bent. I've been taking money from the company for years. From right under her fucking nose! But she doesn't want it investigated because the truth doesn't matter. Only the brand does. Margaret will always turn a blind eye to keep the company's reputation unblemished. And in doing that, she believes she's upholding her fiduciary duty, and maintaining shareholder value.'

Sam didn't think he needed to continue the charade any longer. 'You got that?' he said.

'Got what?' asked Brandis.

'I'm not talking to you, mate. I'm talking to your largest shareholder, two other company directors, your chief creative officer, and two senior detectives.' Sam took off his jacket and undid a few buttons on his shirt to reveal the microphone. 'You're done. And I can't tell you how happy I am about that.'

The door to the meeting room opened and half a dozen police entered the room, followed by Jean Koziol.

Brandis started to hyperventilate. 'What's going on?' he said faintly, sounding like these might be his final words. 'This isn't right.'

'Oh, yes, it is,' said Sam. 'Time for you to pay for all the harm you've done.'

Jean walked around the cops who were busy cuffing Brandis to get to Sam. She reached for his hand. 'Thank you,' she said. 'Your friend Chaz would be proud of what you did today. You made a difference.'

'One guy,' Sam said. 'We brought down one guy, who has done some evil shit.'

'That's how you bring them down,' said Jean. 'One at a time.'

'Thank you, Jean.'

Sam walked down the hallway to the lift. Jono was standing there, waiting for him. He gave Sam a big hug. 'Well done, buddy,' he said.

'Well done, you! Jean and her friends in the police force, getting the warrant, the listening device, and Brandis' words on tape. All thanks to you.'

'There was also a hidden camera in the meeting room,' said Jono. 'I didn't know they'd put it there until a detective mentioned it. They've got audio and video. High def.'

Sam could barely speak. He felt such an overwhelming sense of relief. There had been so many times when he thought Brandis and Viktor and their accomplices had won, that they'd beaten him. Sam thought back to that moment at the strip club when he thought Viktor was going to kill him. He was sure of it. The seconds when all he cared about was staying alive long enough to see Lauren again.

'Guess that calls for a drink,' said Jono.

'I guess so.'

They left the YRG building and began walking towards a nearby bar. Sam rang Lauren and told her what had happened.

'How's your leg?' she asked.

Sam still wasn't walking properly but, with the adrenaline pumping through him, the pain seemed to have eased. 'I'm going to live,' he said.

'When's your flight?'

'Tomorrow morning. I can't wait to see you!'

'What are you going to do now?'

'Take the weight off my feet in some quiet Chicago bar with Jono and chill.'

'I guess you've earned a drink, or two.'

'I guess.'

'Just get home safely.'

'I love you. Everything is going to be okay.'

'Really?'

'Yes, really.'

Chapter 35

When Jono told Sam he was taking him to the Lazy Bird Bar, Sam immediately felt better. He'd drunk quite a lot lately, and he knew his liver could do with a rest, but now was not the time for that. He wanted to clear his head of the most unwelcome images he could ever have imagined. He'd watched people getting murdered, and he didn't know if he'd ever get over it.

The bar was in the basement of a hotel called the Hoxton. Jono called it 'dimly lit' but Sam likened it to a mid-winter night in Antarctica. Not that it was cold, mind you. In fact, it was positively toasty. 'By the way, your mobile won't work down here,' said Jono. 'They're into privacy.'

Sam was okay with that. They grabbed a seat down one end of the blue sofa that ran along the wall opposite the bar. The drinks menu was overwhelming. 'What do you recommend?' he asked Jono.

'Negroni to start?'

'Sounds good to me.'

They were onto their third round when Sam started to think about Margaret's role in what went down. 'Brandis was at the top of my list. And don't get me wrong, I'm bloody glad we got him!'

'Of course,' said Jono.

'But the weird thing is, right now, I'm almost more upset with Margaret. And all the Margarets in this world.' He suspected he was slurring his words. He was tired, and the alcohol was hitting him fast. But he had more to say. 'Brandis is a rare beast, but people like Margaret, who disregard immoral behaviour in the name of – of profit? Furthering their business objectives? They are the enablers. Without them, guys like Brandis can't commit their crimes.'

Jono didn't say anything. He seemed happy to toss back the drinks and just listen.

Sam carried on. 'And what happens to the Margarets? They don't go to jail. They just roll on in the name of capitalism and free markets.'

'Come on, Sam,' said Jono. 'You're an ad man!'

'Okay, maybe free markets are not so bad.'

Sam considered that he might be a hypocrite. He worked in an industry where people spoke and acted like free market evangelists. But he was certain there needed to be checks and balances, for any market. 'I think the problem occurs when your only imperative is money. To increase profits so your stock price will go up.'

'It doesn't have to be that way,' Jono said.

'I know that's not what drives you. You create the most wonderful campaigns. Wonderful because they touch people's hearts. I know you get paid well but you have something else that drives you.'

'That's true. Me and my team…' Jono frowned into his drink. 'We don't know what's going on in the stock market. But we know exactly who has come up with a creative idea we wish was ours. And that makes us try to come up with a better one. And then an even better one after that.'

They ordered two more negronis. Jono's expression softened, and he asked Sam about Lauren. 'I feel awful,' Sam said. 'From the moment I found out the kidnappers had Chaz I've been on some sort of weird trip. A kind of adrenaline rush. And it's screwed up my priorities. I never should have left Lauren alone. Especially not when she's pregnant. I should have kept myself safe for her sake.'

'But Sam…'

'It was great that we got Brandis, but I fucked up,' insisted Sam. 'Big time.'

'You really fucking love her, don't you?'

'More than the air that I breathe.'

'Don't beat yourself up, mate. Lauren's safe, you're safe, Brandis is behind bars. That's not a bad result.'

They managed to throw down one more drink before Sam declared he would fall onto the floor if he did not leave immediately; he needed to get back to the hotel and pour himself into bed. 'I'm done,' he said.

Jono put his hand on Sam's shoulder and smiled. Nothing more needed to be said.

***

Sitting in the waiting area by the boarding gate, Sam was about to pull out a book to read when he received a text from Lauren. She was just wishing him well for his flight. They had spoken an hour earlier. But instead of replying to the text, he got up and walked away from the other passengers to phone her.

'I wasn't expecting to hear from you again so soon,' said Lauren.

'No, I know,' said Sam. 'But I wanted to hear your voice again before I got on the plane. How are you doing?'

'Can't wait to move back home. It's just so good that the nightmare is over, and that you're safe now.'

'Well, in a matter of hours, I'll be back there, by your side. And by Rax's side!'

'We'll both be there at the airport to pick you up.'

'Can't wait,' said Sam.

By the time he boarded his flight, he'd been notified by Zoe that Margaret was gone. She had not been charged with a crime, as far as Zoe knew, but her position was untenable.

Sam still had a few sleeping tablets in his carry-on and spent most of the trip home passed out. He couldn't wait to get to the doctor to get his knee looked at. He didn't just want to be able to walk again, he wanted to make sure he could kick a ball around. That baby boy or girl might one day become a soccer star, or a great football player. Sam needed to start the youngster off with some good practice.

***

He arrived in Sydney tired from the flight but also excited by the fact that he was just about to see his wife. He collected his luggage from the carousel, and pushed his trolley along with all the vigour he could muster, the queue progressing slowly but surely. He looked straight ahead, hoping the Customs guy wouldn't stop him, and – yes – he was through!

There was an expected crowd waiting to see their loved ones in arrivals, faces of all different ages and ethnicities, but no Lauren among them. Sam passed through their gathering, looking twice to be sure. He circled around the café's lounge, returning to arrivals, finding only a few strangers left on the seats. The flight had landed on time, and it was unlike Lauren to be late. He reached for his phone to call her just as a text came through:

WE HAVE YOUR WIFE

Chapter 36

Sam's hand began to shake. 'Fuck!' he yelled at the phone.

He knew there were people staring at him, but he couldn't give a shit. Those snakes had his wife. He could feel his body pulsating, but he was determined to overcome that. He had to come up with a plan. He wondered if the kidnappers knew she was pregnant. She would have told them, surely. If anything happened to Lauren or the baby...

His phone rang. Unknown number. He was surprised to hear DI Reddy's raspy voice on the other end of the line. He tried to steady himself. 'Detective?'

'Mr Pride, I've heard what happened with Brandis, and I'm glad you've had a safe flight home.'

Sam breathed out slowly. 'Thank you.'

'I'm afraid I've still got to talk to you again about what happened in Botany. Can you come by the station ASAP?'

Sam's mind was racing. If he'd involved the police, maybe Chaz's death could have been avoided. He'd been reckless. And going to the States, well, maybe Brandis had been brought to account but that was worth nothing to him if he didn't have Lauren. He'd been a fool to risk her safety. 'I'll be there right away,' he said. 'But there's something else.'

'What?' asked Reddy.

'It's Lauren. They have her. I just – I just received a text. They have my wife.' There was a moment of silence. Sam felt his heart in actual pain, racing against his chest. 'Did you hear me?'

'I heard you,' said Reddy. 'Have you replied to the text?'

'No, I only just got it a minute ago. I was about to and then—'

'Good. Don't answer, Sam. They can't be sure you've actually read it yet. That buys us time.'

'What – what do you mean?'

'Come right to me,' said Reddy. 'Don't touch your phone again until I see you.'

'Won't that seem suspicious?'

'They might know you've landed but that's all. Right now, they think they're in control. They'll wait for you. Now hang up the phone and come to me. I'll have someone from my team ready to greet you at the station.'

'Okay.' Sam walked out of the terminal in the direction of the taxi queue and phoned Kate. He knew Reddy told him to stay off the phone, but he had to act quickly and decisively. It went straight to voicemail, so he left a message asking her to meet him in the station car park. He was pushing his trolley towards the taxi when the phone rang again. Unknown number. Should he or shouldn't he? Was it Kate?

'Hello?'

'It's me,' said Little Ted.

'You're on a burner?'

'Yep. You're in Sydney, right?'

Sam told him what was happening.

'I understand,' said Little Ted. 'But stop at Fred's Café in Crown Street for five minutes first.'

'Why?'

'I can't tell you over the phone. Just five minutes.'

'It can't wait?'

'No, it can't.'

'Aren't you in hiding? Isn't Fred's a bit public?'

'Don't worry about me. It's you and Lauren we need to worry about. I'll be fine.'

***

Little Ted was sitting at a table in the back corner. 'Sit down,' he said.

'I'd rather not but okay.'

Ginny asked if Sam was ready to order.

'Nothing for me,' he replied. 'I'll only be here for a minute.'

Little Ted said, 'I know why you want to, but I don't think you should rely on the cops. Let me call in Bianchi's guys.'

'I appreciate the offer, Ted, but I think this time we should do it by the book.'

'Thing is, Bianchi's guys are better trained than the cops – they're ex-military – and they're paid a lot more. They're the best. You saw the way they took those Triple S blokes out at Botany. How many cops in Australia can shoot like that?'

'I get it,' said Sam. 'But this time – no thank you.' Sam felt a twinge of pain from his knee, but he had to ignore it. He needed it to keep moving. 'Look, I left my taxi waiting outside. Was there anything else you wanted to tell me?'

'Just some army advice: always use the pisser before you start marching.'

**

At the police station, Sam entered the building with Kate by his side. Reddy led them into a meeting room and introduced a detective named Hoskins. Jet-black hair, mid-forties. She had a strong face and there was something high voltage about her.

'I'm here for one reason,' Hoskins said. 'To help you get your wife back.'

Sam nodded. They all sat down.

Reddy explained that DI Hoskins had the training and the expertise to get the result they all hoped for. 'These situations are her bread and butter. This is what she does.'

'How many kidnappings have you handled?' asked Sam.

'More than twenty,' she said without hesitation.

'Success record?'

'Almost perfect. You can't control everything. But you can go close.'

'Okay, then,' said Sam. 'Tell me what I need to do now.'

'Reply to the text,' said Hoskins. 'Ask them what they want.'

Sam did just that. 'Now what?'

'Now we wait. And I need you to relax. Let us do the worrying.'

'Easier said than done.'

'We know,' said Hoskins.

A few minutes later, the reply came through:

> **Meet me at 8 tonight. Be ready to answer your phone at 7. That's when I will tell you the address. You come alone. You tell the police or anybody else about this your wife will die.**

The last four words made Sam shaky. But they also made him angry. He tried not to obsess, and proceeded to show Hoskins the message.

'He hasn't told you what he wants,' she said.

'I'll ask him,' said Sam, and sent a text back.

The reply from the kidnapper was almost immediate:

> **Bring nothing. Just yourself.**

'That's good,' Hoskins said. 'Very clear. Now what you need to do is ask for proof of life.' Sam looked at the message on his phone and tried to settle on the right words. 'If I say something like…' He typed a message and showed it to Hoskins:

> I need proof that Lauren is ok.
> Please let me speak to her.

'Yes, that's fine,' said Hoskins.

Five minutes later they had a photo of Lauren's face. She looked like she had been crying and had marks around her mouth.

'Sam, tell them that you need proof that the photo wasn't taken before...' Hoskins hesitated. 'I mean, they need to show you that Lauren is still alive. Ask if the photo is old.'

> How do I know that's not an old
> photo? I need proof she is still
> alive.

The reply arrived within two minutes:

> That's all you're getting. You want
> to see her alive you answer the
> phone at 7 and be at the location
> at 8.

Sam didn't ask for Hoskins' reply; he knew exactly what he needed to say:

> I will do everything you have
> asked.

***

Sam was at his home in Bondi, with Hoskins and DI Reddy and four other police officers, waiting for the call. The police had done a thorough search of the area before entering the house, fully conscious of the threat the kidnappers had made about police involvement. They found no sign of any Triple S men observing the place. There was a hidden camera that was now being examined by forensics at the station, but no other surveillance equipment.

At five minutes past seven, Sam asked Hoskins, 'What if they don't call?'

'They always call.'

Two minutes later, a text came through:

> 21 Rowe Street Bondi Junction.
> Come alone or she dies.

'Let's not waste time,' said Hoskins. 'We'll have eyes on the house and plenty of officers close at hand.'

Sam tapped his shoe twice, wondering how a listening device placed next to his foot could possibly give as good a signal as one closer to the height of a person's mouth. 'This thing working?'

'Loud and clear,' said the officer sitting a few metres away wearing high tech headphones.

'And you've got one on the car?'

'We do,' said Hoskins.

'Away we go, then,' said Sam.

***

Lauren could not see her captor because of the tape over her eyes, but she could picture him.

'Open your mouth,' he said.

Lauren refused, shaking her head at him.

'Just do it, lady. For your own good.' Australian accent, pitch mid-range, youthful. She imagined a guy who worked at McDonalds but was pissed off about it. There was a niggle in his voice. He wasn't happy with his lot in life.

'Why, what are you going to do?'

'It's just water,' he said. 'You need to drink something.'

'Did you drug me?'

'Yes. And now you need to drink.'

'If I don't?'

'Look, lady, you can die, for all I care. Do you want the water or not?'

'Okay, okay.'

Lauren opened her mouth and felt the glass press against her lips. She began to drink; it was water. Her hands were tied behind her back, so she was relying on him to keep the water flowing gently.

'More?' he asked.

'Yes. Please.'

She drank what she imagined would have been a glassful and then closed her mouth.

'You right?' he asked.

'Why did you kidnap me?'

'It's not about you.'

'What do you want with my husband?'

'You'll find out soon enough.'

'Can you at least take the tape off my eyes. I swear I won't look at you. I'll keep my eyes shut until you leave the room. You tell me when I can open them. When you're out of sight, yeah?'

'Are you fucking kidding me? Shut up or I'll tape your mouth, too.'

***

Sam drove the replacement vehicle he'd been given by BMW to the address in Bondi Junction. Once he'd parked, he phoned Hoskins. 'I guess this will be my last chance to talk to you before – you know…'

'Don't worry,' she said. 'We've got your back.'

Sam climbed out of the car and walked to Number 21, a renovated terrace house. If he was playing Blackjack at the casino, the number would have been lucky. Lucky for him, or for the kidnapper?

He looked up and down the street. Nobody, apart from a couple of electricity workers who he suspected to be undercover cops.

He went to ring the doorbell, only to discover an envelope with his name on it stuck to the front door. He opened it and read the letter inside.

Cross the road and enter the station. Do it quick.

Catch the train 3 stops to martin place.

If you tell anyone your wife dies.

Sam was reluctant to pull out his phone now, in case one of the kidnappers was watching him. But he did read the letter out loud, so that Hoskins, who was obviously listening, would know what was happening. He felt confident that the experts from the police would know what to do. It couldn't have been the first time this kind of ploy had been tried.

***

Sam walked quickly up to the station, glancing around to see if anyone was following. There were no obvious signs. He hoped the cops would have undercover people waiting when he got to Martin Place.

Boarding the train, he observed only three other people in his carriage. One elderly man, perhaps in his eighties, and a couple in their early twenties getting very cosy. They certainly didn't look like kidnappers, at least not the sort you see on TV. One other person, a teenage girl, got into their carriage at King's Cross. She never even glanced in Sam's direction.

When Sam got off at Martin Place, there were about twenty or so people on the platform. He tried to study them all, looking for any obvious signs that they were the *one*. But there were no signs.

His phone rang. Unknown number, yet again.

'Hello?'

The voice was muffled. 'Walk up the steps and take the Castlereagh Street exit.'

'Sure,' said Sam, 'whatever you say.'

'Stay on the phone.'

When Sam got outside, he looked left and right, down towards George Street and back up towards Macquarie. Nothing. 'Now what?' he asked.

'Can you see a black Mercedes SUV?'

'Yes, I see it. It's about thirty metres away.'

'Walk over to it.' The phone went dead.

Sam looked at the phone, making sure that he wasn't the one to hang it up by accident. He then approached the SUV, noticing a driver in the front. Asian guy. Mid-thirties. He was signalling for Sam to get in the back seat.

Sam climbed in and found a big guy waiting for him. This one was younger, but he was tough looking. He had a scar running down the right side of his face. He patted Sam down, even reaching under his shirt to check for a wire.

'Alright, go.' he said.

The driver took off southbound.

'Where are we going?' Sam asked. 'Where is my wife?'

No answer.

'You've got to tell me something.'

The young guy drove like he knew what he was doing. Maybe he'd done one of those advanced driving courses. Nice and smooth, taking the corners like a professional, and checking the rear vision mirror constantly. Sam noticed him slowing down and then taking the traffic light just on amber, making sure the car behind couldn't follow.

They turned left into City Road. Sam wondered if they were heading in the direction of Newtown, but then, suddenly, they pulled over.

'Give me your watch,' said Scarface.

'What?'

'Your fucking watch. You deaf?'

'Okay.' Sam handed the man his watch.

'And your phone and your shoes.'

Sam handed them over, too, hoping the cops would still be able to track him. The big guy opened the door and threw the items he'd taken from Sam out into the street.

'We don't want anyone bugging us, do we?' he said. 'Now, turn your head around.' Sam did as he was told, and Scarface tied a scarf around him as a blindfold. 'Go!' Scarface said to the driver.

They drove for another ten minutes. At one point, Sam could smell the spices coming from what he thought must have been an Indian restaurant. When they stopped, he guessed they'd moved outside the main part of the city because it was much quieter; maybe it was a little side street.

'Get out,' Sam was told.

Sam felt his way as he carefully climbed out of the SUV, missing his shoes. 'Is someone going to—' One of the guys grabbed Sam's arm by the shirt sleeve and led him forward. There was a tap on wood, and then what sounded like a front door opening.

Once inside, the blindfold was removed. 'Hands behind your back,' said Scarface, proceeding to bind Sam's hands with a synthetic cord. 'Now, down the stairs.'

Sam was scared but he tried not to show it, fighting back the shakes. He was in an unknown location, with no guarantee that the cops knew where he was, and he was about to be further cut off from the outside world by walking underground. He'd stepped into a large concrete room that looked like a nuclear bunker. The door was closed behind him. It made him feel like Lauren's death was even more likely. If she'd been killed, they would almost certainly be intending to kill him. But that was of little consequence if Lauren was gone. Don't go there, he told himself. Be present.

The room seemed to be an inverted L shape, though Sam wasn't sure because he could not see around the corner to the right. In the space before him stood a fridge, two sofas, a table and chairs, and a couple of computers with large screens attached.

'Where is my wife?' asked Sam.

'Shut up,' said Scarface. 'Walk.'

Scarface and the Asian driver walked with Sam to the end of the room, the corner of the L, and sat him down on a wooden chair, facing the space that was new to him. It was barren, though at the end he could see two large steel doors meeting in the middle.

A minute later, the doors opened to reveal a Middle Eastern looking man with a neatly manicured beard, wearing dark trousers and a cream blazer. He stepped out of the elevator and approached Sam. His movements were awkward, like he might have been carrying an injury. 'You did as you were told,' he said. 'That is good.' It suddenly occurred to Sam that this could have been the man whom Little Ted encountered in Rose Bay, the bastard who'd gone after his mum!

'Where is my wife?' Sam said again.

'You will see her very soon.'

'Who are you? Why am I here?'

The man picked up a chair from the other side of the room and brought it over so he could sit facing Sam. 'My name is Joseph Khoury. I'm the person who decides whether you live or die, whether your wife lives or dies.'

'And you're connected to me and my wife, how?'

'I run Triple S. I took over from Michael Haddad, who was killed in Botany by – some associates of yours?'

Khoury seemed to be waiting for a response, but Sam said nothing.

'For a long time now,' he continued, 'our business has benefited from our ties to Alliance and Don Brandis. You might have assumed, after the stunt you pulled in Chicago, that Mr Brandis was no longer relevant. But you'd be wrong. He remains just as powerful as ever. He's on remand, but he'll be out soon enough. It's a white-collar crime he's been accused of, so they'll grant bail, and then the case against him will disappear.'

'Just like that,' said Sam.

'You look sceptical, Mr Pride. The case will disappear after the evidence disappears. And you will play a part in making that happen.'

Sam couldn't care less about Brandis right now. 'My wife?' he said.

'We'll get to her. But before that, do you remember, when you were in Chicago, someone saved your life, plucked you from the jaws of death, so to speak?'

'Yes,' said Sam. 'I remember.'

'I think the point would have been made that, as a group, we could reach you anywhere in the world. It doesn't matter that Boris Federova is in Chicago, or that Don Brandis is behind bars. You and your wife remain just as vulnerable.'

'You don't need to do this!' yelled Sam. 'We couldn't care less about your organisation. I only got dragged into this because Brandis was working for YRG. That's over, so we're done. Why can't you just leave us alone?'

Khoury remained unfazed. 'You still have a part to play in securing Mr Brandis' release. Shortly, you will be given a statement to sign.'

'What kind of statement?'

'Does that matter? If you want to see your wife again, you will sign.'

'Of course, I will,' said Sam, trying to control his anger. Lauren's life was hanging in the balance, and here he was losing his focus. 'I'll do whatever you want. But what about the money that went to Premier Enterprises in the UK?'

Khoury smiled, as if made happy by Sam's own submissions. 'Within an hour of Brandis being arrested,' he said, leaning back to entertain the question comfortably, 'the $140,000,000 in the account was transferred by a man named Leo Taylor to a branch in Moscow, where it was subsequently withdrawn. Leo flew to Moscow two hours after that, safe and sound. Premier no longer has a bank account and proceedings have been commenced to shut down the company in the UK.'

Sam was pissed off that Reddy and the other Australian cops had not told him about that. And if they hadn't known, that was equally bad, and Sam was relying on a bunch of incompetents.

'I will be back shortly,' he said, leaving Sam to his chair, hands still tied behind his back.

A few minutes later, Scarface returned and untied Sam's hands, giving him a clipboard with a statement attached. 'Here's a pen,' he said. 'Sign it.'

It didn't matter what the statement might have said, Sam signed it without hesitation.

Scarface took away the signed document, only to be replaced by Khoury a few minutes later. 'Thank you for your cooperation,' he said, sitting down in the chair facing Sam. 'But this was actually less about the statement and more about payback. You defied us. You got Brandis put in jail. There has to be a lesson learned.'

'I've done what you asked,' said Sam. 'Let me see my wife!'

'But that's not enough, Mr Pride. A final decision about you and your wife hasn't been made yet, so, for the time being, you'll remain here as our guest. Well, not right here. In a special room. It's soundproofed. No amenities. But there will be service – of a sort.'

'Where is Lauren?'

'You'll get to see her, all right. Via a video link. But she won't be able to see you.'

'Where are you keeping her?'

'That's all for now,' said Khoury. 'Enjoy the room service!'

Chapter 37

Little Ted stood beside the sofa while Marco Bianchi, patting his Great Dane, looked out across the harbour from his Point Piper mansion.

'How did you do it?' Bianchi asked.

'Sam went to the bathroom at the café. I got the device into the lining of his jacket. It's small enough that Khoury's guy will miss it in the search.'

'He took Sam's shoes, watch, and wallet, but not the jacket?'

'Lucky us. If he had, we'd have had to move in straight away.'

'Putting the wife's life at risk but saving Sam's?' said Bianchi.

'Saving Sam's and giving ourselves a chance at saving Lauren's, too.'

Bianchi looked up at Little Ted, who hadn't moved. 'So, what now?'

'We've got eyes on the exterior, and we've got the council maps of the building, but we can't be sure what they've done inside. The place could have several IEDs.' Little Ted clarified for Bianchi. 'Booby-traps.'

'How many men?'

'We've counted six.'

'They're all from Triple S? The same mob we dealt with at Botany?'

'That's right. Seems the new boss there, Joseph Khoury, has carried on where the last guy left off. He's got some connection to Brandis, who is locked up in Chicago, and Boris Federova, who runs a strip club over there.'

'How do you know all this?'

'Courtesy of your team. One of your guys is a bit of a tech guru. I don't know how he finds this stuff out, but he seems to be able to hack into anything.'

'That would be *Handy*. Oliver Handwell.'

'Right,' said Little Ted. 'You introduced us that day at the café in Darlinghurst.'

'Course I did,' said Bianchi. 'Now, where are the cops in all this?'

'Don't know. Maybe they lost track of him.'

'Should we let them take the glory?'

Little Ted shook his head. 'We're ready to go. Our best chance of saving Sam and his wife is to use your guys.'

'The cops won't like that.'

'Never mind them.'

***

Lauren could feel the blind of tape coming loose. It was risky using the rough corner of her bedpost to leverage it up. She knew it could cost her an eye if she slipped, but she had the right angle; it was working. From the commotion going on downstairs – muffled noises and vibrations that felt like there were people moving about – Lauren figured she had at least a few minutes before her captor returned. 'Ah,' she said to herself as the tape fell away. Her eyes took a moment to adjust to the light, but she could finally see again.

A bedroom. She'd been put onto a queen-sized bed in a sparsely furnished white bedroom; a bed, a cupboard, a window with its blind taped down, a chair by the door. That was all there was, except for the camera up on the ceiling. Was someone watching her?

It didn't matter, she knew what she had to do. If they saw her, they saw her. She had to find something sharp to cut the cord that was binding her hands and feet. It was awkward, but with her back to the cupboard door, she managed to jiggle it open. Inside one of the drawers was a nail file. That would have to do. She twisted her neck around so she could see what she was doing and began rubbing the file against the cord. She had to move quickly. *Faster*, she willed herself. At first, she thought she was making progress. But it was too slow. It would take all day. She needed to find another way. The cord was still wrapped tightly around her wrists.

Click.

What was that? The noise startled her; a key was being used to unlock the door. Lauren quickly lay down on the bed, playing dead. She prayed they wouldn't notice that the tape was no longer covering her eyes. She could hear a man's footsteps approaching, and then she could smell his sweaty aftershave as he moved in close. With her eyes closed, she figured she had one shot. She had to give it a go, regardless of the danger to the baby. Doing nothing would have been a bigger risk to them both. She opened her eyes and slammed her knees up into the man's head with all the might she had in her, shocking herself with the violence of it all. The man fell backwards onto the floor beside the bed, groggy and disoriented.

Lauren climbed off the bed and looked down at him. The job was half done. As long as he was conscious he was still a danger to her. So, she stood right up close to him, feet together, took a small leap into the air, and came down as hard as she could on his head, falling back against the bed as she fell over him.

He was out cold.

'Are you okay?' she said to her baby, her hands touching her belly. Lauren's knees were throbbing, and her feet hurt, but that wasn't about to stop her. With her back towards the man, she managed to lay down at an angle that allowed her to search his pockets. It took a minute or two, but she soon found what she was looking for. A knife. Finally, she had something that would cut through the cord.

And – *snap!* It was done. She used her hands to disentangle the cord from her feet.

Quietly, she opened the blind enough to look out the window. She was on the first floor of a large inner-city house, with another couple of floors above her. She went to the door, pulled it open, ever so slightly, and managed to catch a glimpse of the hallway. Why was nobody else coming for her? Maybe there'd only been that one guy watching the video feed. Or maybe it wasn't working. She stepped lightly into the hallway, trying not to make a sound. She heard footsteps – someone approaching – and quickly ducked behind a cabinet.

***

Scarface rolled a desk with a computer on it over to where Sam was sitting and said, 'You can watch now.'

He typed a few strokes on the keyboard, hitting enter and turning to Sam, only to do a double take at the video feed of a vacant bedroom. 'What the...' He looked over at the Asian, who slowly shrugged. 'Quick!' shouted Scarface. 'Get up there. Tell Khoury she's out!'

Just then, Sam heard a small explosion fire from above.

'Fuck!' said the Asian. 'What's that?'

'I don't bloody know,' said Scarface. 'Get up there and find out. I'll stay with him.' Scarface looked at Sam like he was more of an annoyance than a valuable commodity.

The Asian ran up the stairs and opened the door. Sam could only hear a thud, like somebody had knocked all the air out of a leather bag, until the Asian had landed back on the ground floor, headfirst and out cold.

'What the fuck?' Scarface scrambled out of his chair and hurried behind Sam.

Little Ted pushed into the room, descending the stairs quickly and quietly, his body made impossibly small for a man that size, his gun leading steady, silently negotiating with its target as he closed the distance.

'Stop!' Scarface wedged the barrel of his Glock 34 into Sam's right ear. 'Come any closer and he's dead.'

'If he dies,' said Little Ted, 'you'll die very badly.' Two more of Bianchi's men had descended the stairs and positioned themselves on his flank. 'And I mean *very* badly. One limb at a time. Won't be pretty.'

Scarface grabbed Sam by the arm and dragged him to the elevator. 'Stay back!' he yelled at Little Ted.

The elevator doors opened, and Scarface pushed Sam inside. When Scarface went to press the elevator button to go up, one of Bianchi's sharpshooters blew the gun out of his other hand – an almost clean shot, though Scarface lost his thumb and a lot of blood in the process. Little Ted ran to Sam's aid and pulled him out of the lift, while Scarface lay on the elevator floor, a bloody mess, starting to lose consciousness.

'Let's get you out of here,' said Little Ted, cutting the cord still wrapped around Sam's wrists.

'We've got to find Lauren!' shouted Sam.

He and Little Ted ran up the stairs towards the ground floor, brushing past the Asian who was being held by one of Bianchi's men. The stun grenades had knocked out all the rest of the Triple S operatives, who lay on the ground, face down, with the gun of another of Bianchi's men being waved around over their heads. One of them appeared to have a bullet wound.

The second Sam was past them, he began combing each room on the ground level, searching for Lauren. He shouted her name and pushed open the door to an empty room. No sign. He was standing in the hallway, about to kick open another door, when he heard his name being shouted from the stairwell at the end of the hall. Lauren's face appeared out of the darkness. Sam could hardly believe his eyes. She ran towards him, and they met in a feverish embrace.

'Thank God,' Lauren said.

'I'm so sorry for all this,' said Sam.

'We're alive. That's what matters.'

Sirens were approaching. Sam took Lauren by the hand and walked towards the front door of the house, where Little Ted was waiting. 'Later,' he said, and turned to leave.

Sam said, 'Hey, where is Khoury?'

'I think he took the lift to the roof,' said Little Ted. 'He won't be able to get away from there. The cops can grab him.'

And with that, Little Ted and Bianchi's men were gone.

The Triple S guys who'd been lying on the ground got up and made a run for it, only to be cornered by the police out on the street.

Reddy and DSC Bolton raced through the front gate to where Sam and Lauren were standing by the door; Hoskins and one of her team arrived seconds later.

'Are you hurt?' asked Reddy.

'We're fine,' said Sam.

'Any perps left in the building?'

'A big guy with a scar across his face is injured and semi-conscious down in the basement. We think Khoury, the boss, is up on the roof. There's an elevator.'

Sam noticed Lauren turn and look back inside, no doubt as concerned as he was about the human carnage left in their wake.

'Okay,' said Reddy, nodding to Bolton. 'Let's go.'

***

Bolton raced down to the basement level and immediately took the elevator up to the roof. When Reddy was sure the basement and the ground floor were secure, she followed Bolton up, keen to get her own look at the mastermind behind Lauren Pride's abduction. But when she arrived, the roof was deserted. 'Where is he?' she asked Bolton.

'I don't know, boss. I've looked everywhere.'

'He can't have just vanished,' said Reddy.

'I know. But...'

There were very few places to hide on the roof: a patio area with some weatherproof furniture, a small garden behind that, a satellite dish, a bit of rubbish with a cover over it, and an old-fashioned chimney that was no longer in use. 'Maybe he never came up here?' said Reddy.

'That's right. I was up here quick smart, so I'd have seen him if, you know, if he was still around.'

Reddy took a few steps in the direction of the satellite dish, and then turned around. 'Let's go back down and do a thorough search. Three floors and the basement – there must be a few hiding places down there.'

'I'm on it,' said Bolton, who immediately walked down the stairs to the floor below. Once out of sight of Reddy, who was obviously taking her time, he glanced at his mobile phone. There was a text message from an unknown number:

Thank you – safe now.

Bolton smiled to himself.

***

Reddy was about to walk down the stairs when she spotted the end of a ladder at the far end of the roof, almost entirely covered by a tarpaulin. It was in the pile of what looked like rubbish. She walked over to it and then glanced across at the roof of the neighbouring house. She'd initially thought it would be impossible for Khoury to have jumped across to the other roof. But if he'd used the ladder... Then how would it have been placed so neatly back on the roof after his dash? And there was the tarpaulin covering it, suggesting it had not been touched. Assistance for Khoury? Surely, not.

Following the search of the house, Reddy tracked down Sam and Lauren, who were huddled together out in the street, a few metres from the debris left by the door explosion.

'Take your time,' Reddy said. 'But I need to know what happened here, before we arrived.'

Sam related the events as best he could, but Reddy wasn't satisfied. 'You mentioned this statement that Khoury forced you to sign,' she said. 'A legal document?'

'Yes,' said Sam.

'What exactly did it say?'

'I didn't pay it too much attention in the circumstances. I was worried about Lauren.'

'You've got a photographic memory,' she reminded him.

'Okay,' said Sam, pulling at what little he had glanced over, 'it said something about me denying that Brandis had ever committed an illegal act – to the best of my knowledge – and that I vouched for his integrity.'

'Like a character reference?'

'There were some facts in there – suggesting Brandis had not broken the law – and, yes, also an endorsement of his character.'

'Seems odd,' said Reddy. 'If it was signed under duress, it wouldn't have been legally binding.'

'I know. I guess he had his reasons.'

'What happened to the statement after you signed it?'

'Khoury took it with him.'

Chapter 38

Sam could hardly believe they were back in their own bed. He wrapped his arms around Lauren and kissed her on the shoulder.

She turned to face him. 'I feel like we've lived a lifetime in a very short space of time.'

'It's been crazy, hasn't it?'

'We survived,' she said.

'Only just.'

Despite his dodgy knee, Sam felt like making love; Lauren had a few cuts and bruises from her ordeal, but she didn't seem to be bothered by them either. Initially, it felt like they were strangers getting to know each other for the first time, and perhaps Sam held back because of the baby. But then the intensity grew until they were finally burnt out, collapsing side by side on the sheets.

'I'll have more of this, and less of the other, going forward, thanks,' Sam said.

'Love, not war, hey?'

'Lots and lots of love,' Sam said, kissing her on the lips.

***

Sam would have liked to spend the day with Lauren, but he knew he couldn't. He had to go into work. His staff needed to be briefed and there was nobody else who could do it.

He sent Brie an email from his desk asking her to meet him in the boardroom near Marilyn's office. He had not spoken to her since he got back. When he arrived, she'd been on her break, so he hadn't seen her at reception.

At the appointed time, she came bouncing into the room and ran up to him, arms wide open. Sam didn't push her away, but he felt awkward.

'It's so good to see you,' she said, as bubbly as ever. 'Are you okay?'

'I'm fine,' he said. 'But please, take a seat.'

Brie's expression changed instantly.

'I know what you did,' he said. 'It took me a while. Those occasions when Viktor was one step ahead of me and I couldn't work out why. He seemed to be all-seeing, all-knowing.'

'I don't even know Viktor,' Brie insisted.

'No, but you *do* know someone who gave you drugs on his behalf. And the consequences of your actions, you feeding him information about what I was up to…' Sam felt himself losing his calm, which he intended to keep, so he started again. 'That day in Bondi, with Lauren and I staying at the hotel in The Rocks, and my movements in Chicago…' Sam shook his head at it all. 'Well, Brie, it's probably best we don't go there.'

'Go where? I don't—'

'Brie. That's enough. You could have got Lauren and me killed!'

'But…' Brie was speechless. Sam could see her defences crumbling. He didn't enjoy anything about confronting her. He hated that Brie was guilty, that she'd truly placed him and his wife in danger, but he also hated that he was speaking to a victim, too.

'Anyway,' said Sam, 'the reason I'm talking to you alone, and not with the police, is because I know you've got a health issue to deal with. And I think that takes priority. Your addiction is dangerous, for you and for others.' Sam took a deep breath. 'If you are willing to check into a rehab facility for as long as it takes for you to get well, then that's all we'll focus on for now. Marilyn says there's a top notch one she has in mind. We'll pay. It's not one where you can pop in and out when it suits you. It's full on. If you do this—'

'I'll do it!' said Brie. The tears began to flow freely. 'Anything you say, Sam. Just forgive me for what I did. I'm so sorry!'

'I don't know about forgiveness, Brie. But I do know you need help.'

'I never meant for Chaz…'

'I know you didn't. If I thought you'd intended for him to get killed, we'd be having a very different conversation.'

'Chaz was…' Brie was falling apart. Sam found it hard to hold in his own emotions about it all. 'I really liked him, Sam. I wish he was still around.'

Sam nodded. 'Me too.'

***

An hour after escorting Brie from the building, and asking her subordinate to take the young receptionist directly to the rehabilitation centre, Marilyn stepped out of the lift and marched straight to the desk of Kitty Zhang. By the time she arrived there, several of Kitty's fellow account managers had stopped what they were doing to observe what was about to unfold. Kitty looked startled.

'Kitty,' said Marilyn, 'I'm going to need you to come with me. I'm sure you know what it's about. Could you please gather your personal things?'

'Why? What's going on?'

'Don't act the fool, Kitty. You're better than that.'

It took a few minutes for Kitty to pack her things, and then Marilyn escorted her to the lift and led her to a small meeting room, where one of the finance managers, Isla Colston, was sitting with a laptop open in front of her.

'Kitty, would you like to have a support person at this meeting?' asked Marilyn.

'No. Just say whatever it is you want to say.'

Marilyn sat down. 'As you know, we have been investigating what happened on the night of May the fourteenth. You alleged that the agency's Executive Creative Director, Zoe Barnes, assaulted you. You told us the time and the location of the assault. And you said you wanted $250,000 to compensate you for the alleged behaviour, which you also described as an attack. Without any video footage of the incident, and without any witnesses, it was your word against her word.'

'So, you should be taking my word, not hers!' said Kitty defiantly.

'There are two key things you need to understand, Kitty. The first is that we have recovered the security footage. It clearly shows you accosting Ms Barnes, and not the other way around. Secondly, we have a statement from someone who claims you asked him to delete the footage. The investigation has come to a very clear conclusion. You lied and you attempted to have one of the company's security files destroyed to hide evidence of your deception.'

'What right have you got to judge me?' said Kitty. 'You sit there all high and mighty but – some of us don't – don't get handed things on a—'

'Kitty, I assure you—'

'No! I've had to fight for what I've got. I started with nothing. You don't know—'

'I am sure there are things I don't know, Kitty, but what I do know is this: as of the end of this meeting, you will no longer be working for TBA.'

'What!'

'And while losing your job is a punishment in itself, the thing that most disturbs me, the thing that you will have to live with, is that false and malicious claims like yours do untold harm to the women and men who are genuine victims of sexual harassment and sexual assault, both in the workplace and outside of it. You lied, it would appear, for no other reason than to extort money. A very large sum. Perhaps you also felt slighted by the rejection you received that night, maybe that was also part of your motivation. It matters not.'

'If it'd happened to you...' Kitty's words trailed off as if the fight had been drained from her.

Marilyn continued. 'I'm not going to go into what I've learned about your time at McKenzie and Roberts, but I believe this is not the first time you have made false claims. Isla, please hand Kitty the letter and the file with her severance calculations. Kitty, is there anything you'd like to say before you hand over your security pass and leave the building?'

Tears welled in Kitty's eyes. She took her papers and placed them into the box holding the rest of her personal belongings, quivering as she walked out.

***

All the TBA staff had been sent an invitation and an email about the 2pm meeting on the rooftop. It had to be there because there was nowhere else in the building where Sam could fit everybody. And he didn't want anyone to miss this one.

Sam stood in the same spot where he'd made his speech on May 14, and handed out all those employee cheques. He remembered the way the space had been dressed up for their party's fantasy theme. And looking back, last month felt like a fantasy, like something entirely made up. He certainly couldn't have predicted any of what was to come. The person he'd been closest to that night was the one person who could not be with them now.

He checked his watch. It was a few minutes before 2pm, and the rooftop was looking full. The crowd went back as far as the swimming pool, and there were a few people standing on the white sofas at the back trying for an unobscured view. Sam began imagining Little Ted stepping out of the lift, but he knew that wouldn't happen. His friend was on indefinite leave at an undisclosed location. Marilyn Banks approached him instead, a serious look about her.

'Kitty?' asked Sam. 'It's done?'

'By the book,' she said.

Sam was relieved. He moved to the microphone. It was time to begin.

'It's a while since I've spoken to you all,' said Sam.' The crowd quieted and focused on him. 'The first thing I've got to say is, thank you. There's been some crazy shit going down in the last few weeks, and you guys have kept coming into work, kept being positive, held your heads up high, and continued to do great work. I've said it before but I'm going to say it again; you are the best agency team in the business.

'I know some of you have been worried about me. Thank you for your kind messages. I'm hobbling a little from a bump to the knee, but, other than that, my wife and I are doing all right. And I'm very glad to be back in Sydney.

'The person who cannot be here today is, of course, Chaz Bailley. There'll be a funeral for him tomorrow at the South Chapel of the Eastern Suburbs Memorial Park at eleven o'clock. I find it very strange to be speaking to you here, today, without him by my side. He helped us build this business, this agency, into what it is now. I feel his presence in this building. I suspect I always will. He was my very close friend, as well as a brilliant finance guy. His death, when it occurred, seemed so utterly senseless. He was killed by a man who is himself now dead. Horrific crimes. The sort that you grow up believing would never happen to you or your loved ones. And when they do, it hits you like a tonne of bricks. You have moments when you think you can't cope. You think you'll never get through it. You need help. Support. Love. We all do. We wouldn't be human if we didn't suffer from a loss like this.

'If there's anything you want to speak to me about, at any time, you know where I am. Or if you want to talk to a counsellor, please speak to Marilyn and she'll organise it. I have always said we are a family, and at a time like this we need to come together like a family. We need to support each other. If you need a shoulder to lean on, just look at the person next to you. He or she will be there for you.

'And if you were wondering whether it's okay to attend tomorrow morning, Chaz's family have said, absolutely! Anyone who knew and loved Chaz is welcome. It will be a time, as Auden so aptly put it, to silence the pianos and with muffled drum, bring out the coffin, and let the mourners come.'

There was a moment of quiet, after which Sam asked, 'Now, does anyone have any questions?'

'Is it true that Margaret Whitfield is no longer the Global CEO?' asked Bob Cooper from over near the pool.

'Apparently so,' said Sam. 'I learned of her departure just as I was leaving Chicago. No announcement has been made yet about her replacement, but there's one thing I do know. We have a good contact now in Jean Koziol. Jean is YRG's largest shareholder, and she is an incredibly impressive woman. She also recognises the value, not just to us but also to YRG, in TBA staying true to its values. She doesn't want us to merge with anyone else; she doesn't want us to change the way we go about our business. And whoever the new Global CEO is, it would be a very brave woman or man who defies Jean. She's tough. And, I'm happy to say, she's our friend.'

Chapter 39

After feeding Rax and throwing the ball a few times for him in the back yard, Sam returned to the bedroom to say goodbye to Lauren before heading off for his doctor's appointment. She was sitting on the edge of the bed. He sat down beside her and kissed her belly. Then he looked up and said, 'I'm no good at being noble, but it doesn't take much to see that the problems of three little people don't amount to—'

'A hill of beans in this crazy world? You only wanted us to have a baby so you could use that line!' Lauren pushed him away with a laugh at the Casablanca reference. He might have been a lousy Rick Blaine, but Sam was glad he could still put a smile on her face.

The news from the doctor turned out not to be so great. Sam had fractured his patella and needed to wear a brace for two or three weeks. But it was not the worst either, in that the fracture was only minor and the rehab required was perfectly manageable. Apparently, he'd be as good as new in a couple of months.

Lauren met him at the Memorial Park in Matraville at half past ten, and was clearly surprised to see him standing by the side of the road with crutches. 'It's no big deal,' he said. 'I could walk right now without these ridiculous things, as you know, because you saw me doing it this morning, but the doctor said it'd be better if I stayed off the leg for a few days.'

'Rax isn't going to be happy,' said Lauren. 'He expects you to do more than just hobble about all day.'

'Guess I'll have to make it up to him in a few weeks' time.'

Lauren's mood seemed to shift. 'There's something I need to, um…'

'What is it?' Sam asked.

'I spoke to Noah Campbell.'

'He called you?'

'He rang the other day. I called him back. I felt I had to. He was going to find out about the pregnancy at some stage, anyway.'

'And?'

'I told him that you were the father.'

'Am I?'

'As far as I'm concerned.'

'Did you have the test?'

'I don't need to. I don't care what any test says. I care about you. And our family.'

If he wasn't on crutches, Sam would have taken Lauren's hand. But this was not the time for that. She put her hand on his shoulder for a moment and then they started the slow walk over to the South Chapel. He could see that there were going to be too many people to all fit inside for the service. He said hello to many, introduced a few to Lauren, and eventually they found themselves towards the front. Chaz's father spoke first, then Zoe said a few words, then it was Sam's turn.

'I didn't know Chaz when he was a boy,' Sam began, 'but in the time I have known him, he's been like a brother to me. A crazy irreverent brother, but a brother nonetheless.' Sam struggled to hold back his tears. It felt therapeutic, not only to say his bit, but also to listen to the kind and loving words of others.

***

The service over, when he and Lauren were making their way back to the main road where she had parked the car, Sam noticed DI Reddy lingering in the background. He nodded in her direction, which she seemed to take as an invitation to approach. 'Do you mind?' she asked.

'No, it's okay.'

DSC Bolton remained standing a few metres behind, looking embarrassed that his superior was choosing to have a conversation about their criminal investigation at the victim's funeral.

'We've found some useful trace evidence from the crime scene at Botany,' said Reddy. 'Including DNA that could lead us to Chaz's killer.'

Sam had been shedding tears only a few minutes ago, now he wanted to laugh. 'Sadly, Detective Inspector, Chaz's killer will never do jail time,' he said. 'He lived by the sword, and he died by the sword. Not from my hand, I assure you. His body parts are, I believe, somewhere in Illinois. Possibly on land, or possibly at the bottom of one of those enormous lakes that ice over in winter. I doubt they'll ever be found. But what would I know? I'm just an ad guy.'

'And those other men who died that day in Botany. You've still got nothing to say about them, about who might have been responsible for their deaths? We know exactly what sort of weapons were used and when we track down the men who fired them, you may very well—'

'Sorry, detective. I wish I could help.'

'And the people who miraculously saved you and your wife from your abductors?'

Sam shrugged.

'The Triple S men we're holding don't seem to have any recollection of who blew up the front door of the house and shot two of their lot.'

Sam shook his head. 'As I say, I wish…'

'You know withholding information from a murder investigation is a serious offence.'

Lauren had been standing back, giving the detective and her husband enough space to speak privately for a minute. 'Darling,' she called out, 'shouldn't we be going?'

Sam nodded, and then turned to Reddy. 'Goodbye,' he said.

'I'd love to know what you're hiding, Sam Pride,' said the DI, 'but I suspect I never will.'

Sam smiled at her.

'Oh, and by the way, we haven't found Joseph Khoury yet. But we will.'

That struck Sam as very odd. He had no idea how Khoury could have escaped. But it was not Sam's job to worry about such things. Unless Khoury was coming after him or his wife, he could happily let it go.

Almost all the crowd had moved on now. Lauren and Sam made their way back to the car. It had been a cloudy morning, the sort of day that's forever threatening rain. But to the north, there seemed to be a patch of blue that was growing larger. Lauren opened the back door so Sam could throw his crutches in. She was taking him out for lunch, but he didn't know where.

He'd just sat down in the passenger seat when he noticed his phone vibrate. He removed it from his jacket pocket. It was an email. He had loads of unread ones, and unread was the way most of them would remain. But the most recent one was different. It was from Jean Koziol.

Dear Sam,

I hope you had a safe trip back to Sydney and that your leg is feeling better. Once fully fit, I do hope you'll start planning your next trip to Chicago so we can catch up again. You should bring your wife, Lauren, with you. There is more to do around here than just work!

But on the subject of business, I wanted you to know that as long as I remain a Director of YRG (and I think – unless I suddenly keel over – that will be for quite a few years to come), you will have the support of the Board to run TBA in whatever way you think best. You have my complete trust. And if at any time you start to worry about the ownership and control, despite my assurances, then you should know that you can buy it back from us. I will support you.

Until we meet again.

Best wishes,
Jean

Sam read it out loud to Lauren and asked her what she thought. 'Maybe it would be a good idea to buy it back,' he said. 'Regain our integrity. Take control again.'

Lauren leaned over to him and whispered conspiratorially, 'I say, keep the seventy-four million.'

END